The
Midnight
Side

The Midnight Side

A Novel

NATASHA MOSTERT

wm.

WILLIAM MORROW
75 YEARS OF PUBLISHING
An Imprint of HarperCollins*Publishers*

Quotes from "Phone Calls from the Dead" used as the epigraph are from *Harper's Encyclopedia of Mystical and Paranormal Experience* by Rosemary Ellen Guiley. Copyright © 1991 by Rosemary Ellen Guiley. Reprinted by permission of HarperCollins Publishers Inc.

Lyrics from "Brilliant Disguise" by Bruce Springsteen. Copyright © 1987 by Bruce Springsteen (ASCAP). Reprinted by permission.

HarperCollins books may be purchased for educational, business, or sales promotional use. For information please write: Special Markets Department, HarperCollins Publishers Inc., 10 East 53rd Street, New York, NY 10022.

FIRST EDITION

Designed by Joseph Rutt

Printed on acid-free paper

Library of Congress Cataloging-in-Publication Data
Mostert, Natasha.
The midnight side : a novel / Natasha Mostert.
p. cm.
ISBN 0-688-17385-3
1. Murder victims' families—Fiction. 2. Loss (Psychology)—Fiction. I. Title.
PS3563.O8865 M54 2000
813'.6—dc21
00-025931

01 02 03 04 05 ❖/RRD 10 9 8 7 6 5 4 3 2 1

To Frederick

ACKNOWLEDGMENTS

The Midnight Side required specialized knowledge of the stock market, pharmaceuticals, and patents. Many thanks to my panel of experts: John Plimmer, Lesley Edwards, and the incomparable Robert Swift. They allowed me the benefit of their expertise and gave freely of their time. The responsibility for any errors or excessive leaps of imagination is, of course, not theirs but mine alone.

Many thanks to my agent, Harvey Klinger, for all his hard work on my behalf, and to Lisa Queen, Claire Wachtel, and Jennifer Pooley at Morrow.

Thanks to Dianne Hofmeyr, a good friend and gifted writer. Thanks to my brothers, Stefan and Frans, who stood ever ready with words of encouragement and good cheer. A very special thank you to a remarkable woman, my mother, Hantie. Her imaginative ideas always take my breath away.

To my extraordinary, deeply wonderful husband, Frederick, I dedicate this book. His love and support are at the center of my life.

PHONE CALLS FROM THE DEAD

Literally, a telephone call from someone who has died, usually one with whom the recipient shared a close emotional relationship.

In such a call, the telephone usually rings normally, but may sound flat and abnormal. The connection usually is bad, and the voice from the dead one fades . . .

If the recipient knows the caller is dead, he or she is too shocked to speak, and the call abruptly ends. If the recipient does not know the caller is dead, he or she may chat for up to thirty minutes. Most phone calls from the dead occur within twenty-four hours of the death of the caller, though some have been reported as long as two years from the time of death.

The purpose of these mysterious calls seems to be to leave either a farewell message, a warning of impending danger, or information needed by the living . . .

No satisfactory explanation exists to explain phone calls from the dead . . . In the early twentieth century, investigators modified the telegraph and wireless in hopes of communicating with the dead. Thomas Edison, whose parents were Spiritualists, worked on but did not complete a telephone that he hoped would connect the living and the dead.

> —*Harper's Encyclopedia of
> Mystical and Paranormal
> Experience*

The
Midnight
Side

PROLOGUE

And here the precious dust is layd;
Whose purely temper'd Clay was made
So fine, that it the guest betray'd.

> —"Elegy on Maria Wentworth,"
> Thomas Carew (1594–1640)

THEY HAD SHAVED HER SCALP. ALL THAT BEAUTIFUL RED HAIR WAS gone. Alette's face seemed mottled and bruised in the cool, green dusk of the hospital room.

Four o'clock in the morning. The time when death's angel is walking, as his mother would say.

"Mmmgh."

The sound was tiny—a soft rattle of phlegm in her throat. He leaned over until his face almost touched hers. He gently placed his finger in the soft hollow beneath her eye.

She would be dead soon. "Worm's meat," as the good Dr. Donne wrote so elegantly. But no, she would be cremated . . . she had stipulated it so in her will. No maggots and slow decay for his red-haired love. Fire and cleansing and brittle ashes. "Precious dust," said Thomas Carew. Another seventeenth-century poet with an ear for a clever conceit.

He sniffed gently at the scent of her skin. His lips barely touched the lovely, high ridge of her cheekbone.

He pulled back. Alette was jerking her head and rolling it slightly from side to side on the pillow. Her eyeballs were moving underneath the curved, veined lids.

He wondered if she sensed that she was in danger. Maybe fear was able to breach even the soft, implacable hold of the coma that was shuttering her brain. She had been conscious of danger yesterday just before she drove back to London; of that he was certain. He had watched as she lingered for a moment beside the open car door, slapping her gloves against the palm of her hand: back and forth, back and forth. She had hesitated, he knew, because she sensed a rage in the air.

He always marveled at her psychic abilities. Although she sometimes prostituted herself doing readings for stupid, bored, rich women just like any other common fortune-teller—pandering to their wishes, telling them what they wanted to hear—she was the real thing. She had the gift. He was awed by it and enchanted. Catching a glimpse of this gift was like catching sight of a furtive flame through the closed fingers of a cupped hand.

Back and forth went her gloves. Back and forth. He watched her. He held his breath and his mind silently screamed at her to get into the car.

Get into the car.

To reach this point had taken months. He had engaged in extensive research on how to sabotage the car. Detective novels aside, it's a tricky business: tampering with brakes. It's not easy to get it just right. To inflict just enough damage so that the brakes would keep functioning normally and only give way once she steered the car through those hairpin bends. Of course, he had also ensured that her seat belt wasn't working.

Get into the car.

With a slight shrug of her shoulders she turned her body side-ways, pulling both her legs into the car with one feminine, grace-ful motion; her skirt riding up slightly against her thigh.

What was it Alette had said during their last conversation? "My life is obsession. At times I'm obsessed with keeping my own free-dom. At other times I'm obsessed with robbing someone else of theirs."

She had spoken slowly, sounding almost puzzled. The light streaming in through the window had blanked out the expression in her eyes. Her face had the flawless, un-human look of a face caught in the cold shock of a flashlight.

Obsession.

Obsession is an open wound; a trickle of rotting pus. Only a clean cut can stop the green poison from spreading. Amputation. Severance. Brutal, uncompromising, and quick. Soft hands make stinking wounds, as his mother was fond of saying, and she's right. A break has to be clean and absolute. Final.

With no possibility of a comeback.

FIRST ENVELOPE

ONE

I long to talke with some old lover's ghost . . .
　　　　—"Love's Deitie,"
　　　　　John Donne (1572–1631)

WHEN THE PHONE RANG ISA WAS DREAMING.

She was dreaming of a funeral: the funeral of her love. The funeral to which she was not invited, to which she dared not go.

Wind in the trees, white flowers on black mud. The widow's dress billowing at the hem.

At the widow's side stood Mark. Isa recognized him instantly, although they had never met. In a few years' time Mark would lose the graceless, gawky gestures and the outsized nose of adolescence and become the image of his father. At this moment his hand was protectively draped around the shoulder of his mother, who was weeping with wild abandon, without any thought of propriety. Her face was screwed up into an ugly grimace of woe and her mouth was open. To her left were the two younger girls—twins —Cecily and Anne. Their long, blond hair was pulled back behind their ears with crimson velvet ribbons.

Isa wanted to join them. She wanted to take the widow's slack hand into her own, and kiss the smooth cheeks of the little girls.

She wanted to say, "Please talk to me. I want to talk about him. I have no one to talk to about him. I have no one with whom to share my grief."

Isa started to speak but the wind blew the words from her mouth. She started to walk toward them but her legs dragged, heavy as lead.

Then she felt a tug at her sleeve. She looked down and saw the hand resting on her elbow. As always, this hand was small, much smaller than her own square, capable-looking hands. And as always, Isa was unable to see the owner of the hand although she could sense her presence, and on the edges of her peripheral vision hovered a shape . . .

The phone rang: the sound a long, long chain dragging her back to consciousness.

She fumbled for the phone, her fingers slipping and then clumsily gripping the receiver. Behind her eyes was a sense of flickering nausea. The ringing of the phone sounded odd: flat, atonal; strangely off-key.

"Isabelle, is that you?"

The connection was poor. But the voice could only belong to Alette. There was no mistaking that whispery voice. And only Alette ever used her full name: Isabelle. Or rather I-I-sabelle. Alette always pronounced her name with the first syllable slightly drawn out: "I-I-sabelle"—like a child calling out the name of another child during a game of hide-and-seek.

Isa struggled to concentrate. She had difficulty hearing. And her mind was still stupid with sleep. The phone call seemed almost an extension of her dream. In her dream she had sensed Alette beside her, had felt the pressure of her hand, and now, only a waking moment later, here she was talking to her. The switch from dream to reality was so abrupt, her brain was struggling to cope with the transition.

Isa knew her cousin was calling from London, but although the satellite hookup between the UK and South Africa was sometimes poor, this connection was particularly bad. Some words came through as clearly as though Alette was standing next to her, while other words were drowning in a sea of scratchy noises. The words faded away but it sounded as though Alette was constantly repeating, "Isabelle, is that you?"

Isa pushed herself upright and pulled a pillow into place behind her back. "Alette, it's me. Listen, we have a terrible line. Let me call you back."

"No." The word came over the line with the force of a bullet. "Don't do that. Don't hang up."

"What's wrong?"

Silence. But the noise on the line was lessening.

Isa looked out the window. The curtain was open. She must have forgotten to close it when she went to bed last night. Actually—she could hardly remember the previous night. The sky outside her window was gray, streaked with pink. Leaning over, she picked up her wristwatch from the bedside table. Five A.M.

She ran her tongue over her lips. Behind her eyes lurked a wicked ache, which no doubt had something to do with the wine-glass that stood next to the telephone. But it wasn't the aftereffects of the wine that made her feel suddenly apprehensive. Something was wrong. London was two hours behind Durban—it was three o'clock in the morning for Alette.

"Alette—what's wrong?"

"I couldn't sleep." The ghost of a laugh. "Sorry I woke you."

Isa shifted more comfortably against her pillow. "It doesn't matter."

"You were having a nightmare."

Isa hesitated. "Yes." She didn't ask how Alette knew. Alette always knew.

"Do you want to talk about it?" Alette's voice was clear. The noise on the line was now hardly noticeable.

"No. I'm okay." For a moment she considered asking Alette about the hand in her dream. But no, then she'd have to discuss with Alette the rest of it—her distress at not being able to attend Eric's funeral; her insane desire to approach his family—and she most certainly did not want to discuss Eric with Alette. The last time they had talked about him the discussion had deteriorated into a row. Alette had not approved of Eric. "He doesn't even make a pretense of ever leaving his wife," she had said vehemently. "Thirteen years you've given him. How could you do this to yourself?"

That conversation had taken place three months ago; only ten days before Eric's death.

Isa repeated the words to herself silently: Eric's death. Eric was dead. Death. Such a tired, dusty word. It hovered on the lips like a poisoned sigh.

"Isabelle . . . Isabelle, I may have to ask a favor of you . . ."

"What is it?"

"I've always been able to count on you."

"Yes?" Isa wondered where this was going. She pressed the phone close to her ear. The noise was picking up again.

"Can I count on you—will you promise me that if I need you, I can count on you?"

Isa frowned. "You should know the answer to that."

"Watch out . . ." Alette was talking, but her words were fading in and out. Something about fear, Isa thought, about being afraid. Something about danger.

Isa spoke loudly and deliberately into the receiver. "Alette, I'm losing you. I'm hanging up. I'll call you right back."

She didn't wait for an answer. She replaced the receiver briefly and then started to dial Alette's number in London.

She listened for the first loud click that always follows the country code, then the second click after she had dialed the code for London. While dialing, she cradled the phone in her neck and picked up the wine bottle from the bedside table. It was almost empty. She never used to drink by herself.

The phone was ringing in her ear. No one picked up. Isa waited, baffled. If Alette wasn't at her home, where had she called from at this time of the morning? The phone kept on ringing. No one answered.

She slowly replaced the receiver. Maybe Alette would call back. If not, she'd have to try calling her again later.

She yawned. Yes. Later. Turning onto her side, she pulled the pillow into her arms and closed her eyes.

When she opened her eyes again the pink sky had turned to blue. The two weaver birds outside her window were engaged in a noisy marital spat. She reached for the robe at the foot end of the bed. The robe was thick; too heavy to wear at this time of the year. Even this early in the morning the air was already soft with heat and humidity. But the robe was his robe. She needed to feel it against her skin before facing the day. She rubbed the flannel between her fingers. It had his smell on it still.

As she got to her feet, she saw herself reflected in the tall standing mirror next to her closet. The robe was too wide for her, she could wrap it around her almost twice, but otherwise it was a good fit. She was thin, almost hipless, but she was tall and had broad shoulders for a woman. As a child she had felt ashamed of her skinniness and her height: she had been the tallest by far in her class. She remembered the first time she had met Alette. They were both thirteen, but Isa had almost reached her full height. She felt unattractive, clumsy.

"Why, she's a giraffe." Those were Alette's first words upon being introduced to her lanky cousin. And then, "Don't slouch,

Isabelle. Don't you know how important it is for a woman to carry herself well?"

Blinking back fierce tears, Isa had glowered at her smiling, pretty, red-haired cousin. But she had taken Alette's advice, as she would take her advice in so many other things over the years. She taught herself not to stoop and to walk with more confidence. She developed a sense of style: severe but chic. She never outgrew her shyness, though, her natural reserve—but a smart jacket, a classy haircut: these had become her defenses.

The mirror glimmered white in the half-light. Isa drew the cord of the dressing gown tight around her waist. The woman in the mirror repeated the action. A woman with black hair cut mannishly short. Wide mouth. Gray eyes under straight brows. Outwardly composed and sure of herself. Her hands a dead giveaway with their raw nails bitten to the quick.

She turned the knob of the bedroom door and stepped out into the living room. This room smelled stuffy and airless. Dust motes flickered in the broad wedges of light falling through the panes of the window. She opened the French doors that led onto the patio garden, and as the doors swung wide, the scent of honeysuckle drifted inside.

For a moment she paused beside the two chairs drawn up next to each other in front of the television set. She leaned over and plumped up the crimson pillow on the one chair. She left the other chair as it was with its seat cushion sagging, the indentation of a head still clear against the top of the down-filled headrest.

It was an old chair with an old-fashioned footstool. The fabric had been expensive when she had had it covered almost twelve years ago: a Clarence House silk, imported from England. It wasn't really the right kind of fabric for a chair that took a lot of wear. The silk was now shiny with age and starting to fray. But she had bought it because of Eric. He had picked it out himself. It was an odd choice for him; he was very much a corduroy-and-tweed man. But he had liked the feel and texture of the rose-tinted material: "like water." And then he had claimed this chair as his chair, flopping into it with a satisfied air of ownership whenever he visited. She'd get on his lap, curling her long legs beneath her as if she were just a little girl, while he stroked her hair and touched her face. It was a ritual. Just the two of them sitting there together for the longest time, simply holding on to each other, not speaking. And then he'd cup her face in his hands and ask with the formality of a first-time lover: "May I kiss you?"

Eric.

She placed her hand on her breast. Oh. Her heart was sagging. She could feel it tilting slowly; dragging, dragging at her chest and her heart was so heavy.

Such pain. Such terrible pain.

The parking bay at the end of the row was still empty. Obviously Eric's colleagues were still battling it out as to who was going to get that coveted space. Isa pulled her car into a bay close to the elevator.

She had applied more makeup than usual that morning. Bathing her eyes in cold water hadn't really helped either. She kept her dark glasses on after she got out of the car.

It was a small building, housing only a start-up computer company, a publishing house dealing in purple romances, Eric's accounting firm, and her own office. Since Eric's death, she had been thinking of moving, of starting fresh somewhere else. Somewhere she wouldn't unconsciously listen for his footstep on the floor above her; wait for him to casually bump into her in the elevator or car park. She should make an effort to get on with her life. But she seemed to have no energy, no energy at all. It was too easy to give herself up to a kind of mental drift. She was unable—

maybe unwilling—to free herself from the flaccid but relentless grip of lethargy. She went to bed tired; she woke up tired.

Isa pushed open the glass doors on which the words ISA DE WITT INTERIORS: ARCHITECT AND DECORATOR were stenciled in black letters. Cindy, her secretary cum receptionist, had the phone to her ear and a resigned expression on her face. When she saw Isa walk in, she rolled her eyes and made a cutting motion across her throat.

"Who is it?"

Cindy placed her hand over the receiver: "Mrs. Marais."

Isa sighed. "Let me talk to her."

She wasn't looking forward to the conversation. Anna Marais was a client who took up a lot of time and energy. As a favor to one of her other clients, Isa had taken her on: redesigning and redecorating the woman's bedroom for her. But there always seemed to be something wrong. The trim on the curtain was not the exact shade of mink Mrs. Marais had stipulated. The builders were rude to her and would have to be replaced. The chest of drawers that was delivered to her house yesterday showed a scratch and why hadn't Isa come herself instead of sending her assistant?

The woman was more trouble than she was worth and Isa had yet to get a check out of her for services already rendered. But she forced herself to keep her voice even. Yes, she would stop by today to take a look at the bureau and yes, she could assure Mrs. Marais that the work would be done well before the start of the Christmas holidays.

A large design easel was situated in front of the window on the far side of the room. Isa walked over and for a few minutes she looked at the sketches for the De Vere project. The skylight in the entrance hall was too small: maybe she should splay it out at angles to make the volume appear larger. And she still wasn't happy with the client's preference for a large, round-headed window in the living room: it was all wrong for the visual drama created by the other slim, twelve-foot floor-to-ceiling windows. Still, this was the kind of project she enjoyed, creating a space from scratch; not having to fuss and fumble with ill-proportioned rooms devoid of light and symmetry.

Turning her back on the sketches, she moved closer to the window. The view from here was not inspiring: industrial warehouses with dust-covered windows and corrugated iron roofs. But if she looked down the narrow opening between the two unlovely buildings opposite, she could see the fierce blue water of the Indian Ocean. At the moment the ocean looked like a painted strip of color, but later in the day the sun will beat down with such frenzy that the blue would splinter into a million blinding, diamond sparkles. Isa opened the window and breathed in the peculiar smell she associated so strongly with the city of Durban and its harbor: a hushed smell; a smell of salt, musk, and secret decay.

She glanced at her watch. Maybe she should try calling Alette again. It would be almost noon in London. But just as she stretched out her hand to the receiver, the phone buzzed sharply.

"A call from London," Cindy said in her ear.

Isa smiled. "Put her through."

"It's a him. A Mr. Darling. He's says he's a solicitor."

The name was unfamiliar to Isa. A solicitor?

The voice that came on the line was very British. Very Received Pronunciation English: the cut-glass accents of the upper classes. The words were uttered neatly, precisely, and they shattered her world.

"I'm so sorry to have to convey the news to you over the telephone," Mr. Darling said. "I did not myself know of the accident until after Mrs. Temple passed away. As executor of her estate . . ." His voice carried on and on, but Isa didn't hear him. Accident.

Alette has had an accident. Only a few hours ago they had spoken together on the phone and since then . . .

"I don't understand." Isa's tongue felt heavy in her mouth. "She's an excellent driver. What happened?"

He coughed. "A wicked stretch of road, that. Very easy to lose control of the wheel. And she wasn't wearing her seat belt." He paused delicately. "As I was saying, Miss de Witt, I do believe it would be of great help if you could fly over to London for the reading of the will. I can tell you now that you are the sole beneficiary. . ."

Eric. Now Alette. She placed her hand to her mouth, and when she took it away a long, sticky string of saliva clung to her palm.

"Miss de Witt? Are you there?"

She forced herself to speak. "Go to London? Why should I go to London?"

"Well, she left you the house and you might like to take a look at it before deciding on how to proceed. It is still on a long lease, you know. Sixty years, fifty-three unexpired," he added. "Furthermore . . ." He paused and she could hear him take a deep breath. "Furthermore there is a quite unusual clause in the will, which would require you to be in town."

Cold, she was cold. She placed her one arm over her chest, hugging herself.

"What clause?"

"Really, it is rather difficult to explain and it is not something I would care to discuss on the telephone. It would be much better if we could meet face-to-face. I thought as Christmas is almost upon us, you might be able to break away perhaps? Would it be a great inconvenience to fly over?

"Is there anything important keeping you in South Africa right now?" he tried again when she did not respond.

Isa thought of the bottom drawer in her closet: boxer shorts and T-shirts and socks rolled into neat bundles. White handkerchiefs and a pair of cuff links. She thought of his toothbrush in the cup on the top shelf in the bathroom. She thought of what it would be like to simply switch off the light and pull the door shut behind her.

"No. There's nothing keeping me here."

"Are you all right, Miss de Witt?" The solicitor's voice was tinged with genuine concern.

"It's just . . . I spoke to Alette only this morning."

There was a long pause. The solicitor spoke slowly, warily. "Miss de Witt, I'm afraid you must be mistaken. You could not have spoken to Mrs. Temple today. Mrs. Temple died two days ago."

TWO

Quit, quit, for shame, this will not move,
This will not take her;
If of her selfe she will not Love,
Nothing can make her:
The Devill take her.

—"Song,"

Sir John Suckling (1609–1642)

THE GROUND WAS SOAKED WITH THE RAIN OF THE PAST WEEK. AS HE
let himself into the front garden, his shoes sank deeply into the wet
mulch of leaves and dirt. He didn't close the small, black gate
behind him. That gate always creaked on the back swing, and
though it was late and not one window in that entire street of terraced houses showed a light, he did not want to take a chance on
waking any of the neighbors.

A gust of wind shook the branches of the tree above him and a
spatter of wet drops chilled the back of his neck. He moved closer
to the house, looking up at the pale, uncurtained window on the
top story where her bedroom was.

For a moment he felt his breath catch—he could have sworn he saw something moving up there: shadow on glass. But then he shook his head and blinked deliberately. No. He must stop this. It was over. She was gone.

The spare key should still be in its usual hiding place behind the loose brick, guarded by the climbing hybrid musk roses. There were no roses in bloom now: just a tangle of tough stems. But come summer, he knew, the pink and apricot buds of "Buff Beauty" and "Cornelia" would scent the garden with a dreamy fragrance.

Roses had been her passion. And she loved the old varieties: "Gypsy Boy," "Grüss an Aachen," "Madame Isaac Pereire." "The most sweet-smelling rose in the world," she'd say, her red hair pushed up underneath the wide straw hat, the large pruning scissors moving through the foliage with unsentimental vigor. She believed in cutting back the roses hard, so hard that he had protested. But she merely laughed at his concern. "You have to be cruel to be kind. If you give it a good pruning now, you'll see. It will reward you with hundreds of blooms in years to come."

Cruel to be kind. Those were the exact words that had gone through his mind during the service. Cruel to be kind. Nip in the bud. Close the book. Drop the curtain.

Put the lid on.

He smiled. His fingers searched in the hollow behind the brick and withdrew the two keys tied to each other by a simple piece of string. For a moment he stood staring at the keys, absentmindedly wiping away the dirt clinging to them, his mind still on the service. He had never been to a cremation before, hadn't quite known what to expect. But it had all been done very tastefully. He was a little surprised at how few people there were. Two of the neighbors, some clients, a woman she had befriended at her aerobics class—and that man, of course.

At the end of the service the funeral director had asked them all to sign the funeral book. In a cramped fist Alette's neighbor had written in the comments column: *I will never forget her smile. God bless.* He had written two words only: *Precious dust.* His epitaph for her. It amused him to think that she had read these very words only a few minutes before the crash. And what a delicious irony that her epitaph should be words from an elegy written for a woman who had lived more than three hundred and fifty years ago: a chaste woman, a woman of virtue: "*filia praemortua prima Virgineam animam exhalavit.*" A woman with a virginal mind. Whereas Alette had been a slut. Wanton and hard of heart, to borrow a phrase of his mother's. In no way like the sainted Maria Wentworth, who died in 1632, and of whom could be said, ". . . a Virgin, yet a Bride / To every Grace, she justifi'd / A chaste Poligamie, and dy'd."

He placed the key in the lock and turned it noiselessly. He wasn't going to disturb anything. He merely wanted to touch her things. Maybe lie in her bed for a brief moment, touch his cheek to her pillow. It would be his own private way of saying good-bye to her. A small act of self-indulgence.

THREE

She, she is dead; she's dead; when thou know'st this,
Thou know'st how wan a ghost this our world is.

"The Anniversaries,"

John Donne (1572–1631)

THE PRE-CHRISTMAS RUSH CAUSED MOST FLIGHTS FROM SOUTH
Africa to England to be fully booked. Isa was unable to get a direct
flight to the UK and had to settle for a connecting flight via
Frankfurt. This would have worked out fine, allowing her to
arrive late morning in London, but her plane was delayed before
takeoff from Johannesburg and she missed her connection. She
arrived at Heathrow sore and weary to the bone; seriously wondering whether the whole trip was a huge mistake. By the time she
had struggled through the long line at immigrations and retrieved
her luggage, the watery sunshine that had greeted the plane on its
arrival had disappeared. Isa emerged from the airport building into
a chilly, dark blue dusk.

She pushed herself into the corner of the roomy backseat of the
taxicab and buttoned her coat up to her chin. The cold weather
was a shock to the system after the moist heat she had left behind

in Durban. The cabdriver, fortunately, was not the chatty type. After asking her for the address, he closed the small window behind his head and she could hear, very faintly, the sound of his radio: Bob Dylan knocking on heaven's door and sounding indescribably weary.

Alette's cremation had taken place two days before. She had told Mr. Darling to go ahead with the service and not to wait for her arrival. At the time she wasn't sure when she'd be able to get a flight out, and truth to be told, wasn't she looking for an excuse not to be there? After Eric's death she had longed to be part of a ceremony; a ritual. But with Alette . . . no.

Tomorrow she was to meet with Mr. Darling at his offices. She wondered if he was feeling apprehensive about meeting her. Poor man. He probably thinks he has a nutcase on his hands after listening to her telling him of her phone conversation with a person who had died forty-eight hours before.

After learning from him of Alette's death, she had immediately contacted the phone company and had, with the greatest difficulty, persuaded them to check on whether she had received an incoming call in the early morning hours. There was no record that such a call had been placed.

Outside it had started to rain. Drops of water, stretched into impossibly long pear-shaped streaks, clung for a brief moment to the windows of the cab before being blown away by the wind. She really was extremely tired. So tired that she did not properly take in the rain-swept road, the yellow smears of headlights. With a faint start of recognition, though, she identified the rectangular bulk of Buckingham Palace. She had always thought of it as a place constantly flooded with festive light, but tonight the building was dark. And then the taxi was leaving the busy main street, turning and twisting; weaving through tiny, narrow streets lined with terraced houses and red-brick mansion blocks. She caught a brief glimpse of the cold gleam of the Thames before the taxi driver stopped the car in front of a dark house. With a cheery, "Here you are, then, love," he helped her unload her suitcase. Isa watched the black cab until its tiny orange taillights disappeared from view. She turned to face the house in front of her.

It was a narrow, terraced house on three floors, sharing its party walls with two identical-looking houses on either side of it. Alette once told her that all the houses in this street had been built in the thirties. Their facades were simple and uncluttered, with no decorative flourishes: no cast-iron fencing, no white-and-cream stucco pillars like the period houses Isa had noticed on her way in. But the street was tree-lined—probably delightful in summer—and every house seemed to have the luxury of a small front garden that set it back from the road. At the moment, though, the soft, sifting rain gave the street a forlorn, abandoned air.

Isa had never visited Alette in this house. The last time she was in London was five years ago for Alette's wedding and by then Alette was already living with Justin. It was only after the divorce that Alette moved to this place. There was talk of Isa flying over for a visit—helping out with the refurbishment—but somehow that never happened. At the time Isa hadn't felt confident enough to be away from her office. Her business was not yet established and was balanced on that precarious edge between success and sudden collapse. And then there was Eric. Their life together could be measured in stolen hours over lunch or after work: passion and desire and togetherness squeezed into small, furtive chunks of time. The idea of leaving him for two or three weeks had been unthinkable.

And the years went by. And every year over Christmas they'd tell each other that yes, this was the year they really had to get together. But they never did. And now she hadn't seen Alette in five years. And now it was too late.

The tiny black gate stood wide open. Isa walked through and pushed it shut. It creaked dismally and she shivered slightly at the wet feel of the wrought iron against her palm. She walked up the small front garden, tripping a little over some broken flagstones; her suitcase dragging in her hand. As she climbed up the two shallow steps leading to the front door, she started to rummage in her shoulder bag for the keys. The super-efficient Mr. Darling had had them couriered to her in South Africa.

The locks were oiled and the keys turned without any trouble. The door swung open into darkness. Keeping the door open with her shoulder so that the entrance hall could be lit by the feeble light of an outside lamppost, Isa groped against the wall in search of a light switch.

The light came on. She blinked for a moment in the sudden, bright-edged glare. Moving away from the door, she allowed it to swing softly shut behind her.

As in most London houses, the hall was narrow, opening up immediately into a balustraded staircase leading to the second story. A rear door, which she assumed led to the kitchen, was directly ahead of her. On the console table flanking the left wall was a bamboo tray with some unopened letters. On the right-hand wall were mounted hooks from which hung an array of scarves, hats, and jackets.

One hook only was empty. Isa thought of Alette running down the stairs; casually pulling a coat from that hook, selecting a matching scarf. Then stepping outside and closing the door. And never thinking that she would not again return to her house.

Cold; it was bone-chillingly cold. Isa placed her hand against a wall-mounted radiator. It was icy to the touch: the central heating had been switched off. She reached for the round knob of the thermostat that was set into the wall and turned it all the way up.

Ignoring the closed door to the rear, she started to mount the stairs. Her feet made no sound on the dark blue carpeted runners. Alette loved comfort. She craved thick carpets, soft rugs, cashmere throws: opulence and luxury. Isa's own taste was more minimalist. She dreaded clutter; abhorred fussy walls and floors. But as she walked through the tall, graceful doors of Alette's living room, the chandelier bursting into a shower of gold above her head, she had to admit that Alette's love of lavishly layered patterns and textures made the room appear like some exquisite jewel box.

The down sofas were covered in an overblown rose-printed fabric. Cushions in a variety of stripes, checks, and patterns, ranging in color from sweetest strawberry to deepest aubergine, were scattered throughout the room. Throws in a muted mossy green were draped over the backs and arms of the deep-buttoned chairs. Seagrass mats, ruggedly tactile, rubbed against a soft-piled Oriental rug. An eye-catching lacquer screen with a wild profusion of birds and flowers gleamed in the one corner of the room. On the mantelpiece was a charming, enameled carriage clock and next to it a big ten-by-six studio photograph of Alette.

And there were books. Books everywhere. Books lining the walls; books piled on every available surface. Novels. Nonfiction. Volume upon volume of poetry. Each of those books, Isa knew, would bear in its margins evidence that Alette had pored through its pages. Alette never read a book without a pencil in her hand. She scribbled in the margins, underlined and circled words; annotated every book she read with her own private thoughts. There was a time when she had stopped borrowing books from Alette, because reading a book of Alette's made for a very different experience than reading it in its virgin form—simple black on white— unsullied by any of Alette's scribbles and asides.

A soft, thudding sound—more felt than heard—made Isa turn her head to one side and listen. She walked out of the room and onto the landing and peered over the balustrade to the floor down below.

After a moment she straightened slowly. It was probably just an echo from one of the radiators. Since turning on the heat, she had been aware of the odd, clanging noise as the radiators throughout the house started to fire up.

She suddenly noticed the bleak stare of the uncurtained windows at the end of the passage. But when she tugged at the elaborately swagged drapes, they remained fixed. These curtains were for show, they would not close. As she turned around and started to walk up the last flight of stairs, she wondered at the self-assured ease of a city that allowed the people who lived within it to live their lives without shuttering themselves from outside eyes. She had noticed this on her previous visit to London as well. Everywhere you looked, the windows were uncurtained; families living their lives in full view of any passerby who'd care to stop and watch. So unlike home. In South Africa windows were covered by thick drapes at night, and veiled by day with opaque voiles. Fear made people withdraw behind high walls and live in rooms where they were followed by the blinking red eye of alarm systems on standby.

The door to Alette's bedroom was closed and the catch was stiff. She had to rattle the handle and put her shoulder to the door before it would open.

The first thing she noticed was the scent in the air: rose and patchouli. *Rosa abyssinica,* to be precise. A fragrant rose from Ethiopia. Alette used it for potpourri. *To remind me of Africa,* she had once written to Isa in a letter. *I am surrounded by all these English beauties, but I need an African rose to remind me of home.*

Isa moved toward the bed to where she could see the outline of a lamp in the gloom. Her fingers groped, found the switch. Soft light reached out and touched the walls.

This room was unabashedly romantic. A huge four-poster bed, extravagantly hung with some soft, white, diaphanous material, dominated the room. The bed was made, but she could see the imprint of a body on the subtly textured fabric of the bedspread. One of the pillows had been removed from underneath the bed-spread and placed on top. The soft down was dented in the middle where a head had rested.

On the bedside table stood many, many photographs in silver frames, but Isa did not allow her eyes to more than skim over the images. She recognized herself in two of the pictures, but she wasn't yet ready for a full inspection. She would leave that for the next day when there was sunlight in the room and few shadows.

An old-fashioned dressing table stood in the corner. The silvered texture of the mirror was flattering to the viewer—it smoothed out imperfections, muted bruises under the eyes. But to Isa the sight of her own face seemed wrong inside that gleaming reflection. The face of another woman used to look out from its depths: a face surrounded by red curls; long tendrils like the hair of those sublimely feminine figures in a Burne-Jones or Rossetti painting. Proserpine; Lady Lilith. Isa imagined Alette sitting on this kidney-shaped stool, impatiently twisting her thick hair into a French twist, her mouth full of pins. And then picking up the heavy, embossed hand mirror to examine her profile; the long-lidded eyes softening contentedly.

In this room, too, there were books. One entire wall filled with them. But the books in this room reflected Alette's preoccupation with mystical phenomena. There were books on tarot reading, the interpretation of tea leaves; books on premonitions, omens, symbols, psychic powers. Books on the occult and paranormal. Books on African rituals and mystical ceremonies.

Spread-eagled on the seat of the one armchair in the room was a book, which Alette must have been in the process of reading. Isa was just leaning forward to pick it up, when that indefinable feeling of being watched prickled the skin on her arms. She turned her head and looked out the back window. On the top floor of the apartment block opposite, a figure—a male figure—was clearly outlined against the yellow light streaming through the window. He was looking straight at her. Just as her brain registered the figure, the light in the window was abruptly switched off. But she had the feeling that the figure was still there, still watching from within that dark oblong.

At least Alette's bedroom had curtains that could be drawn tight. Isa yanked the drapes closed, shutting out the presence of the watcher outside. But she felt unnerved. She looked toward the other end of the room. She'd better close the curtains in those front windows as well.

This window looked out onto the street where the taxi had dropped her off earlier tonight. The houses opposite were one story shorter than Alette's house. She was able to see clear over their roofs to where the spires of a church stood elaborately fretted against the night sky. There was a light on inside the church and the stained-glass windows glimmered with purple-and-green prisms and diamond squares of ruby. It should have been comforting: the dark, patient shape of the church—black against the lesser blackness of the sky—but it wasn't. As she watched it seemed to her as though the windows were starting to glow with a demented energy. Even after she had drawn the curtains; even after she had remade the bed with some fresh linen she had found in the closet and had slid between the cool sheets, even then; the image of that glittering window stayed with her: a bloody jewel invading her dreams.

FOUR

Yet Lord, instruct us so to die,
That all these dyings may be life in death.
> —"Mortification,"
> George Herbert (1593–1633)

Isa woke up feeling disoriented. She struggled upright from amid the welter of pillows and grabbed for the alarm clock, suddenly panicked that she had missed her appointment with Mr. Darling. But it was only eight A.M.

She padded barefoot to the back window and drew away the drapes. It had stopped raining and the sky was a watery blue. Isa looked up at the corner window on the top floor of the small apartment block across the street. She almost expected to see the same figure staring at her from the window, but there was no one there. From where she stood, she could make out a lofty ceiling and some brightly colored curtains tucked to the side. She turned away. In the light of day her apprehensions of the night before seemed silly.

Her suitcase lay open, its contents spilling out in disarray. She had been so tired the previous evening that she hadn't bothered unpacking. She had simply grabbed her toiletries and nightdress after a quick shower in the tiny attached bathroom. But this morning she felt like taking a proper bath. There was another bathroom farther along the passage, and like every other room in the house, it was sumptuous. Wheat-colored Egyptian-cotton towels were stacked neatly on top of each other on the seat of a wicker chair. Highly scented oils in silver-stoppered glass bottles were arranged on the washing table.

Isa sank into the hot water. As she lay looking at Alette's silk robe hooked to the back of the door, she tried not to feel like an intruder. But she couldn't help it; it was like breaching a private sanctuary. She could never see herself living here. Alette's presence was so strong.

She wasn't sure what to wear. She finally settled on a gray suit with black pumps: elegant, reserved. Mourning. The solicitor would expect that. She glanced at her watch. She was going to have to hurry.

She walked quickly down the two flights of stairs. In the hallway she hesitated: the rear door was slightly open. She could have sworn it was closed when she arrived here last night. But maybe she was mistaken. This was the one room in the house she had not yet explored. She leaned her shoulder against the door and pushed it fully open, almost tripping over a pair of mud-caked Wellingtons parked right inside the door. As she expected, it was the kitchen cum dining room. Or rather office. Upstairs, in Alette's bedroom, was an exquisite, antique Regency writing desk of coromandel wood inlaid with ivory, but it was clear that Alette had used this sturdy dining table as her real place of work. On top of the table were a closed laptop computer, stacks of papers, an in and out tray. A box of tissues and a telephone. An iron gimbal swung from a butcher's hook dangling from the ceiling. Inside the window hung a wind chime, its five chimes deadened by a thin, silver restraining chain wrapped around their base.

Isa rifled through the papers on the table. They all seemed to be letters that Alette was planning to send out to her clients: a small, select group of extremely wealthy people. Alette ran a tiny but very lucrative business of "interpreting the future": fortune-telling, not to put too fine a point on it. It was all done in very good taste: no crystal balls and gypsy head scarves, only a lightly scented piece of notepaper forwarded once a month to some very exclusive London addresses. Alette had been quite cynical about the whole enterprise. "I tell many of them only what they want to hear," she used to say. "That's what they pay me for. They won't thank me for anything else and they can't handle anything else, anyway." Alette was a pragmatist, always had been. Isa remembered Alette as a young girl, reading the tea leaves for the blue-haired ladies of her mother's knitting bee. "Do you really believe in all that stuff?" Isa had asked her. Alette's answer was: "It's not whether I believe; it's whether they do."

Isa was aware that there were people who, although admiring of Alette's business instincts and her razor-fine intuition, dismissed her as a master manipulator. Isa knew there was more to it than that. Alette had a gift. Isa had seen it at work. Catching sight of it was like witnessing that fleeting moment when flint strikes fire from stone.

Isa pushed the letters to one side and turned away from the table. All these people would have to be contacted and informed of Alette's death. Or maybe they already knew. She'd have to ask Mr. Darling about it. She stepped into the kitchen area and opened the yellow fridge. There was a champagne bottle, half-full, with a ragged piece of paper towel stuck into its neck, and on the bottom shelf a Marks & Spencer ready-prepared dish still untouched in its original wrapping: duck à l'orange and well past the sell-by date stamped on the cover. Next to it was a tray of chocolates. One of the chocolates had been bitten in half and then discarded. The sight of the food was disturbing, but still she felt herself smile. The discarded piece of candy looked like a chocolate-covered toffee. Alette preferred soft centers.

She straightened. She'd have to get rid of the food, but there was no time for it now. She wasn't sure how long it would take her to reach Mr. Darling's office and she'd rather be early than late. She hoisted her handbag over her shoulder and picked up her coat. As she left the house she carefully shut the door and made sure to lock both the top and bottom locks.

She managed to hail a cab almost immediately as she stepped into the street. The cabdriver identified her accent without any trouble and took it upon himself to point out the sights as they drove down the Embankment, the slate-gray water of the Thames on their right. Isa dutifully nodded as he gestured at the cob-webby outlines of the Albert and Chelsea bridges, the Oxo Tower, and the South Bank Centre: monument to an architect's sad love affair with concrete. Sometimes she thought her profes-sion should adopt some adapted version of the Hippocratic oath: *First, do no harm.*

At any other time she would have enjoyed the tour, replied to the taxi driver's comments with more kindness and interest, but the tension inside her was rising. Up till now she had not thought too much about the upcoming meeting; had not allowed herself to speculate on what it was that was so sensitive that Mr. Darling would not discuss it with her on the phone. But she was just about to find out.

Once inside the warren of tiny streets close to St. Paul's Cathedral, traffic stalled. When the cabdriver finally deposited her at the entrance to a stone building, the time of her appointment was less than five minutes away. Although the facade of the build-ing was imposing and although Isa knew that Alette would make sure of the very best legal representation, the long, dingy corridors leading to Mr. Darling's door were unimpressive. The occupants of this building were obviously united in their distaste of any ostentatious display of wealth and influence: a kind of inverse snobbery that nevertheless made a very definite statement.

Mr. Darling's office itself was positively Dickensian in its decor, with flocked wallpaper and tired curtains edged with grime. Mr. Darling, though, was a surprise. Tall, tanned, and blond, he looked like an Australian surfer. His smile was easy and he used it often. His manner as he offered her a seat and a cup of coffee was decidedly laid-back despite the public school accent and meticulous phrasing. After asking her a few polite questions about her trip, he opened the drawer and took out a thick file in a green folder.

Isa had half expected him to read the will out loud to her, as in a detective story, but he merely handed her a slim document threaded through on the spine with a blue ribbon. "You can read this later at your leisure," he informed her, "and then, if you have any questions I shall be happy to answer them. In short, I can tell you that Mrs. Temple left you all of her possessions. You are her sole heir. It is a not inconsiderable estate, even without the house. She's made some very shrewd investments over the years and she recently sold all her shares in her former husband's company. She still received maintenance from him—that, of course, will now cease."

Isa looked at him directly. "When exactly did Alette draw up her will?"

"She first came to my office three months ago. She was very insistent that the will be drawn up as soon as possible. I do not want to upset you, but she seemed to think that there would very soon be call for the existence of such a document. It's almost as if she had a . . . a premonition." He flushed slightly, as though he had uttered a remark in poor taste.

"You said the road where she had the crash was a dangerous one?"

"Certainly in bad weather, yes. And the road conditions were exceptionally poor that night. Fog. Ice on the road."

"I can't understand what she was doing there."

"I do know," he replied unexpectedly. He hesitated and then continued slowly, obviously picking his words with care. "She told me she had . . . business . . . to discuss with her former husband. Mr. Temple was visiting his mother at the time and she drove out to the north coast of Devon to meet with him."

The way in which he hesitated before saying the word "business" made Isa wonder, but before she could pursue the matter, he continued, his voice suddenly brisk. "Anyway, Mrs. Temple left very detailed instructions for her funeral, which, I assure you, I have followed to the letter. She stipulated that she wanted to be cremated and she wished to be buried along with"—he paused and picked up a sheet of paper from which he read painstakingly—"two African idols—a male and a female figure—carved from Cape Stinkwood, dating from the late nineteenth century."

Mr. Darling lowered the paper and looked at Isa. "She actually left the carvings in my possession when she came in to sign the will. I kept them in my safe."

Isa leaned forward. "These figures, were they very smooth, very polished, both about twenty inches high?"

He nodded. "Indeed. Are you familiar with them?"

"Yes." Isa did not elaborate but she remembered them well. They were made from a very tough wood; darkly patinated by the touch of many hands over many, many years. The two dolls represented "spirit marriage partners." They had been a gift to Alette from Siena, Alette's former nanny. Siena had explained that they were symbols of the perfect union between man and woman and of a love that happens only once in life. Actually, she had been present when Siena had given Alette the little idols. And after all these years she was still able to recall the cool gloom of Siena's room; the smell of the Zambuk ointment that Siena used to rub into her body. Siena handing Alette the wooden carvings. The skin of Siena's hands so black it seemed almost blue but her palms pink as a rose. She also remembered vividly, and with embarrassment, her jealousy as Siena handed the dolls to Alette while she, Isa, stood by, receiving nothing. Many years later Alette would give the dolls to Justin as her wedding gift.

She opened her eyes to see Mr. Darling looking at her rather anxiously. She'd better watch it. He already thought she was slightly unbalanced.

"You should also take this with you." He withdrew an over-size manila envelope and handed it to her. As she took it from him, she could feel the outline of something square and hard against her fingers.

"What is it?" She withdrew the contents: a large book covered in fake leather and a brass box.

"It's the, um, ashes." He gestured awkwardly at the box. "And this—he tapped the cover of the album—"is the funeral book. I thought you might like to have it."

She opened the book. The names were unfamiliar to her. The remarks in the comments column seemed awkward and self-conscious: *We'll miss her; A darling girl; May she rest in peace.* On the very last line someone had printed in block letters: PRECIOUS DUST. The words were unaccompanied by a signature.

"Was Alette's ex-husband present?"

He coughed. "Yes. Mr. Temple attended the ceremony."

Isa skimmed through the handwritten names. Justin had not signed the book.

She closed the album carefully. "You said there was an unusual clause in the will, which you needed to discuss with me in person."

"Yes." He seemed reluctant to continue. When he spoke his voice was hesitant. "Miss de Witt, I have to stress that you are not legally obliged to follow the instructions set out in this clause. If you decide against it, it will in no way affect your status as the heir. You will still receive the full inheritance. This last clause is in the form of a request. But Mrs. Temple seemed very sure that you would accede to her wishes."

He opened the green folder again and took out another, but medium-size, manila envelope from it. "Once a week, for the next three weeks, I am supposed to give you one of these." He slid the envelope across to her. Her name was printed in the center of the envelope and at the top right-hand corner were the words *First Envelope.*

"No, please don't open it here." He stopped her as she made to open it. "I myself have no knowledge of the contents and Mrs. Temple was adamant that the information within should be strictly between you and her." He rubbed his hands together in a Pontius Pilate gesture, as though to absolve himself of all responsibility.

Isa looked at the envelope in her hands. Alette had certainly made sure that no one else would be able to open it. Not even her attorney. The flap was not only sealed with blue wax, but the wax held in place a label on which Alette had signed her name. Anyone opening the letter would automatically tear through the signature.

She looked back at Lionel Darling. "Why not give me all the envelopes now? I'm leaving for South Africa again as soon as I've found an estate agent to take care of the house and—"

"Unfortunately, that would create somewhat of a problem. Mrs. Temple stipulated that you were to receive the envelopes one by one in the order specified. She also indicated that she would like you to remain in London for the next month. She said it would simplify the entire process. Although, if you absolutely had to return to South Africa, she seemed to think that you might still manage to follow the instructions—or rather requests—contained within these letters."

Isa stared at him. "Well . . ." her voice faded. She fingered the envelope. "Maybe I should read it first."

"Yes, I suspect that would be best. No doubt the letter will clear up everything. But as I said, she seemed very sure that you would comply with her wishes?" The solicitor's voice ended in a question, leaving the observation hanging in the air.

Isa looked up to meet Lionel Darling's puzzled eyes.

"We were close," she said.

THE COFFEE SHOP WAS CROWDED AND OVERHEATED. STEAM PEARLED down the inside of the dirty windows. The only empty table was squashed into a corner next to a coat stand weighed down by countless coats and jackets.

But even in an unglamorous little place like this, they knew how to serve a good cup of tea. A friendly waitress brought her a pot of tea brewed with proper tea leaves. Isa sipped the warm liquid slowly. In front of her on the table was the still-sealed manila envelope. She was reluctant to open it.

She finished her tea and looked into the cup. She wondered what Alette would have made of the pattern of tea leaves at the bottom. Surely that cluster of leaves clinging to the side formed an anchor—or was it an hourglass? What did the hourglass stand for again? Imminent peril or some such nonsense. Maybe it was an anchor after all. That at least would signify constancy in love.

Isa tilted the cup. It was no use anyway. The cup had almost perpendicular sides, which made it unsuitable for leaf reading. She replaced it in its saucer and pushed it to the far side of the table. It was time she faced the envelope.

She slid her forefinger underneath the flap and the waxed seal split and broke and Alette's signature deteriorated into two fragments. Isa placed her hand inside and drew out the sheaf of papers fastened with a simple paper clip.

The letter was written in Alette's sloping hand and started off without an address or date at the top:

Dear Isabelle,

First, the ashes. I hope you're not totally spooked, but this is what I'd like you to do. Take the urn or vase or whatever it is they use, and when you return to South Africa, take me with you. I want to go home; I mean really home. I crave a truly blue sky. I don't want the sun to shine, I want it to burn. I long for a landscape that is wild, not manicured. Please strew my ashes on the farm—in the cleft of the great Yoni stone—you remember: Siena's secret place.

Oh, Isabelle. Where to begin. I am going to ask a favor of you: a big one and you probably won't like what I'm asking, but hear me out, please.

My life over the past three years has been a horror. Actually, make that five years, because the story really starts on my wedding day. You remember that day, don't you? White veils and lace and Justin looking so handsome.

I had such high hopes, Isabelle. I thought I had finally found a man who truly understood me, who loved me for who I am. A man to grow old by my side, someone who can go the distance.

But things started to go wrong almost immediately. Justin became insanely possessive. His jealousy was a fearful thing. I felt as though I were under constant surveillance: he was always checking to find out where I was, calling me from his office obsessively. If he couldn't get ahold of me right away, he'd start calling my friends and clients. He was smothering me; sometimes it felt as though he was sucking the very oxygen from the air. If I so much as looked at another man he flew into terrible rages. He was convinced that I was being unfaithful to him. Now, you know me, Isabelle. I'm the first to admit that I haven't been very . . . well, constant in my relationships with men. Love 'em and Leave 'em Alette, right? But not with Justin. With Justin it was different. I really can't blame myself for the breakup of this one.

Justin became immensely critical of everything I did. He belittled my interests, ridiculed all the things I'm passionate about. During our courtship he had often quizzed me about my fascination with mystical phenomena, but with a kind of affectionate amusement, or so I thought. Now all of a sudden he made me feel like a kook, a flake of the worst kind. And then there was the garden. It became a tremendous bone of contention. For some reason, which is beyond me, he found my love of gardening immensely irritating. Oh, I know what you're thinking. This is all trivial, petty stuff: the kind of irritations that plague every marriage. But you don't know what it's like, Isabelle: a constant barrage of criticism, a relentless assault on everything you hold dear. I started feeling worthless, a failure. The person I used to turn to for comfort had now become the source of my deepest distress. I can't begin to explain to you what that did to my perception of myself and the world I've created for myself.

The situation went from bad to worse. Justin would set these arbitrary little rules, which I was not supposed to break. I was not allowed to move as much as a picture out of its place without his approval. I was not allowed to wear the color green anymore. He censored my reading. When I listened to a CD from our collection, I had to replace it exactly where I found it. If I was in breach of a rule he would become enraged and refuse to speak to me for days. When he entered the room, I had to stop whatever I was doing and give him my full attention immediately. He even interrupted my sleep. If he felt I was sleeping too soundly, he would wake me on purpose. I was constantly exhausted and becoming disorganized.

Even my memory became impaired. Justin forced me to cut my ties with my friends. And finally he made sure I gave up my business. He wanted me completely isolated.

Isabelle, you know me as someone who does not take things lying down and who can give as good as I get. But one day I woke up and realized that I had turned into a person I did not recognize at all. The sad truth of it was that I had become a willing participant in his mind games. I had enabled Justin to do to me exactly what he wanted and was even trying to find excuses for his behavior by being critical of myself. I had allowed myself to become a victim. I had to get out.

So I asked for a divorce. He refused, of course. He couldn't actually stop me from leaving, but he promised he'd make sure I'm financially ruined and tied up with lawyers for years to come. He also threatened to wash our dirty laundry in the tabloids. You can imagine the interest there'd be in Justin Temple's story.

But I had one foolproof way of freeing myself. When I realized that there was no other way I'd be able to escape, I threatened Justin with the one thing in the world he could not afford. And so, he let me go. I'll tell you his secret later on, Isabelle. It is very much an integral part of the favor I am going to ask of you. By the time you receive the third envelope, you will understand exactly what it is all about.

Escape. It felt so wonderful to move out of the apartment and into my own place. Getting reacquainted with the old Alette. Going about my business, reaching out to the world again. But I had rejoiced much too soon. Ending my marriage still did not bring an end to the particularly perverse and poisonous relationship that existed between Justin and me.

He wanted a reconciliation. He sounded sincere in his apologies. He promised to give me space, to respect my boundaries. He used my sense of fair play against me, appealed to my sense of loyalty. I am the kind of person who believes that everyone deserves a second chance and here was a man I had cared for deeply, whose regret seemed absolutely genuine. You have to remember: although I've been involved in many, many relationships, Justin was the first and only man I had ever really loved. So, for a very brief time, I decided to try again. But I realized almost immediately that the attempt at reconciliation was a mistake. I felt trapped. After only a week I asked him to leave and told him we had to face up to the fact that it was over once and for all.

And so, the nightmare started again. He refused to accept that he would be unable to win me back. Justin and I have been living apart for three years now, but I have not been free of him for even one day. I'm his captive. It's claustrophobic, immensely tiring.

Where he had battered me with criticism while we were married, now he was killing me with kindness.

Imagine waking up in the morning and finding not one, not two, but twenty romantic cards shoved through the mailbox in the front door. The envelopes have no stamps on them, so you know they must be hand-delivered. Every card has a sentimental message and a plea for forgiveness.

Imagine having lunch with a friend in a restaurant and a smiling maître d' brings a bottle of Krug champagne to the table: compliments of Mr. Temple. Oh, and he also asked to have a crème brulée prepared for your dessert. Actually the menu does not feature crème brulée, but the restaurant understands from Mr. Temple that it is your favorite dessert and of course they'll be happy to prepare it specially.

Imagine returning to your home and finding a repairman on a ladder outside your house, attending to the leaking gutter, which has been troubling you for so long. And when you ask him how he comes to be there, he replies that Mr. Temple has arranged it and is also taking care of the bill.

The next morning you open the door to find that every single flower in the garden has been picked and arranged into a lovely bouquet, which is lying on your doorstep, fastened with a gorgeous bow. Beautiful, yes? But the garden is denuded, not one single bud has been left. So you go to the police station and tell the absurdly young desk constable that you are feeling harassed. And he looks at the flowers in your arms and says, "We can hardly arrest someone for sending you flowers, ma'am."

Justin is so clever. He is terrorizing me, but he knows it will be very difficult for me to convince anyone that his motives are malignant. This new behavior of his is just another way of exercising control over me. His constant attention is intruding into my life, keeping me from returning to an ordinary existence. The never-ending intrusions are a subtle way of assuring me that he remains a presence in my life. Things would be quiet for a while, and then just as I would start to relax, something small and not at all threatening would remind me that he's still out there. I'd return to the car and there would be a red rose under my windshield wiper. Or I'd receive in the mail the latest book on some or other topic he knew I'd be interested in. These are not expressions of love, Isabelle. They are expressions of a terrible anger. Sometimes I wish he would rather explode into violence— threaten me with physical harm—beat me. I want bruises, scars, something tangible to prove to the world what kind of man he is and the evil game he is playing. Instead I get chocolate, flowers, a string quartet on my doorstep. And the sick feeling that his hold on me will never ease.

Obsession is a terrible thing. Do you remember that day we saw the flamingo and the eagle? You remember: that day we visited the Etosha pan and we saw those hundreds and hundreds of flamingo taking flight—one moment dragging their wings through the water and the next moment turning into a pink-and-white cloud.

You remember how beautiful that was? And then there was this one bird. She couldn't take flight because a Fish eagle had spotted her as his prey and was hovering just above her. Just high enough to allow her to leave the water, to flap her wings a few times—but not high enough to allow her to fully take flight. And this beautiful bird would almost become airborne and then crash back into the water. Again and again it happened. Again and again. Until, finally, the bird was so exhausted that it put up no fight when the eagle came in for the kill. I feel like that bird, Isabelle. I can never get away. I can never free myself.

I live with a kind of free-floating anxiety these days. I can't explain why, but I feel threatened. I feel as though I'm being constantly watched, as though I have no privacy left, as though Justin knows about my every move. Maybe I'm becoming paranoid. Maybe this sense that I need to be eternally vigilant is impairing my judgment. But that, you see, is the real horror. Justin has succeeded in making even a normal environment feel hostile. Seemingly insignificant things now make me wonder and worry. When I return to my house, I think: Did I leave on that outside light? When I look out the window I hesitate: Is there someone watching behind that tree?

Why haven't I ever told you about this, you ask. I couldn't. The entire situation made me feel ashamed. And I'm used to taking care of you, not the other way around.

Justin keeps telling me how much he loves me, but love does not behave this way. He hates me, I know that well. No tears from him when I'm no longer around. And as I write this, I know death is close. The feeling is so strong: the strongest feeling I've ever had. I'll be gone soon and not only will Justin not have me around to torture anymore, but now it's going to be my turn. He made me his captive; now he's going to find out what it feels like to be rendered helpless, to lose everything that gives you a sense of control in your life.

I want to leave him a little keepsake. Something for him to always remember me by. And I need your help, Isabelle. I will explain exactly how, in this and in the following two letters you will be receiving.

I don't know how much I told you about Justin's business affairs, about Temple Sullivan, his company. When Justin and I first met, it was still a pretty shaky concern, but over the past few years the company has been going from strength to strength. Temple Sullivan is tiny compared to the other pharmaceutical giants, but its fortunes have skyrocketed because of Taumex.

Taumex represents the most important development in the fight against Alzheimer's. Not only can it arrest the development of Alzheimer's to a remarkable degree, but it also has the potential to stave off the onset of the disease altogether. Temple Sullivan holds the patent for Taumex. In the U.S. a patent is valid for seventeen years from date of grant and in Europe it is valid for twenty years from date of application. It took Justin eleven years to steer Taumex through the clinical trials, which means that he has approximately seven years left in which to make a massive profit. Holding the patent for Taumex is a license to print money. It is the cornerstone of Justin's success. It also holds the seeds of his downfall. You see, Justin has made the mistake of putting all his eggs into one basket. Temple Sullivan is basically a one-product company: no matter that Taumex is a very sexy product. This is not a diversified company and that makes it vulnerable.

My plan is this: Over the next three to four weeks you and I will orchestrate an offensive against the company, which will cause its stock price to fall dramatically—to such an extent that Justin will be removed as CEO. I give you my word that the drug itself is not the target: it's Justin I'm after.

Justin is a driven man. He has always felt the need to prove himself. His father was disapproving and critical and I won't even begin to tell you about his mother. A coldhearted bitch if ever there was one. She hates me and I truly detest her. Between the two of them, his parents did a bang-up job in assuring that Justin fears failure above all else.

Your first assignment will be relatively simple. We're going to start a rumor. It's easy: here's how.

I want you to call three brokers—you'll find their names and the houses they work for at the end of this letter. Call them and tell them that you have some inside information on the company. Don't give your real name. You can use any name you feel like, of course, but it would be nice if you would identify yourself as Sophia. (Don't ask: private joke.) Tell them that Justin has been experiencing supply problems for quite some time now. This, by the way, happens to be true. One of the ingredients for the drug is sourced in Madagascar—there really is no alternative source available. Justin has had some run-ins with the local officials there and there are a host of other problems.

Keep in mind that in England, British Telecom offers a service that allows you to find out the number of the last person who called. Obviously, you don't want that to happen. There is a way to get around this, though, so make sure that when you place your calls to the brokers, you enter 141 before dialing the number. This ensures that if these men should try using the callback service, they will be unable to trace you. Furthermore, my number is unlisted. You're safe.

The three men I want you to call will be skeptical and probably won't act on what you have to tell them. However, they will act when later they read a report on this in the financial pages. Thereafter, when Sophia calls again, they'll be sure to pay attention. You will notice that I've enclosed two smaller envelopes under cover of this letter, addressed to Dan

Harrison of the Financial Times and Martin Penfield of the London Post respectively. The Financial Times probably won't print the story until after they've done some investigating of their own—those guys are careful and responsible—but when they do, they'll find that the story pans out. Next time they will act more speedily on information coming from Sophia. As for the Post, Martin Penfield is an aggressive city editor and I'm sure he'll run the story on the basis of the information I'm sending him. So we can expect a quick turnaround time from his paper. In the letters to Penfield and Harrison, I'm referring them to Simon Fromm, a former employee of Justin's. He and Justin had a tremendous row a year ago and he's still holding a grudge. With enough persuasion, he'll open up and confirm the rumor.

Temple Sullivan's stock price is likely to dip—but not by much—and will then most likely recover. But we will have drawn attention to the company and at present that's all that is necessary.

Next week we will turn up the heat.

I'm not insane, in case you're wondering. George Herbert said, "Yet Lord, instruct us so to die, that all these dyings may be life in death." Well, Herbert was deeply religious and I'm not, and revenge is not the most noble of motives, but with your help my dying can be life in death. The balance of power was always with Justin during our relationship. Now it will change. Revenge is an immensely empowering emotion, and Justin can't get to me. How do you punish a ghost?

Isabelle, this is me talking. Not some crazy woman. You're my cousin. Blood of my blood. I love you like a sister. I really, really need you to do this for me. If I've hurt you with my attitude toward Eric, I'm sorry. I still think he used you, but you loved him and I accept that. Please, please do this for me. I *have suffered. It sounds melodramatic when I put it like that, but it's true.*

I've always watched out for you, ever since you came to the farm—so quiet and angry. I've looked after you, watched over you. In return I've always been able to count on you. I know I can count on you now. You'll do this for me, won't you. Won't you?

Come on, Isabelle. I dare you.

FIVE

But Death will lead her to a shade
Where Love is cold, and Beauty blinde.
> —"The Philosopher and the
> Lover: to a Mistress dying,"
> Sir William Davenant
> (1606–1668)

"I DARE YOU."

The girl who spoke had braces on her teeth and a malevolent gleam in her eye. Her school uniform showed a stain just below the collar. She looked at Isa for a moment and then turned to the girl at her side. "I knew it, Alette. Your cousin's chicken."

"No, she's not." Alette spoke calmly. "Come on, Isabelle, it's not so bad. I'll show you."

Alette dipped her hand inside the shoe box and removed a fat caterpillar from among the velvety mulberry leaves. Without any change of expression she stuck out her tongue and placed the silkworm on top of it.

Isa felt sick. She looked at the glistening pink tongue, the silkworm's soft, crumpled skin. The grayish-white worm was mov-

48

ing sluggishly but deliberately toward the back of Alette's tongue.

Alette closed her mouth. For a few seconds she stood without moving. Then she opened her mouth and took out the worm again, balancing it on her finger.

"Here." She held out her hand to Isa. "Take it."

Isa held out her hand hesitantly. The dazed worm plopped onto her palm.

She looked into Alette's eyes. Her cousin had a slightly quizzical expression on her face: a kind of could-I-have-been-mistaken-about-you look. It chilled Isa's heart. If she failed this test, it would be over. It would forever jeopardize her chances to become friends. And she did so want to be friends with this stunning girl.

The worm was moving from her palm toward her wrist. Isa placed the forefinger of her other hand directly in its path. For a moment the caterpillar hesitated. Then it gripped her finger with its tiny, hairy legs.

Isa deposited the worm on her tongue. She closed her mouth and blanked out her mind. After a few seconds she took the worm out and dropped it among the other silkworms in the box.

Alette smiled. "Well done," she said.

UNTIL A MONTH BEFORE, ISA HAD NEVER REALLY GIVEN MUCH thought to the fact that she had a cousin. On top of the piano in the drawing room was an out-of-focus photograph of two bald-headed babies in elaborate christening dresses. Isa knew that the baby on the right—the one who was crying—was herself. The other baby, she had been told, was Alette, the daughter of her mother's brother who lived in Natal. But Isa's mother died when she was two and her father had not bothered keeping in touch with her mother's side of the family.

Then, a day before her thirteenth birthday, Isa's father crashed his car, killing himself and a young couple and their little boy.

On the day of the crash, he was quite drunk. This was not unusual. He was intoxicated almost every single day of his life, although Isa never heard her father slur his speech or saw him stumble when he walked. It was a matter of pride to him that he carried his alcohol well. After an especially fierce drinking bout, his smile might become a little wider and occasionally, but not often, he became violent. Isa learned to recognize the signs. When his smile faded and he became quiet, she made herself scarce.

On the day of his death, as he got behind the wheel, he was— by his standards—fairly sober. Isa smelled the alcohol on his breath, but that morning he had been especially affectionate toward her and she was grateful. And then he went out and killed an entire family and left her with the guilt of not having tried to stop him.

Her uncle Leon drove up all the way from Natal to attend the funeral in Johannesburg. He was a mild-mannered man with vague eyes. After the funeral he took Isa to one side and told her that from now on she would be living with him and his family on their sugar farm near the Tugela River in Natal. "You'll like it there," he told her. "The farm is called Kleingeluk, that means 'a small dose of good fortune.'" He looked into her mistrustful eyes and touched her shoulder briefly, awkwardly. "You'll like it," he repeated.

Natal was a shock to someone used to cool, crisp Highveld air; arid colors and the purity of dust. Natal presented itself to Isa as an onslaught on the senses: steaming heat, flowers in outrageous colors, the air vibrating with screaming cicadas. The sweet stickiness of sugarcane permeating everything, giving life here its texture. The homestead surrounded by sugarcane and the fields stretching as far as the eye could see. To Isa it felt as though she might be swallowed, devoured by all that poisonous green. A mere thirty kilometers to the south was the ocean. But there was not a hint of brine in the air; not a suggestion of a cooling breeze.

The heat seldom eased. Isa had to become used to waking up in the mornings with sweat on her forehead. It seemed to her as though people here breathed more slowly, as though the humidity in the air made even breathing an effort; a conscious act. Women talked softly, without energy, and there were moist patches on their dresses under their arms. In Natal everything was bigger. The insects were large and fearless. The farmhands who cut the cane wore boots up to their knees to guard against the teeth of enormous cane rats. It was a powerfully feminine landscape, with its rolling hills and in the air the sweet stench of decaying flowers. The cycle of birth and rebirth was as tangible as a slow, sensuous heartbeat. It was Alette's milieu. It was her setting. It was perfect for her.

Alette. Alette with her small limbs and fragile bones and heavy woman's breasts. Alette, at age thirteen, already utterly and uncompromisingly promiscuous. "Why?" Isa once asked her after Alette had sneaked back into the room after yet another amorous tryst—this time with a smitten boy who lived on a neighboring farm. "You don't even like him."

Alette arched her back tiredly. "I like being held."

At first, the two girls hadn't bonded. The atmosphere between them just after Isa's arrival on the farm had been tense. Isa felt clumsy and rawboned in the presence of her cousin. Alette seemed intent on baiting Isa; subtly needling her and then sitting back to enjoy the spectacle of Isa blinking away angry tears and responding in a voice that trembled horribly.

Alette challenged Isa not to be timid. "I dare you" were words that Isa came to know well; words she came to dread.

There was the time Isa watched disbelievingly as Alette lay flat on her back beneath some power lines that were strung dangerously close to the roof of the house. Alette slid slowly back and forth underneath the lines, the cords only inches away from her body.

"I dare you."

The blood rushed in Isa's ears. In her mouth was the prickly taste of fear. As she slid her body underneath the lines, she was shivering, even though the corrugated iron of the roof was hot enough to scald the skin on her back.

There was the time they swam the river. The honey-colored water was blood warm on the skin. The weeping willows on the other side of the riverbank seemed very far away. Something cold brushed against her leg and Isa was afraid. The cane cutters swore there was an immensely old *ingwenya,* 'crocodile,' haunting this part of the river. In front of her Alette seemed to be floating, her hair dark and stringy, her limbs pale shapes in the muddy water. Isa's arms were getting tired. For one dreadful moment her head dipped beneath the water and it became dark around her. By the time they reached the bank, she was swimming without thinking, her mind numb; her body aching and exhausted, her lungs burning up.

Isa did not share Alette's liking for the thrill of risk. But she had no defense against Alette's raised eyebrows and half smile. And even though she tried to fight it, she realized that the more she got to know Alette, the more she craved her approval. Alette was testing her and Isa was determined that her cousin would not find her wanting.

Things were starting to change between them.

THE RELATIONSHIP CHANGED FROM THE ADVERSARIAL TO THE symbiotic. Alette became Isa's protector. At the school where Isa and Alette were students, their classmates were mostly children from a small cluster of villages and from surrounding farms, and they had all known one another since infancy. The children formed a tight clique and without Alette, Isa would have been lost. But Alette assured Isa's popularity. She exaggerated Isa's academic achievements at her old school. She admired Isa's drawings and sketches and expected her circle of friends to show admiration also. And in return Isa gave her loyalty to Alette utterly and without reservation.

At the farm, the two girls were pretty much left to their own devices. Her uncle Leon and her aunt Lettie were kind to Isa but not especially interested in her. Her uncle doted on Alette, but Isa had the feeling that Aunt Lettie was slightly jealous of her daughter.

She and Alette became as close as sisters; closer. And yet they were so different from each other: different in temperament, different in what they wanted out of life.

Alette stated often and with conviction that she would never marry. "Marriage turns women into drudges," Alette said in that calm way of hers. She didn't speak aggressively, just with total certainty. "I don't see myself in that role. What about you, Isabelle? Would you want to marry?"

And "yes," said Isa meekly, "I would." And yes as well to children, a house in the suburbs and a husband who came back from the office at five, loosening his tie and asking what's for dinner. She looked into Alette's incredulous eyes and said defensively, "I'm not a romantic."

"Then why are you reading this?" Alette picked up the paperback romance, which Isa had borrowed from her friend Barbara, who, in turn, had stolen it from her mother's stash.

Alette looked contemptuously at the cover, which depicted a swarthy man and a swooning female striking an unlikely pose against his shoulder. Alette flicked open a page and started reading a passage out loud. Before she had finished, Isa was convulsed with laughter. Alette was substituting all the male pronouns with female pronouns and vice versa.

"Her muscled arms were like steel bands around his fragile shoulders," Alette read in a high, affected voice. "She placed a fin-

ger under his rounded chin and tilted his small, expectant face up
to hers. 'You light my fire,' she growled huskily, and pressed her
lips against his moist, half-open mouth. He smiled tremulously
and bravely offered himself to her rough passion."

Alette threw the book away from her and it skidded across the
table. "Of course, you're a romantic. But your need for security
and stability is stronger. And so you'll willingly settle for a life of
comfortable boredom. Whereas I want delirium and protracted
desire. A man who'll eat oysters off my breasts—like Casanova,"
she said, laughing at Isa's repulsed expression.

"And what about the heartbreak?" Isa asked, a little stung by
the contempt in Alette's voice. "Feelings that strong usually end
in tears."

Alette looked at her with amusement. "There's always the one
who kisses and the one who is being kissed. I'll be the one who
turns the cheek. But I need the man I'm with to ache and burn. He
should want me more than anything. That kind of infatuation is
not possible in marriage. And anyway"—she made a dismissive
gesture with her hand—"playing house is not in my nature and
character is destiny."

Many years afterward, Isa would think back on these words
and wonder at the strangeness of life. Because Alette did get married, while she, Isa, did not, but went on to occupy for years that
much more tenuous and shadowy position of the other woman.

IsA WOKE UP SWEATING AND NAUSEOUS. THE FARM WAS DEAD QUIET.
It was late and her room was dark and it took her a brief, terror-
filled moment to realize that the person standing next to the bed
was Alette. Dressed in a white cotton nightgown, Alette seemed
as ephemeral as a ghost.

"What . . . ?"

"Bad dream," Alette said matter-of-factly. "Wait, I'll be right back." She turned around and padded almost noiselessly out of the room on her bare feet. Isa heard a stair creak as Alette carefully negotiated her way downstairs in darkness.

Isa rubbed her eyes tiredly. This was the fourth time in a week that she had had the same nightmare. And every time Alette was there to wake her up, to rescue her from the dream's insistent grasp. She did not know how Alette knew. They didn't share a room, but somehow Alette seemed able to sense her distress.

"Here, drink this, you'll feel better." Alette had returned to the room carrying a glass of her mother's homemade ginger beer.

The tart bubbles tickled Isa's nose and she sneezed.

"Shh." Alette closed the door and then walked over to the window, pulling back the curtain. Moonlight flooded the room. The two girls sat down on the wide windowsill and Isa drew her knees up to her chest and hugged herself. The night was warm but she was feeling cold.

For a while it was silent between them. Outside everything was bathed in a milky light. White banana trees, white sugarcane, black shadows.

Isa glanced over at Alette. She was leaning forward, her forehead pressed against the pane of glass.

"Alette . . ."

"Hmm?"

"How come you know?"

"Know what?" Alette pulled away from the window.

"How come you know every time I have a bad dream. Do I shout in my sleep?"

Alette shook her head

"So then how?"

"I just know. It's like I'm dreaming and you're dreaming and somehow I manage to wander into your dream. No, that's not quite right." She frowned. "I don't know how to explain it. But I know that I can see you in there although you're not able to see me yet."

"Yet?"

Alette shrugged. She blew her breath against the windowpane. In the gray patch of moisture, she traced with her finger three words: NON OMNIS MORIAR.

Isa leaned over to take a closer look. "What's that?"

"Something we learned in Latin class last week."

Latin was not one of Isa's electives. The words made no sense to her. "So what does it mean, then?"

"It's a quote from Horace," Alette said dreamily. "It means, 'I shall not altogether die.'"

Isa stared at the three words. The letters were already disappearing—only the M of MORIAR standing strong and clearly etched.

Alette spoke again. "Siena says our dreams live on after we die. Even when our bodies are cold, our dreams are still out there and will haunt the dreams of the living."

Isa shivered. "That's creepy."

"No, it's so cool. It's like we're never really gone. All our passions survive. All our desires and fears, the things we care about the most. And we can influence those who are still alive."

Isa didn't answer. She watched as Alette reached out her hand and wiped the pane of glass clean with the side of her fist.

"Are you okay now?" Alette looked at her. "Do you want to talk about your nightmare?"

"No. It was the same one." Broken bodies and mangled cars. Death and guilt. The little boy had been only three years old.

"You sure you're okay?"

"I'm sure."

Alette got to her feet. "So let's go back to bed then. It's late."

She waited until Isa got under the covers and touched Isa's forehead briefly. "Call me if you need me."

"I will."

"Although I'll probably know anyway."

"Yes." Isa smiled. She suddenly felt immensely comforted.

"Do you want the door open or closed?"

"Open, I think." Isa watched Alette as she walked toward the door. "Alette . . ."

"Yes?" Alette was looking back over her shoulder. In the uncertain light her eyes were black.

"Thanks."

"Sure. Sleep tight now."

Isa pulled the sheet up to her chin. She was just about to turn over when she became aware that Alette was still standing motionless in the doorway, watching her.

"What is it?"

Alette hesitated. "These dreams I . . . we . . . have. Maybe we should talk to Siena about them."

"Okay. If you want to."

Alette nodded. "I want to."

SIENA WAS ALETTE'S AIA; HER NANNY. SHE WAS A ZULU. HER SKIN was deeply black and her voice as deep as a man's. She was the one person, Isa always thought, who truly had a hold on Alette's affections. Alette was dismissive of her mother and tolerant of her father's adoration. She was certainly very fond of Isa. But Siena she adored. The only time Isa would ever see Alette weep would be after Siena's death.

Siena had looked after Alette since the cradle and as such occupied an important position in the household. But it wasn't her role as caretaker that made her a person of influence on the farm and in the larger community. Siena was a mystic; a diviner—or, as people like Aunt Lettie insisted with obstinate European arrogance and ignorance—a witch doctor.

Siena had children of her own: two boys, both grown. The one

worked in a restaurant in Johannesburg, the other was a lab assistant at the University of Natal. Neither one seemed quite at ease
with their mother's pursuits and Siena had told Isa that in many
ways Alette was closer to her than her own sons. It was from Siena
that Alette got her interest in all things mystical. And Siena recognized Alette's psychic abilities. "This one," she'd say, "this
one has the power."

When she first entered the household, Siena had been only a
twasa or initiate, but since then she had fully entered the world of
the *isangoma*. The farmhands would consult with Siena first before
going to see Doc Smith with their medical problems. If you needed
help in locating a missing item, Siena was the one to ask. She
could identify witches and was in intimate contact with the ancestral spirits. And even those who scoffed at her powers could not
deny her insight into human nature. She was an excellent judge of
character and she made it her business to know as much as she
could about the lives of the people who lived on the farm. Much
of her success as a diviner was based on the fact that she could
shrewdly manipulate those who sought her advice by knowing a
great deal about them. It was a lesson she made sure of teaching
Alette: to know her friends well . . . and her enemies, very well.

SIENA'S ROOM WAS DARK AND COOL. IT WAS QUIET: ONLY THE
despairing buzz of a bluebottle, trapped between the pane of glass
and the mosquito-wire screen, disturbed the silence. Isa felt her
eyes grow heavy. It was *tjaila* time—the hours between two and
four in the afternoon, when all activity on the farm ceased. Aunt
Lettie would be taking a nap, balancing on her forehead a cooling
handkerchief dipped in rose water. Uncle Leon was in his study.

Alette was lying on her stomach on top of Siena's bed, looking
down. Siena's mattress was balanced on a number of bricks that
were stacked below each corner of the bed. These bricks raised the

bed to a lofty height. The reason, as Alette had once explained to Isa, was to keep Siena safe from the *tokelosh*: a malevolent little man with a large head. However, as his legs were very short, the *tokelosh* could not get on top of a bed that was raised in this way.

On the other side of the room Siena was sitting cross-legged on the ground. She was a large woman but moved with ease and could fold her limbs into impossible positions. While Alette had been talking, she had seemed almost asleep, her lids drooping low over her eyes. She hadn't interrupted Alette's flow of words even once.

Now she stirred. "Soon you will stop dreaming on your own and have a shared dream," she said. Her hand gestured from Alette to Isa. "And the shared dream will lead to a waking dream."

"What is a waking dream, my *ousie*?" Alette's voice was respectful. Her manner toward Siena was always one of affection tempered with deference. Alette showed scant regard for the authority figures in her life, but Siena was the exception. Siena was able to shame Alette to tears with a single glance.

"In a waking dream you will know you are dreaming and you will have the power to change your dream. You will walk through your sleep and your mind will be awake."

Isa regarded the old woman dubiously.

"In the Kalahari desert," Siena continued, "the San people say we are all part of the Great Dream which dreams us."

Alette understood immediately. "So the real world and the dream world are one. There is no true distinction between them."

Siena nodded. "Life itself may be a dream. And sleep a quick death and death a long sleep."

Siena suddenly turned toward Isa. "I am afraid for this one," she said, and looked at Isa directly. "You do not have the power to change the dream. You can only take the hand and follow."

Isa's throat felt dry. "The hand?"

"Yes, you must take her hand." Siena pointed to Alette. "But take care . . ." She hesitated as though searching for the correct word, and then continued in rapid Zulu.

Alette was fluent in Zulu. She grew up hearing Zulu spoken by Siena and by the cane cutters on the farm, but Isa did not speak the language. She looked questioningly at Alette, who was listening carefully. "What is she saying?"

Alette hesitated. "I don't know. I don't quite follow." But Isa had the feeling that Alette had in fact understood every word.

Only many years later did Isa learn what Siena had warned her about: "Take care that you do not get lost in there," the old woman had said. "And take care that the dream does not take possession of you."

BUT THE DREAMS SHE SHARED WITH ALETTE DURING THOSE FIRST few years did not seem sinister at all. In fact, they were joyous and magical: liberating beyond imagining.

Her memory of the first time she and Alette had consciously walked through a dream together would never leave her.

She had just made the transition from waking to sleeping. One moment she was lying in her bed, aware of the cool bed linen beneath her palm, the room silvered by a pale wash of moonlight, the far-off chatter of the radio in the living room floating up the staircase. The next moment she was standing in an open field. Her dreamscape seemed deserted, but she knew she was not alone.

She turned her head and Alette was at her side. She knew it was Alette, although in those first initial moments of the dream she was able to see only a hand protruding from the shadowy fall of the wide sleeve of Alette's nightdress. The hand was held out at her, outstretched in invitation, palm turned upward. *Take my hand.* And trustingly, without any hesitation or fear, Isa placed her hand inside Alette's.

The dreamscape around her suddenly bunched like a muscle, folding in on itself before unfurling again in a giant spasm. Her eyes were dazzled by a million colors that would be impossible to imagine upon waking. Trees exploding into vivid colors like burning torches. Transparent skies and clouds of solid rock. Weeping stones and sugared stars. Flowers imbued with an inner life. But despite the ecstatic blend of form and color, the world around her seemed stupendously real and minutely detailed. More real, in fact, than the real world.

But what made her shared dreams with Alette truly magical was that Alette was able to *control* the events in the dream.

Alette taking a key from her pocket, opening a door, and peeking into the blackness behind it. "No, we won't go in here. Let's try the next door."

Alette throwing herself backward, her long red hair streaming past her shoulders. "Don't let go of my hand, Isabelle." And Isa falling, falling: a long vertiginous drop with the walls of the cliff so close if she reached out her hand she could touch them. The wind thundered in her ears—her eyeballs felt dry and tearless. She turned her head and saw the white blur of Alette's teeth. And suddenly she was gripped by fear and cried out and Alette said, "Don't worry, we'll stop this. We'll go back." And the next moment they were standing again safely at the top of the cliff, looking down at the void beneath their feet; as though just by imagining or thinking about it, Alette had made it happen immediately. This became the magic phrase in all subsequent dreams: "Don't worry, we'll stop this. We'll go back." And the monsters would retreat, the shadows disappear.

It never occurred to Isa then that this was in any way unusual: this ability to enter the dreamscape in full consciousness, to have in you the power to direct and change the stuff of your dreams to fit in with your desires: to mold it to your hand. She did not understand then how extraordinary it was not to be at the mercy of whatever your unconscious decided to throw up at you; to free yourself from the demons stalking the world of sleep. Only many years later, as an adult, when she had started to read up on the phenomenon of alert dreaming, did she realize how rare it was—the ability to consciously manipulate and interact with the events in your dreams.

Her research taught her that this was a phenomenon known to science and that it had even been given a name: *lucid dreaming.* Though lucid dreaming could—with great difficulty—be learned, less than five percent of the population were natural lucid dreamers with the power to consciously take control of the events in their dreamscape. She learned that children and adolescents were more likely to dream lucidly and that the most advantageous time for lucid dreaming was close to dawn when the cycle of sleep is near its end and REM sleep at its most prolonged.

Lucid dreaming had a tradition stretching back over millennia. Shamans and mystics considered it an integral part of their existence. In the East it has always played an important role in meditative practices. But in the West, especially during the Catholic Inquisition, lucid dreaming became part of a hidden, furtive world allied to alchemy, freemasonry, and witchcraft: a perverse practice that could only be whispered about and hinted at. It was not until the early eighties when Stephen LaBerge at Stanford University managed to induce lucid dreams in laboratory conditions that respectability returned to the field and science started to take the phenomenon seriously.

Power over dreams. Of course, she, Isa, did not have that power. Alette did. She was merely the companion. As long as she held on to Alette's hand, she could share in the adventure. The only thing within her control was whether to hold on or whether to let go. If she let go of Alette's hand, the dream ended and she woke up. But she seldom let go.

Until she met Eric. At first, he had been fascinated by what she told him about her night visits with Alette. But then he became critical. There was something "unhealthy" about it, he said. He wanted her to stop. And she, so in love, so afraid of losing him, had decided the time had come to cut that shimmering link with her cousin.

The next time she saw the hand appear in a dream, she ignored it. It was not easy, everything inside her wanted to feel those cool fingers folding around her own. She knew she was cutting herself off from a parallel existence in which she could escape the Isa who lived on the margins, who looked in on life. She knew she was losing the Isa who was bold and intrepid. But she was in love. She was weak.

The hand returned in subsequent dreams and every time Isa turned her back on it. And finally the image of it started to fade and flicker like audiovisual signals sent to earth by astronauts who were drifting farther and farther into space. And then it disappeared altogether. She and Alette had not had a shared dream in more than twelve years.

So was that what it was, then? The telephone call from the dead? A return to an old childhood practice—merely part of a conscious dream? There was, after all, the hand. It was the first time the hand had appeared in her dreams in a very, very long time. But you couldn't share a dream with someone who was dead . . . could you?

Maybe she had succeeded in deliberately inducing this dream. Words imagined; a familiar, loved voice willed into being. Perhaps she had had an unconscious wish to hear Alette's voice: that low, whispery voice that makes you feel as though you were about to listen to a most exciting secret. Her days were so gray now, so deadened. Maybe she had needed to be touched by Alette's vitality, her restlessness, her jarring common sense.

It was a comforting explanation, but Isa knew in her bones that it was not the correct explanation. There was more to it than that.

To begin with, during that phone call, she had not experienced the feverish texture and richness that characterized the lucid dreams she had shared with Alette. She might not have experienced a waking dream in almost twelve years, but she could still vividly recall the feel of it: the opulence, the glow of energy and light that animated every single object.

But there was another, more compelling reason why the phone call could not have been part of a lucid dream. Alette's hand had always been the trigger that started every one of their shared dreams. The flat monotone of an ordinary dream could only be transformed into a lucid dream after she and Alette had linked hands. But that night when she had dreamed of Eric's funeral, she had not taken the hand, which had tugged at her sleeve so insistently.

No, the phone call was real. The phone call was part of the waking world, not the sleeping world. And somehow, she did not know why or how, it was tied in with Alette and Justin's destructive relationship and with a letter: a vengeful letter, which describes in careful and loving detail the blueprint for one man's destruction.

SIX

"HELLO, HELLO. WHO IS THIS?"

Robert Geissinger's voice sounded irritated. Twice now Isa had called him on his extension and twice she had hung up just as he answered. His name was the first of the three names that appeared at the end of Alette's letter.

We're going to start a rumor. It's easy: here's how.

Isa tried to speak but her throat closed. The receiver clung to her sweaty palm.

"Oh, sod off," the broker said vehemently, and the phone clicked in her ear as he hung up on her.

Isa replaced the receiver slowly. She was sitting in Alette's bedroom at the Regency writing desk that faced the back window. On the wall next to the fragile marquetry table were shelves housing a large variety of antique perfume bottles. The sun was streaming in through the window, warming the bottles and causing a faded fragrance to scent the air.

Propped up against the tiny, galleried drawers of the desk was Alette's letter. The pages were dogeared. She had read and reread the document so many times that she knew almost every word by heart. Isa looked at her hands. Her fingernails had taken a beating again. She just couldn't seem to stop chewing her nails. The least bit of stress made her revert to a habit that was childish and disgusting.

She couldn't believe that she was seriously contemplating doing what Alette wanted. She hardly knew Justin. She had spent a few days with him and Alette in London the week before the two of them got married, and from what she recalled, he couldn't have been more pleasant. Dark-haired, sophisticated, and attractive, he and Alette made a striking couple. They seemed so much in love. Alette looked serene and calm. In her eyes was the contentment of someone who has reached a goal long sought after.

And when Alette walked down the aisle, hadn't she, Isa, felt just the faintest pang of jealousy? Orange blossom, white veils, iced cake. All the trappings and trimmings of a ceremony she felt she herself would never experience.

Three years ago, when Alette first told her that she was planning to divorce Justin, Isa had pitied Justin just a little. He had the distinction of being married to Alette, but obviously he was merely the last in a line of lovers with whom Alette shared her time before moving on. Alette was kind to former lovers and usually the parting was amicable. Of course, if Alette had told her what the real state of affairs was, she certainly would not have wasted her pity on Justin. But Alette had never said a word.

Please, please do this for me. I have suffered. It sounds melodramatic when I put it like that, but it's true.

Isa shivered. Alette never begged for anything. It distressed Isa, made her feel insecure. Alette had always been the fearless one. Alette was the one who could cope with any situation. Isa still couldn't believe that one man had managed to so traumatize her cousin.

Isa looked again at the names of the three brokers with their telephone numbers, which Alette had carefully printed one below the other. Maybe she could do what Alette wanted. It did not seem as though telling these men of Temple Sullivan's supply problems would have consequences that severe. Alette herself said in the letter that the stock would dip but probably recover again. Maybe she should call the brokers, send those two letters to the newspapers, and see what happened. Next week she'd take a look at what the second envelope contained. She could always back out of the whole thing then.

Isa placed her hand on the receiver; hesitated.

I've always watched out for you . . . I know I can count on you now. You'll do this for me, won't you. Won't you?

Isa picked up the receiver and started to dial. When Robert Geissinger answered, she spoke in a clear, strong voice.

"Mr. Geissinger, you don't know me but I have some information which you might find interesting. It concerns the pharmaceutical company Temple Sullivan . . ."

SIX MILES AWAY, ROBERT GEISSINGER HUNG UP THE RECEIVER AND looked at the piece of paper on which he had doodled during the conversation. He had written the words *Temple Sullivan* and surrounded it with lots of smiling "have-a-nice-day" faces. Rather symbolic, he thought. And appropriate. Only happy thoughts where this company was concerned. Talk about your super growth stock.

Way back when he was still squeezing pimples and trying to look down Susan Curtis's blouse in science class, Temple Sullivan was just another small company with a promising but problematic product. The drug had to jump the twin hurdles of getting FDA approval and EMEA marketing authorization; formidable obstacles both. But even in those days, the company had caught his interest.

Geissinger had been an unusual teen: apart from an abiding love for Manchester United football team, his passion in life was the stock market. By the age of thirteen, he was checking closing prices on CEEFAX. By the time his voice broke, he had a phantom portfolio of stocks he would have invested in if he had the money and the means. Topping the list was Temple Sullivan. He had told his father, a long-distance truck driver, to get into the market, but the old man had refused. A real shame that was. In those days you could buy Temple Sullivan stock on the London Stock Exchange at seventy-five pence per share. Today the stock trades at twenty-two pounds per share. If his Da' had invested only one year's fag money, he would have been able to buy a house by this time.

A few years later Geissinger had joined Devereaux as a broker. He didn't have much by way of higher education, but he had smarts and he was hungry. And he was still interested in Taumex. He knew in his gut that this was the next big thing. Bigger than Zantac. Bigger than Prozac. He kept the faith, despite some setbacks in the early in vitro and animal clinical trials. Forget cancer and heart attacks, he told his mates. Growing old is the big fear. Growing old gaga is the Godzilla of fears. If you could swallow a pill to stop that from happening—well, that was the pot at the end of the rainbow. Furthermore, apart from the product, he was impressed by Justin Temple and the management team he had put together. Temple had managed to coax Gabriel Perette, a man who commanded a lot of respect in the City, out of early retirement and had persuaded him to become Temple Sullivan's finance director. Patience was all that was needed. This company was a winner, he was sure of it.

He was proved right. He had used every penny he had, and a lot he didn't have, to buy as many additional shares as he could when the company made a rights issue. Taumex sailed through the Phase II clinical trials. The number of prescriptions during the first week after its launch dwarfed even that of Viagra —the male impotence wonder pill—and up till then the fastest-selling drug in the history of pharmacology. Temple Sullivan stock soared. It had made his reputation and his fortune—was still making it. And now this woman with the odd accent who had just called him was trying to rain on his parade.

Geissinger swiveled his chair around to face the prematurely balding man behind him. "Hey, Cueball."

Charles Quest was speaking into his telephone and did not answer. He simply raised a long finger in warning. Then he said, "Certainly, I'll hold." He looked up at Geissinger. "Watch out. If you persist in calling me that, I simply won't talk to you."

"A real blow that would be." Geissinger grinned. Actually it would be. Charles Quest had the reputation for keeping his ear close to the ground. If there were any rumors floating about, Quest would know. "Seriously, Charlie, have you heard anything about Temple Sullivan—anything about possible supply problems?"

"Hmm. Hmm. Where did you hear that?"

"This woman just called me out of nowhere with some cockamamie story about Taumex and sourcing problems in Madagascar."

"What woman?"

"I don't know. She calls herself Sophia."

Quest turned sideways in his seat and spoke into the phone again. "Well, could you tell him Charles Quest from Devereaux has called. Yes, thank you so much." He hung up. "I love this man," he said, and gestured to the phone. "When other investors get jittery and jump out, this one jumps in. And if you make him a little money he actually says thank you. Anyway, Sophia. Never heard of her." He sighed deeply and stared at the rapidly moving tape as though he might find inspiration somewhere within the glowworm-green alphabet soup. "Why don't you give that pretty pharmaceutical analyst a call. You know, the little blonde with the punk hairdo. Ask her if she and her playmates have anything to share."

Geissinger crumpled up the piece of paper with the doodles and lobbed it in the direction of the wastepaper basket. "Sophia—it sounds like a character from a sitcom. She's probably a loony."

"Probably. But call the little analyst anyway. I hear she has a pierced navel."

Geissinger grinned. "Maybe I will at that."

By the time Isa had finished calling the three men on Alette's list, her neck felt stiff with tension and she had a crick just below her shoulder blade from sitting perched on the very edge of the seat.

One of the men she had called had refused to speak to her when she would not give her full name or the name of the "company" she represented. The other two had listened politely but had not sounded exactly startled or in any way worried by what she had told them. They had been quite civil and quite noncommittal.

Well, that was that. Now she only had those envelopes to send to the two newspapers. And then wait.

She glanced out the window and stiffened. On the top floor of the apartment block opposite, in the corner window, was the watcher from the other night. He was looking in her direction. When he saw that she had noticed him, he lifted his arm and waved.

Isa got out of the chair and walked to the other side of the room to get out of his line of vision. But almost immediately the phone started ringing. Isa hesitated, then walked back to the desk and picked up the receiver.

"Hi. I'm just trying to be friendly." The voice at the other end of the line sounded amused.

"Who is this?"

"The guy you just turned your back on. Yes, that's right, up here. See, I'm waving at you again "

Isa looked at the corner window. He was a big man with heavy shoulders. He wore a crimson sweater and held a cordless phone to his ear.

"Look," he said, "I'm coming over there to talk to you. I was a friend of Alette's."

"No, wait . . ." Isa felt almost panicked.

"See you in a minute," he said cheerily, and disappeared from view.

When the doorbell rang five minutes later, Isa was already waiting apprehensively in the entrance hall. Apprehensively, but also angrily. She didn't like being thrust into this situation.

He was even bigger close up. His dark blond hair was thick and long and untidy. He was not handsome: his features were far too irregular and he had an odd-shaped nose—*squishy* was the word that popped into her head. Still, he was attractive in a sort of rumpled way. On the front of his red sweater was knitted a design of flying reindeer. Very much in the Christmas spirit, Isa thought sourly.

He stuck out his hand. It was huge. "Hi, I'm Michael Chapman. And you must be Isabelle."

She looked at him surprised. He grinned. "It can only be you. Alette described you perfectly."

"I'm Isa. How can I help you?" Nervousness made her sound brusque.

He gazed at her for a moment. "Look, you don't know me from Adam and I can see you're not at your ease. But there's a really nice little place just around the corner from here where they serve good tea and great scones. What do you say?"

"I don't know . . ."

"Oh, come on. I can't look that dangerous." When she didn't answer he said, suddenly somber: "Please. Alette and I were good friends. I'd love to talk to you about her. I still can't believe she's gone."

Isa remembered her dream about Eric's funeral. Her illogical desire to talk to Eric's wife and family; to share with them her grief.

He was waiting for her reply, eyebrows lifted inquiringly. He had kind eyes, she thought.

"Let me get my coat."

On the way over, she studied him from the corner of her eye. He didn't walk, he shambled. He was swinging his arms in a disjointed kind of way. His shoes were good shoes, but dull and unpolished. He was not fat, just very heavily built. He reminded her a bit of a shaggy Saint Bernard.

Inside the tiny tea shop, he dropped the menu twice. Either he was clumsy, or he was more nervous than he was letting on.

"I appreciate this, you know." He folded the menu and placed it at the edge of the table, where it seemed in danger of falling off again. She had to stop herself from pushing it back to the middle of the table.

"You and Alette were friends?"

"Good friends. We were never intimate," he added awkwardly. "But we shared the same interests: the same taste in books. We met three years ago at the Chelsea Flower Show. I recognized her immediately as the beautiful girl living opposite me."

"So you introduced yourself."

"Actually, no. I was looking at some roses and she came over to me and told me that I'd do better with another variety. The rose I was interested in had no fragrance." He smiled. "She said roses that had the scent bred out of them were vulgar. So that was another thing we shared: we're both gardeners."

"But you live in an apartment block."

"My mother, my sister, and her little boy live in Putney and they have a proper garden. I look after it for them."

"So what is it you do exactly?" Isa suddenly realized that it sounded as though she were interrogating him. But if he resented being questioned like this, his face didn't show it.

"I'm a photographer and artist. Photography's the bread; art is the candy." He grinned. "The Tate is close by and every Monday you'll find me there, copying the artwork. It keeps my eye in. The rest of the week I'm a photographer: everything from baby pictures to weddings. I'd love to be able to paint and sculpt full-time, but a man has to eat."

He inclined his head slightly to one side. "But I seem to remember Alette telling me that you're an artist as well."

"Not really. In my spare time I sketch a little. It's just a hobby. Not important."

"Hobbies are always important. They represent the true passions in someone's life. I've always thought that if I couldn't be an artist, I'd want to be an astronomer. If I were younger I might have trained for it properly. As it is, I just dabble." He shrugged. "Of course, living in London is not the ideal place to observe stars. Too much ambient light. I have to go out to the country and I don't often get the chance. It's a pity. I'm passionate about binary stars."

"Binary stars?"

"Two suns caught in each other's gravity. Two suns spinning together for all eternity."

"That's rather . . . romantic."

"I like to think so." He smiled. "It could also be terrible, I suppose. The idea of never being able to break free."

They were quiet as the waitress brought them their tea. Michael slowly stirred the tea in his cup, the spoon almost disappearing inside his hand. Isa noticed that his eyelashes, though fair, were long and thick.

"You know." He hesitated. "You scared the stuffing out of me the other night."

"I scared *you?*"

"Well, yes. First the lights went on inside a house where the person who might have switched them on couldn't possibly have done so. And then imagine how I felt when I saw a woman moving around inside this house where the occupant is supposed to be dead. For one awful moment I thought you were Alette."

"I was pretty spooked by you as well. I saw you watching me and the next moment you switched off your light. Why?"

He smiled wryly. "Frankly, I was embarrassed that you'd caught me staring."

"Well don't do it again. It's creepy."

"No, ma'am." He smiled again; an easy smile this time.

After taking a sip of his tea, he said, "You were very close to Alette, weren't you? She told me you grew up together."

"We were like sisters."

"I rather expected to see you at the funeral."

"You were there?"

He nodded and for a fleeting moment there was genuine distress in his eyes.

Isa thought of the funeral book Mr. Darling had given her. She couldn't remember seeing Michael Chapman in the list of names.

"You didn't sign the book."

For a moment he looked confused, then he said, "Oh—no. No,

I didn't. Couldn't think of anything to write, really. Everything I thought of sounded so trite."

"Her ex-husband didn't sign his name either." Isa didn't know why she felt she had to mention it. The words left her mouth as if of their own volition.

"I saw him there." Michael's voice was colorless.

Isa watched him fold his arms across his chest and thought: He knows. He knows about Alette and Justin.

"You don't like him, do you?"

She couldn't believe herself. Under normal circumstances she would never ask such a question of someone she had just met. But after Alette's letter she felt as though she were flying blind. Anything he could tell her would be important.

"He's a prick," Michael said calmly. "Sorry. That was crude. But it's the truth. Alette's life was a living hell because of him."

She made a noncommittal gesture with her head. "I gathered that where Alette was concerned, he was very . . . possessive."

"Possessive?" Michael was silent for a moment, his gaze vacant. Then he shook his head slowly. "Possessive is not the correct word. It went beyond that. Alette was the most independent-minded person I knew, but Temple destroyed her self-confidence. Some guys don't know how to accept no for an answer. He was obsessed with her. Besotted. He couldn't deal with the fact that she was no longer interested in him."

Isa frowned. "There is something that troubles me. Her attorney told me that on the day of her death she had driven all the way to the north coast of Devon to talk to him. Why would she do that?"

"Her attorney told you this?"

"Yes. Why, what's the matter?"

Michael lifted his eyebrows. "I find it odd that he would know about it, quite frankly. I wouldn't have thought that Alette would have taken him into her confidence to such an extent."

"I'm not quite sure what you mean. He said she had business to discuss with Justin."

"Oh. Well, maybe that's what she told him . . . but still, I wouldn't have thought she would even have mentioned the meeting at all."

Isa suddenly remembered the slight hesitation that had marred Lionel Darling's smooth voice as he uttered the word "business."

"So the meeting with Justin wasn't about business."

"No. On the day she died she was going to have it out with him. She had asked my advice, and to tell you the truth, I was dead set against her talking to the man. It was only going to fuel his obsession even more. But Alette had had enough. He was visiting his mother and she drove all the way out there to confront him. On her way back, she had the accident. So I suppose we'll never know whether she managed to talk some sense into him. My guess is not."

Isa looked past Michael out the window. The burst of sunshine that had seemed so bright and cheerful that morning was gone. The sky was gray. The wind whipped up stray papers and debris and tugged at the coats of passersby.

She realized that Michael had asked her a question and was waiting for an answer.

"Pardon?"

"I asked how long you'll be staying here," he repeated again patiently.

"I'm not sure yet. I have all these arrangements to make."

"She left you the house?"

Isa nodded. She pushed her chair back and got to her feet. "I have to get to a post office. Could you direct me?"

"Sure. There's one just a block away from here." His eye fell on the two envelopes she had taken out of her bag.

"That's Alette's handwriting." He sounded shocked.

"Yes. She asked me to send these off for her." When he looked at her strangely, Isa tried to explain. "She left me some instructions in her will . . ."

"Oh. Well, then." He sounded almost at a loss. "If you need any help, let me know." He took his wallet out of his back pocket. "Here's my card. I mean it. Anything I can do—just name it."

She looked up into his eyes. He really did have kind eyes. "Thank you."

She turned around and allowed him to help her with her coat. He was such a big man, he made her feel quite fragile. It was an unusual feeling. She was so tall, she was usually able to look most men straight in the eye.

On the sidewalk outside, he held out his hand. "Well, so long, then."

"Good-bye." She watched as he crossed the road right in front of an oncoming car. He was walking with that peculiar shambling gait she had noticed earlier, but he was also surprisingly quick. He reached the other side of the road unscathed and turned around to give her a final wave before disappearing around the corner.

Isa pushed her fists into her coat pockets and turned in the direction he had pointed out to her. She found the post office without any problem. After buying stamps, she pushed the two envelopes through the slit of the post box one by one; holding on to them until her hand had fully disappeared from view.

For a moment she stood looking around her irresolutely. The weather had deteriorated badly. But she couldn't face going back to the house.

Fulham Road was busy with shoppers. Christmas lights in the shape of Christmas trees were draped around every lamp pole. In the freezing fog the tiny white lights seemed to be floating. Movement and noise were all around her, but still Isa felt isolated from it all; as though she were an invisible woman with those around her heedless of her presence. She tried to make eye contact, but people were looking straight through her. She passed by a pub and the door suddenly opened with a rush of warm air. The sound of laughter floated out at her and she stopped for a moment to listen.

She turned off the high street into a residential street. It was quiet here. It must have started to rain again, because when she touched her hair she was surprised to find her hand wet with moisture. It was so peculiar, this English rain. One moment the street was dry and then all of a sudden there was water underfoot and rain glimmered on the black tree trunks. The rain was quiet; almost unnoticeable. How did Alette stand its soft, insidious presence day after day? In Natal the rain was heavy and dense and the drops so big they made the leaves on trees droop.

Isa could never understand why Alette hadn't returned to South Africa after the divorce. Alette loved Natal: its sensuous heat; the promiscuous growth of the vegetation. When she asked Alette if she'd ever go home again, Alette said no. "I can't live there anymore," she said. "Everything has to do with race. It's too tiring living there. In South Africa your every act, your every thought has a moral dimension. It's hard enough as it is just to build a life. The guilt and the fear—I can't handle it any more." Isa accepted that explanation without comment but it never really satisfied her. Alette was not a quitter or a coward. And she truly loved the place. Something else must have influenced her decision.

Isa was beginning to tire. Her aimless wandering had taken her up the Exhibition Road and she was now walking through large, cast-iron gates into Hyde Park. A swarm of birds flew up from the trees in front of her, their wings black crescents against a cold sky.

Isa stopped dead in her tracks. She knew this place. She had been here once before. She had a vivid picture of that day: the day before Alette's wedding. They had just left a restaurant where

Justin and Alette had held a late lunch for out-of-town guests. It was a snowy day, with all the enchantment of white sidewalks and streetlights throwing shimmering circles on the ice. Justin and Alette had insisted on walking her back to her hotel and they had passed by Hyde Park, stopping for a few moments at this exact same spot.

And all of a sudden, as though music were playing for their ears alone, Justin and Alette had started to dance. Isa remembered the two figures twirling silently, locked in an embrace. Alette's red satin pumps: the thin, high heels sinking into the soft snow; around one slender ankle a gold chain from which dangled a tiny rose-shaped charm. Justin in his long, dark overcoat cradling Alette in his arm. Her hair: long, red tendrils clinging to his shirtfront.

Five years ago. Five years in which love turned to hate: gold turning to lead. An experiment in emotional alchemy that went horribly wrong.

Isa turned around and walked out the gate. She hailed a taxi, and as she got into the cab, she gave a last look back over her shoulder. That silent dance underneath the hushed trees was haunting her still.

By the time she unlocked the front door of Alette's house, the light was fading: the day turning to dusk. Isa did not switch on any lights, even though it was almost dark on the staircase and she had to guide herself by gripping the balustrade firmly.

The late afternoon gloom had drained all color from Alette's bedroom. The sheer white drapes trailing from the posts of the bed; the moon glint on the silver frames on the bedside table; the dark shadows in the folds of the drapes: they had the muted clarity of a black-and-white photograph. Isa kicked off her shoes and lay down on the bed.

She made a conscious effort to relax. Her gaze came to rest on one of the photographs on the bedside table. It was a picture of

Alette and herself on their confirmation day: demure faces, high-collared suits too grown-up for fifteen-year-olds. The suits were identical. For some reason Aunt Lettie had insisted on it. Next to this photograph, captured in a carved wooden frame, was a dreadful picture of Siena, eyes narrowed into suspicious slits, her mouth doubtful. But it was the only photograph Alette had of Siena. Siena hated having her photograph taken. She feared the camera: believed it might spirit her very soul away. She had only acquiesced to having this picture taken because Alette had practically begged her. And at the time Siena had already been very ill.

Isa could still recall the last time she had seen Siena alive. It was during one of her weekend visits to the farm after she had started college. She had walked into the house, happy and excited to be home, and had come upon Siena and Alette unexpectedly where they were sitting together on the outside veranda. They hadn't seen her and something made Isa hesitate, made her hover just inside the doorway out of sight.

Siena was sitting cross-legged on the ground, huddled in a brown blanket. Every so often she would cough. In her hand was a piece of chalk with which she was drawing on the cement floor in front of her.

The chalk scratched noisily against the concrete. Siena was drawing a large triangle.

"Here." Siena tapped a spot at the apex of the triangle. "Here is God, the creator. And here—" she leaned forward and pointed to one leg of the triangle—"are the ancestral spirits. They are very important. The ones who have died recently are still close to us. If you ask them for help they will give your message to the more important spirits who died long ago. And those very important ancestors will give it to the Godhead."

"What happens to the important ancestral spirits?" Alette's voice was low.

Siena closed her eyes briefly. "After a long, long, long time the spirit can return to its tribe and live again. If it so wishes."

"So they never really die," Alette said slowly.

Siena did not answer. She gestured at the opposite leg of the triangle. "These are the forgotten ones." She looked at Alette and her voice sounded remote. "They have died violently and far from home."

"The forgotten ones?"

"Their link with their people is broken."

"So they are lost?"

From where she stood behind the door, Isa was unable to see the expression in Siena's eyes, but the weariness in the old woman's voice cut her to the heart.

"They become nature spirits," said Siena. "Like the nature spirits of flowers, and rivers and rocks. But they will not acquire a new life on Earth."

It was very still. Not even a birdcall disturbed the silence.

Siena sighed. "Yes. Maybe that is right. Maybe you can say: They are lost."

THE PHONE RANG. THE MEMORY OF SIENA AND ALETTE SITTING SIDE by side on the sunbaked veranda, the branches of the acacia tree throwing sharp shadows on the wall, faded from Isa's mind. She stretched out her hand to pick up the receiver.

But suddenly she didn't feel like talking to anyone right now or having to explain why Alette wasn't the one who was answering. She looked at the phone, willing it to stop, and after a few long moments the ringing ceased almost abruptly.

On her return to the house it had been dusk, but now the sky outside the window was black. She was cold and stiff from lying on the bed for so long. Maybe she should run herself a bath.

The sound of the front door banging shut made her sit up with a start. She swung her legs over the side of the bed and walked silently on stockinged feet out onto the landing outside the room.

For a moment she thought she had been imagining things because the house seemed almost peculiarly silent, but then she clearly heard the rustle of clothes and the sound of a footstep on a stair.

She moved back into the room and grabbed the phone. But as she stood there with the receiver in her hand, the dialing tone finally turning into a long, monotonous stuttering noise, she realized that she had no idea whatsoever what the police emergency number was in the U.K. Back home the emergency number was branded into every South African's memory. But over here she just did not have a clue.

She could hear the sound of breathing and a male voice swearing under his breath. Quietly she slid behind the bedroom door. Her fingers curled around the base of a charming little statuette: Cupid, the archer, with his full quiver of arrows. She picked it up. There was a satisfying heft to the little figure. She lifted it in the air and readied herself.

The intruder stopped just inside the bedroom door. Through the opening between the door and the jamb, Isa could make out a dark raincoat and the outline of an arm.

He stepped fully into the room. Isa pushed herself away from the wall and rushed at him, the statue already swinging down in a vicious arc. He must have heard her a split second before she moved, though, because he swung around and his uplifted arm deflected her blow.

"What the hell—" He swung his arm violently backward against her and the force of his movement drove the air from her body and made her stumble badly. Her knees buckled, and as she fell to the floor, she gasped as her elbow connected painfully with the side of the table.

The pain was so sharp and severe that it stunned her for a moment. From the floor she looked up into the intruder's face.

He had aged. Five years ago his hair had been black, showing no untidy patches of silver or any thinning at the temples. His jaw, once firm and taut, had slackened, but there was a new tightness at the corners of his eyes and mouth. He was still an attractive man.

He stared at her. "Isa. God, I'm sorry. Here, let me help you." He leaned forward and held out his hand.

She hesitated for a second, then placed her hand in his. She felt a tiny shiver of apprehension—revulsion?—running through her body as he pulled her to her feet.

She straightened her back and looked him full in the face. "Hello, Justin."

"Are you okay? Are you hurt?"

She shook her head and moved away from him. "What are you doing here?"

He had the grace to look embarrassed. "I did call just now. There was no answer and the house was dark, so I thought I'd take a chance and sneak in here before you came back."

"You knew I was here?"

He sighed. "To be honest, I saw you the other night. I passed by here and saw you through the window."

He turned around in sudden irritation. "Why are we standing here whispering at each other in the dark?" He reached with unerring certainty for the light switch behind the door. "There."

He looked over to where she was standing, warily watching him. "I know. This is unforgivable. I should have just knocked the other night. The truth is, I wasn't sure whether you'd want to see me. You and Alette were so close. God knows what she told you about me after the divorce."

"She didn't tell me that much." Which was, technically speaking, true.

His eyebrows raised incredulously. But before he could speak she said, "So what is it you're looking for?" In the bright glare of the overhead light, she could see deep creases on his forehead.

"I'm looking for a ring . . ."

Isa stared at him disbelievingly. "Alette's wedding ring?"

He made an impatient gesture with his hand. "No, no. It's an enameled gold ring. It belonged to my mother. I gave it to Alette shortly after our engagement. I've always wanted it back."

Isa gestured to the dressing table. "Go ahead."

"Thank you," he said in a subdued voice. He slid open the drawer and took out the rosewood box in which Alette kept her jewelry. After opening a few of the small chamois pouches, he extracted a thin golden ring. "This is it."

"May I see it?" Isa held out her hand.

"Of course."

It was a "poesy" ring. She had seen others like it in the Victoria and Albert Museum. These poetry rings were always inscribed with a romantic message. She turned the ring around. This one's message read "As true to Thee as Death to Me."

"It's pretty." As she gave the ring back to him, she realized that her hands were trembling.

"It's valuable. This ring is not the original ring, which dates from 1662—it's a copy. But it is over two hundred years old. Alette should have kept it in a safe." He frowned. "I'll reimburse you for this, of course."

"No. Please take it." Isa turned around and started to walk out of the room, forcing him to follow her. As she passed by the rearview window, she looked out. A yellow wedge of light was coming from the corner apartment on the top floor of the building opposite. Michael was at home.

She was acutely aware of Justin behind her as they walked down the stairs. In the entrance hall he stooped and picked up his briefcase. It had a zippered top and was open. Isa recognized the salmon-colored pages of the *Financial Times*. The paper was folded at the page that listed the day's stock prices.

Her stomach suddenly felt hollow. She opened the door quickly and stood to one side so that he could leave.

He lingered on the door step. "Listen. I want us to see each other again. How long will you be staying?"

"Awhile longer. But, Justin . . . I don't know about this."

"I'm not taking no for an answer. I'll pick you up for dinner Sunday at eight."

She opened her mouth to protest, but as he shifted his briefcase from his left to his right hand, she caught another glimpse of the newspaper, and the knowledge of what she had done earlier that day suddenly struck her forcibly. Who knows what might be printed in that newspaper tomorrow?

She looked back at him. His eyes were a clear blue. Underneath there were black shadows.

She took a deep breath. "All right. Eight o'clock."

It was only after he had left that she realized she hadn't asked him how he had gained access to the house.

SEVEN

Too late hee would the paine asswage,
And to thick shadowes does retire;
About with him hee beares the rage,
And in his tainted blood the fire.

> —"The selfe-banished,"
> Edmund Waller (1606–1687)

LOVE IS VIOLENCE. SHE SAID THAT. VIOLENCE AND LOVE: LINKED together as through some diseased organic tissue.

Love is torment. Love is emotional incontinence. We seek desperately to suffer, she said, because love without suffering is love without ecstasy. And for ecstasy we'll do anything. To experience that extreme friction of the senses, to arrive at that moment when all the faculties are heightened; for that, we'll willingly seek to be violated, to meet any of love's rough demands.

Isn't it telling, she said, that unneurotic love—the love of the sane and levelheaded man—is seldom, if ever, celebrated? Think Lancelot and Guinevere. Think Abelard and Héloise. To prove her point she'd read to him out loud passages from her favorite poems. Tales of forbidden love, fatal love, unrequited love.

He adored it when she did that. It took him back to those early, early years when his mother read poetry to him at bedtime. Not nursery-rhyme books. Not Jack and Jill went up the hill, but real, grown-up books. How important that made him feel. Almost as if he were his mother's confidant. And what a privilege to drift to sleep, teased by thrilling thoughts he did not fully comprehend.

His mother preferred the work of the Metaphysical poets: that clubby, elite group of men who wrote for each other's intellectual gratification and who lived in a time of plague and war and instability. She taught him to appreciate poetry in which love and carnal desire exist in a world shadowed by death and corruption; by fleabites and maggots; carcasses, dissections, fever, palsy, quicksilver sweat, and bracelets of bright hair about the bone.

Violence is love. Didn't he, through violence, make the ultimate sacrifice? Wasn't there something heroic in an act which terminated so abruptly the cancer of obsession?

But he was concerned about his compulsion to return to Alette's house again and again. It was going to get him into trouble. That night, when he had heard the key scrape in the lock, he had had just enough time to slip into the kitchen and close the door. He had been confused by his brief glimpse of a tall, slim, female figure in the doorway, but then he had noticed the suitcase and he knew it had to be Isa. Or rather Isabelle, as Alette always insisted. She must have just arrived from the airport. What he would have done if she'd decided to explore the kitchen first, he did not know.

In the end it had been quite easy to slip out unseen. And later he had watched her through the window. He had relished her unself-conscious vulnerability: the vulnerability of a woman who was being observed without her knowledge.

He hadn't expected it to be so thrilling, finally, to talk to her. Face-to-face, he was able to see a lost look in her eyes. She had lovely eyes. She wasn't a beauty, not like Alette, but there was something at the corner of her mouth—something sad and soft—which touched him.

Still, he had problems with the fact that she was living in Alette's house. And sooner, rather than later, he would have to find out why she was staying on.

EIGHT

We by this friendship shall survive in death,
Even in divorce united.

"La Belle Confidente,"
Thomas Stanley (1625–1678)

ISA SCROLLED SLOWLY THROUGH THE MENU ON THE COMPUTER SCREEN; past the entries for "Market at a Glance" and "What's Hot/What's Not," until the cursor came to rest at "StockFind." Then, as she had done several times a day for the past week, she typed in the words "Temple Sullivan" in the space left for the company name and double-clicked on the yellow-and-red Go Find It icon. The screen turned blue.

There was a fresh item on Temple Sullivan in the news section: a brief discussion of a promising, new-generation anti-inflammatory drug in the company's pipeline. But not a word about Taumex or any potential sourcing and supply problems. Not a word. She had not really expected to find anything. She had already scoured the pages of the *Financial Times* and *London Post* and they hadn't carried any stories either.

Since making the phone calls to the brokers and mailing

Alette's letters to the newspapers, she has been monitoring Temple Sullivan's stock price with the zeal of a lottery-ticket fanatic. But so far there had been no unusual price move.

She had also accessed past news stories on the company and details of financial performance. Until only fourteen months ago, the stock had been volatile in the extreme; at one stage falling a vertiginous twenty percent before rallying again. In the past fifty-two weeks, however, the stock was headed in one direction only: up. And according to the analysts, its dizzying upward trajectory seemed set.

Isa moved the cursor to the icon that would allow her access to real-time stock quotes and tapped the enter key. The screen blinked and current stock prices and trading details started flowing across the screen. As she watched, a small green arrow appeared next to the trading symbol TMPSUL and the entries for "last price," "last change" clicked over. Temple Sullivan stock was up forty pence on the day.

She leaned back in her chair. She didn't know whether to feel relieved or disappointed. But one thing was clear.

Alette had it wrong. No one was taking any notice.

SHE SHOULD HAVE CANCELED HER DINNER DATE WITH JUSTIN. WHY hadn't she?

Isa looked in the mirror as though she would find the answer there. But the sight of her anxious eyes and pinched mouth only made her more nervous than she already was. And she was nervous. She was very nervous. Her hands wouldn't stop shaking. She glanced at her watch. She had exactly thirty minutes to pull herself together before meeting Justin.

She needed some color in her face: she was too pale. She picked up the blusher and dragged the soft brush in generous strokes across her cheekbones. Now she looked like a clown. Strained eyes and apple cheeks. She'd have to go wash it off.

More than once this week she had thought of canceling. But it was imperative that she find out more about what had happened between Alette and Justin. She owed it to herself. After all, she had now become an invisible partner in that relationship.

A relationship dictated by the wishes of a dead woman.

Her hands trembled as she stretched the sheer fabric of the panty hose over her toes. Justin had called earlier that day to ask if she'd mind meeting him at the restaurant. She preferred it. The idea of again meeting him at the house made her feel short of breath: this house where Alette looked out at her from every photograph, where she could imagine turning around suddenly to find Alette curled up in an easy chair, yawning and stretching unashamedly, still sleepy after a long nap.

She couldn't understand why she hadn't yet made any effort to pack up Alette's things. She should start making arrangements for storage; consult with an estate agent. Instead she has left everything virtually untouched. Alette's garden shears, gloves, and mud-caked boots were still lying in an untidy heap just inside the kitchen door. Every time she entered the kitchen, she had to step over them. The laundry bin was filled with Alette's underwear and some of her lace blouses that required hand washing. In some ways she, Isa, felt like the ghost: a creature of no substance who was haunting a house that was waiting breathlessly for the sound of other, quicker footsteps on the stairs; for another hand to turn on the lights. Even now, as she pulled the front door to and placed the key in the lock, she did it without any sense of ownership. This place would never be home.

Justin was already waiting for her at the table when she entered the restaurant. He got to his feet and pulled out the chair with old-fashioned courtesy. For a few moments as he spoke to the waiter about menus and drink orders, she was able to study him. The other night in the house, he had seemed to her not only grayer, but somehow grayed: as though the energy she had always associated with him was there no more. But tonight he seemed closer to the charming, darkly handsome man she remembered. His most outstanding characteristic used to be a decisiveness of manner, and an air of barely contained enthusiasm. The intensity with which he approached life, the speed at which he made his decisions, had been seductive.

He was looking at her appraisingly; probably noticing quite a few changes as well.

He picked up the menu. "So what do you feel like? The fish is good here."

They discussed menu choices, mentioned preferences in food. They both spoke tentatively, hesitantly; circling each other like wary fencers. The conversation was punctuated by fractional hesitations; by their eyes meeting and then sliding apart. She realized that they had too much to say and too little to say. At times the conversation flowed easily: a tide of inane, safe nothingness; but then a chance remark would suddenly—dizzyingly—open up the possibility of accessing the store of shared memories regarding Alette.

Alette. She could just as well have been sitting at the table with them, her chin propped up on one hand, her eyes narrowed dreamily in that way she had when she was relaxed and enjoying herself.

He was now telling her about his business. He probably thought it a topic admirably suited to keep dangerous emotions from crowding in on them. What could be more innocuous than talking about work, what could be less messy. He spoke animatedly, seemingly quite at ease, while she clutched her fingers under the table, felt a nerve tighten inside her forehead.

He was explaining to her some of the early difficulties they had faced in the development of the drug. "Diagnosis was the major problem. With Alzheimer's it used to be that it was very difficult to diagnose properly. Brain scans as well as blood and spinal fluid tests were of only limited use. And as long as doctors weren't sure of their diagnosis, the possibility of prevention and cure was remote."

She was surprised. "I always thought the symptoms of Alzheimer's were unmistakable."

He shook his head. "Only after the patient had died and a post-mortem performed could a physician be sure whether it was Alzheimer's or not. Only after." He added slowly: "The only certainty was in death."

He stopped speaking and for a moment his face relaxed into an odd, close-lipped smile.

"Has that changed?"

He looked back at her, his gaze suddenly focused again. "Oh yes. An American drug company funded a project at Oxford University called Optima. Their studies pinpointed massive tissue loss in the brain as a marker for Alzheimer's. No other kind of dementia shows such visible tissue loss. And a host of other studies have been done worldwide, which have all helped to dramatically cut the error rate in diagnosis. They also managed to pinpoint the beta-site APP-cleaving enzyme, BACE: one of the two enzymes responsible for plaque formation in the Alzheimer brain. All of this paved the way for the development of Taumex."

"Why Alzheimer's? Why didn't you choose something else. Cancer, AIDS?"

"No." He shook his head emphatically. "Nothing fascinates like dementia. It is the ultimate puzzle. Think about it. Think what it must be like to lose sight of the memories and sensations of a lifetime. Think of your desires becoming colorless: your most intense passions of no more value to you than an empty paper cup."

He was leaning forward, his hands restlessly playing with the utensils on the table. His eyes were fixed solidly on her face, but she had the impression that he wasn't noticing her. "Of course, even in our daily lives we have brushes with dementia. We become demented with grief. Or crazed with love. We become enraged and lose our grip on reality." His mouth twisted. "A different type of madness, I grant you. But possibly just as nightmarish."

The intensity in his voice made her uncomfortable. "Tell me about the company," she said. "Business is good, then?"

"Touch wood." He knocked lightly with his knuckles against his head. "No, seriously, the company's doing fine. The good times are here, finally. It took us eleven years, you know, to get to this stage. With pharmaceuticals it's a crap game. It was touch and go for a while: the first clinical trials were a nightmare. But Taumex is now out there, being prescribed. And we now have the capital to start pushing some of our other drugs that are in development. There's a central-nervous-system drug we're working on—an antidepressant—which is looking good, and I'm very excited about our research into a new anti-inflammatory drug."

She took a deep breath. "You love your job."

"I do." His voice was almost subdued. "This sounds pretty mawkish, I know, but it's a job worth doing. Taumex is a good product: it's helping a lot of people. In the U.K. alone there are one hundred thousand people diagnosed with Alzheimer's every year. That's a planeload of people every day."

He lifted a self-mocking eyebrow. "And, let's face it: I'm making real money. But that's enough about my affairs." He gave her an uncomplicated smile. "Let's open another bottle of wine. Then I want you to tell me all about your job; what you do."

He seemed genuinely interested. And after a while she could feel herself starting to unclench. The wine was relaxing her, making the blood run through her veins warmly and sleepily. The background noise in the restaurant was a benign, soothing hum. She could almost forget about Alette; about the letter. She could almost enjoy herself. This was a man who knew how to charm and he was a good listener. He had a way of seeming to concentrate intensely on what she was saying. It had the effect of encouraging her to talk more about herself than she would have thought possible. Maybe it was the wine. Maybe she was a soft touch, taken in by the compliment he was paying her by giving her his undivided attention. Paying attention was, after all, the greatest gift you could bestow on anyone. Whatever the reason—and later she would have great difficulty explaining it to herself—he had managed to get her to talk about Eric.

"What do you miss most about him?"

She thought for a moment. "He asked good questions."

It was quiet between them, then he nodded as though what she had said made perfect sense.

"How did he die?"

"He was hijacked in his car. And then they shot him. My worst nightmare was always that something might happen to him without my knowing. And that's the way it turned out in the end. I didn't know he had died until two days after."

The memory of that moment was still vivid as a wet burn wound. She had heard about it in the ladies' room, of all places. She remembered herself applying fresh lipstick and listening with half an ear to the banal conversation between two pretty secretaries. Hearing his name. Her hand holding the lipstick slackening and then jerking; leaving a bloody mark across her cheek.

Justin touched her hand: a butterfly touch. "I'm sorry."

She shook her head. "We had twelve years. That's more than most people have."

He gazed up briefly, then down again. "You accepted the fact that he would never leave his wife and children."

"Yes."

"You weren't hoping? Not even in your heart of hearts?"

"No. I wasn't proud of coming between him and his wife. The guilt was always there. But I could see myself living like that for the rest of my life. The only regret I had was that I might never have a child of my own. But I was willing not to make that demand."

"Not making demands. That does seem to be the magic formula."

"I know Alette thought I was playing a loser's game. But the truth of it is, even if I were, I didn't care. I would do it again, if I could only have him back this minute."

And there, she had done it. And the mention of Alette's name chilled the air between them.

He leaned back in his chair. "I've always wondered what it must have been like growing up with Alette." He made it sound as though she had been part of a dubious experiment.

"What do you mean exactly?"

He shrugged. "Well, Alette had a way of simply dragging one along in her wake. It must have been overwhelming at times for someone . . ." He didn't finish the sentence but Isa knew what he was thinking. For someone like herself.

"Alette always looked out for me."

His face stayed smooth, unemotional.

"She was the one who encouraged me to go to graduate school: to study architecture. And if it weren't for her, I wouldn't have my own business now. After her parents died she used some of the money they left her to help me with start-up capital."

It suddenly became important to her that he should understand how much she owed Alette; what Alette meant to her.

"She saved my life once."

There was a pause, then he said simply, "I didn't know that."

"We were fifteen. We went hiking and I stepped into the path of a mamba. Most snakes are shy; but not black mambas. They're incredibly aggressive. I wasn't wearing hiking boots, Alette was. So she decided to take the risk. She deliberately moved and distracted the snake's attention. It attacked her, not me."

"But she was okay?"

"No. Actually she wasn't. What she didn't know was that mambas rear up when they attack. They can rear up to a height of three feet and they bite several times in rapid succession. Alette got bitten in the arm repeatedly. She should have died; you don't survive an attack like that. But a medical emergency helicopter happened to be in the area and they got her to the hospital within thirty minutes. Against all odds, she pulled through."

"So she was close to death."

"She managed to beat it."

And then Alette's dad had gone out to search for that snake. He had found the mamba in a hole in the ground, next to eleven perfect, white, oval eggs, and had shot it. After that he had smashed the eggs. For years afterward the snake lay curled up inside a glass canned fruit bottle on a shelf in Uncle Leon's study. Every now and then Isa had climbed on top of a chair to stare at that glass bottle and its contents: the oily coils; the fangs inside the half-open, black-lined mouth; the formaldehyde, at first clear, then slowly yellowing with age.

She looked up to find Justin watching her. "That's quite a story."

Isa replaced the wineglass with a sharp little bump. "Isn't it."

"Don't be so defensive, Isa. Just because Alette and I had our differences"—for just a second something flickered behind his eyes—"it doesn't mean I'm going to sit here bad-mouthing Alette to you. I know the two of you had a special relationship."

"We did, yes." Correction—wrong tense—she thought silently. We do.

He sighed. "So when are you planning on going back to South Africa?"

"I'm not sure. There are a lot of loose ends to tie up." She tried to sound less evasive. "The house and so on."

"Well, if you need help with anything, I'm available."

"Thanks. Alette's attorney seems very capable. I'm meeting him again tomorrow afternoon, as a matter of fact. And Alette's affairs are in order. She left detailed instructions for me to follow." As the words left her mouth, Isa blushed, suddenly aware of their double meaning.

He lifted a quizzical eyebrow at her obvious discomfort. Then he said idly, "What are you doing for Christmas?"

"Christmas. I haven't actually thought that far ahead."

"Well, listen." He stopped and took out his credit card to give to the hovering waiter. "I have to go to the country. I'm spending Christmas with my mother. But I'll still be around until the twenty-third. Why don't we have a drink together before I leave?"

She made a sharp, negative motion with her head. "That's okay. I'll be fine, really."

"There are still some of Alette's things in my apartment. Alette and I somehow never got around to sorting them out. You ought to have them. Actually, I seem to remember seeing some photographs amongst all of that stuff. And books. Why don't you come by and take a look. Pick what you want and I'll dispose of the rest."

"I'd like the photos."

"Fine, it's settled then. Stop by next week. Wednesday at around seven." He rummaged inside his wallet and took out a small, buff-colored business card. *Justin Temple. Chief Executive Officer. Temple Sullivan International Ltd.* Both his home and business addresses were on the card.

When she got up from the table, he placed his hand on her elbow. Through the fabric of her dress she could feel the pressure of his fingers. "I'll drive you."

They didn't speak inside the car. He steered the car smoothly, competently, through the blur of traffic. She leaned her head against the neck rest, her eyes looking out at the black night beyond the window. The ghostly outline of a face glimmered for a moment against the glass and she blinked. But it was merely a glimpse of her own reflection.

Justin stopped the car in the street outside Alette's front door, not parking it. With the engine still running, he got out and opened the door for her.

"Thank you."

As he slammed the door shut behind her, Isa saw Michael Chapman getting out of an ancient Mini Cooper farther down the street. It was a slightly comical picture: this large man sticking out his long legs from within the tiny interior of the car. The light from the street lamp turned his fair hair white. As he turned around, he spotted Isa and gave her a quick salute.

"Who's that?" Justin was staring at Michael's retreating back.

"Someone I've met."

"You make friends easily." Beneath the bantering tone, there was something else in his voice, something edgy. "Wait a minute, I know him."

"He was a friend of Alette's."

"Of course. Now I remember. The brain-dead finger painter."

"Actually," she said primly, "I think he's a nice man."

"Nice man." He smiled, his eyes suddenly amused. "Yes, I can live with that. It makes him sound sufficiently boring." He made to get behind the wheel, but she stopped him.

"Justin. I'd like the keys."

He frowned.

"The keys to Alette's house. The ones you used to get inside the house."

"Oh, yes. Sorry. I still feel terrible about creeping in there like a thief. What you must think of me." He reached into the inside pocket of his jacket. "Here you are. I meant to give them to you earlier tonight, but I forgot."

She took the two keys from him. "How did you come by these?"

He shrugged. "Alette gave me a spare set."

Isa could feel the disbelief turning down the corners of her mouth. He shook his head. "It's true. She gave them to me of her own free will." A sudden gust of wind blew his hair into his eyes. He put up a hand to push it back. "We tried to reconcile once." She had the impression that he wanted to add something to what he had said, that he was hesitating. But then the troubled look left his eyes and his face assumed its habitual expression: not guarded exactly; not wary but . . . watchful.

"Thank you for dinner." She held out her hand.

"It was good to catch up. I'll see you next week, then." Before she could react, he leaned forward and gave her a light kiss on the one cheek: his lips barely brushing her face.

She had been so keyed up for her meeting with him that it was now almost an anticlimax to watch him drive away before she sedately walked back into the house. It was quite late. Although there really was nothing left to do but get ready for bed, she was wide awake.

Her eye was caught by the book with its pebbled leather cover that Alette must have been reading, and which was still, like that first night when she had come upon it, lying spread-eagled and facedown on the easy chair. She picked it up.

It was a book on alchemy and its symbolic significance in spiritual evolution. She paged listlessly through the densely printed pages. As usual, Alette had marked many of the pages in pencil. Exclamation marks, wavy lines, and double vertical lines abounded in the margins. One entire paragraph was shaded: *Solve et Coagula: determine all your elements, dissolve that which is diminishing, even though you may self-destruct in doing so; then with the power gained from the preceding process, congeal.* A few pages on, another high-lighted sentence: *In the Tradizione Ermetica, Evola teaches that alchemy is the transformation and change of one being into another being, one thing into another thing, weakness into strength, the physical into the spiritual.* The words *weakness into strength* and *physical into the spiritual* were heavily underlined and in the margin next to it, Alette had printed: *How to help myself? How to empower myself? How to save myself from myself?*

Isa rubbed her thumb against the page, as if by doing so she could fathom those questioning marginalia. The words stared up at her: dead sentences only.

She was finally beginning to feel sleepy. She took off her dress and underclothes and opened the closet to put them away. And there it was—as immediate as a favorite thought—the faded, elusive scent of rose and jasmine that perfumed all of Alette's drawers and closets. Isa pushed the door even wider and reached for a cedarwood hanger. Her hand brushed against a white, lacy night-dress. The fabric was filmy. It clung to her skin for a brief moment: a secret, hidden caress.

She withdrew the nightdress from among the folds of the other garments. It was one of Alette's antique pieces. The embroidery was slightly frayed, and the collar had yellowed with age. Alette loved vintage clothes. She used to scour antique stores for just the right garments. How many times had she accompanied Alette on these shopping expeditions and watched her pick through crumpled velvet hats, lavishly embroidered blouses, and dresses in drop-shoulder style.

Actually, as she looked closer at the garment in her hand, she recognized this nightdress . . . and she had a clear memory of the day Alette had bought it. Alette holding the Victorian negligee with its mauve ribbons against herself. "Think of the stories this can tell, Isabelle. Think of all the emotions: the desire, lust . . . the heartbreak." Alette touching the low-scooped neck, the tiny silk-covered buttons; a slow smile on her lips.

The dress was long and wide. Alette must have drowned in it. But it would be a perfect fit for herself. Without thinking, without hesitating, Isa slid the cool folds of the nightgown over her head.

The softness of the fabric felt pleasant against her skin. For a moment she stood looking at herself in the mirror. Clothes maketh man? No. One was born beautiful. The seductive power of a lovely face was a birthright, not something that could be acquired by simply wearing a pretty nightie. She remembered what her aunt Lettie used to say: Women fall in love by listening. Men fall in love by looking. Isa placed her hands on both sides of her face, pulling the skin back so that her eyes lifted with an Oriental slant. Her face remained stubbornly unremarkable.

She sighed and switched off the lamp next to the bed before pulling back the covers and sliding under the sheets. For a while she lay on her back, her eyes adjusting to the dark. She moved her leg, her foot exploring the cold expanse of bed stretching to the one side of her. She wondered what had gone through Alette's mind every night before she closed her eyes to sleep. Did she also stretch out her hand toward the other side of the bed—like this? Did her hand also encounter only vacant space? Probably not. Alette, so truly solitary by nature, usually had someone in her life. And during the brief time Justin and Alette had tried to reconcile, he would have slept in this bed, his head might even have rested on this very pillow.

Tomorrow afternoon she would be picking up the second envelope from Mr. Darling's office. What was it Alette had said in her first letter? *Justin can't get to me. How do you punish a ghost?*

Alette would expect her to collect the envelope tomorrow and continue their partnership. Although the first envelope's instructions hadn't led to anything, who knows what the second might hold?

Should she go through with it? She did not want to let Alette down, but she was starting to have a very bad feeling about this. And after meeting Justin tonight, Alette's plan seemed insane. The evening had not turned out the way she had expected. Probably she had had an infantile wish to see a monster looking out of the eyes of the man sitting opposite her. A vampire whose cheek might crumble to dust at the first ray of sun touching his face. Instead she had spent the evening with an attractive and very charming man. It wasn't that she didn't sympathize with Alette. Of course, she did. Alette's life had been a misery for years and Justin was to blame. But could anything warrant destroying a person's life's work?

Revenge is an immensely empowering emotion.

No. Isa closed her eyes tight. No more. She couldn't do it.

"I'm sorry, Alette." She spoke out loud. Her voice did not carry. It was deadened by the weight of the heavy drapes; the many pillows.

She turned over on her side. She was so tired now. The flesh felt heavy on her bones, she was so tired.

Her legs were like lead and she would not be able to run away from the snake, which suddenly reared up from the grass in front of her. The black, round-pupiled eye. The flickering tongue. The smooth scales prettily patterned against the olive-brown body. She could hear Alette's voice. She was speaking calmly but the words made no sense. And then Alette moved her feet decisively, deliberately; kicking straight at the coiled body, which reacted with a deceptively sluggish, ill-tempered sprawl, the head striking at Alette with astounding speed.

Alette's face so white and frightened. "Isabelle, I'm scared."

The sun spinning, and her breath fire inside her chest as she ran for help. *Hurry, hurry.* She had to get help fast, because if she didn't Alette would die. And it would be her fault, she'd be to blame. *Hurry, hurry.* She stumbled, and a fierce pain shot through her ankle. *Hurry, hurry . . .*

And then, suddenly it was dark as though the sun had been shut out by a tremendous fist and Isa knew she had stepped out of this dream into another. From the corner of her eye, she saw a shape moving slightly behind her. And the shape became a shadowy outline, a figure. And the figure held out her hand.

Take my hand.

Isa stared at the hand. If she took it, she would be instantly transported into the magical reality of a lucid dream. She could sense this parallel reality pulsing softly—insistently—like an undulating web of light just underneath the fabric of her present dream. It's been so long, too long . . .

She slowly lifted her hand, reaching out, her fingers stiff and outstretched. Her fingertips were almost there . . . almost touching. . . . She stretched out her entire arm and felt the muscles pull in her shoulder. . . almost there. . . almost. And then, with no effort at all, she placed the palm of her hand against Alette's.

The fear that slammed into her like a rush of wind was so unexpected it took her breath. The surface under her feet was whipped away and she was hurtling forward, forward—out of control. She was inside the close confines of a car: the glowing green needle on the speedometer was rising steadily. A jumble of impressions battered her mind. The headlights burning into the fog. Trees spinning blackly past the window. The sound of a distressed engine.

She threw her head back on her neck and screamed and her lips drew tightly across her teeth. She turned to the shadowy figure beside her, expecting at any moment to hear Alette say, "Don't worry, we'll stop this. We'll go back." But the words did not come and she looked down at her hand still clasped in Alette's and she jerked it away, and with a sickening, almost physical thud, she tumbled out of sleep.

Her eyes flew open.

She was lying on her side and the pillow underneath her chin was wet with saliva. It was dark, but the room was filled with noise.

The phone was ringing. The ringing sounded odd, flat, strangely off-key. The sound seemed to trigger in her a sense of fluttering nausea.

As if in slow motion she reached for the receiver.

"Is that you, Isabelle?" The voice was low and whispery, almost drowned out by a noise that sounded like the wind blowing through a million leaves.

"Isabelle? Isabelle is that you? . . ." Again the voice faded and she heard only the sound of those restless trees.

"Isabelle . . . don't let go of my hand. Send . . . letter. Isabelle . . ."

Isa tried to speak, but her voice failed her. And then the phone crackled violently and the next moment all she heard was the long, dull tone of a disengaged line.

Isa slammed the receiver onto the phone. Groping behind the bedside table, she gripped the telephone extension cord and ripped it out of the telephone jack.

Somehow she had found her way to the bathroom and was now standing with her hands clamped to the sides of the washbasin, her stomach heaving dryly, eyes straining in her head.

When she finally straightened—the back of her hand pressing against her lips, the inside of her mouth tasting rancid—her eyes locked onto the image in the bathroom mirror opposite her.

For just a moment, for just a splinter of time, the surface of the mirror rippled like wind writing on water. And the face in the mirror blinked her green eyes and shrugged away the heavy fall of red hair from her forehead.

SECOND ENVELOPE

NINE

Darkness and Death lyes in my weeping eyes.
— "The Change,"
Abraham Cowley (1618–1667)

"WHO THE HELL'S SMOKING IN HERE?"

The voice was strident and a fist banged on the outside of the lavatory cubicle's door. Daphne Campbell almost swallowed her cigarette. She quickly stubbed it out in the toilet-roll dispenser and flushed the butt down the drain. She smoothed her hair and pulled at her skirt before opening the door.

The woman on the other side of the door was glaring at her. Not that that was unusual. Brenda Munion always glared. She had feverish eyes and a permanently pugnacious expression. In the newsroom she was known as "Gotcha." But she seemed especially irked right now.

"You know I get fucking asthma from cigarette smoke. This is a smoke-free building, may I remind you. Why aren't you having your fags outside?"

"Have a heart, Brenda. It's minus two below."

Brenda Munion snorted and ripped open her handbag. All

Brenda's movements were always frighteningly abrupt: as though she was having difficulty clamping down on some inner well-spring of violence. Daphne watched as she took out a lipstick and a powder compact and smashed them down on the side of the washbasin.

"I see Martin gave you the Temple Sullivan story."

Daphne nodded listlessly. As far as she was concerned, it was a totally bogus story. And boring. And not the kind of thing she wanted dropped in her lap a week before Christmas.

"So what's happening there?" Brenda was rubbing the lipstick onto her mouth as though trying to erase her already thin lips. And the color. The woman should stay away from cola-colored lipsticks. It made her complexion look even more muddy than it was.

"Not much. It's a load of BS if you ask me. I called this guy— Fromm, I think his name is. A former employee. Very sorry for himself. He told me he has some documentation, which can back up the whole story, but when I asked him to fax it through, he suddenly became coy."

"I interviewed Justin Temple last year," Brenda said. She had taken a pair of tiny tongs from her purse and was now trying to curl her eyelashes. Daphne looked away. This was too much. She had had a disturbing glimpse of the underside of Brenda's eyelid.

"Temple. You remember," Brenda was saying impatiently. "That profile we did on him."

"Oh yes. What's he like?"

"I thought he was really glam."

Glam? Daphne grimaced. "You liked him, then."

"I always have a soft spot for a man who's rich and looks like Heathcliff." Brenda dropped her lipstick into her bag. "But I'll tell you one thing. He runs a tight ship. So what did this Fromm character have to say?"

"Oh, just that there's this one species of plant, which is a vital ingredient in Taumex, and that they've had some problems trying to grow it in a greenhouse environment. And he said something about the authorities in Madagascar threatening to put the plant on the endangered-species list." Daphne shrugged. "So they'll just harvest it someplace else, right. Someplace not third world. It doesn't sound like that much of a problem to me."

Brenda Munion turned around slowly. "Are you stupid, or just ignorant?"

"What's with you?"

"Madagascar has a unique ecosystem. They have plant and animal species there you don't find anywhere else in the world. You may have a real story on your hands. You need to do some digging. It's called investigative journalism." Brenda spoke with exaggerated patience. "Maybe you've heard of it."

Daphne stared at her resentfully. But before she could respond, Brenda said, "I'll take this story. Let me speak to Martin."

"No." Like hell was she going to give this bitch anything. "I'm on it."

"If you change your mind, let me know." Brenda walked to the door. Just before exiting she said spitefully, "You may have to give up your weekend in Ibiza. Pack away the Speedo, darling."

Daphne stared at her reflection in the mirror. She noticed the tiny red veins in her eyes. Too many end-of-the-year office parties will do that to you. And now she'll probably have to get in her car and drive out into the wilds of Gloucestershire to talk to this man Fromm. Shit. Shit. Shit.

THE WHITE MARBLED FLESH OF THE LOVERS GLEAMED WITH A COOL pallor. His hand, large and beautiful, rested on her hip. She was leaning forward, straining to press her mouth against his. Their lips met in an endless kiss; a kiss that was eternal.

"She's more eager than he is."

Isa turned around. Behind her stood Michael Chapman. His hair was as untidy as the first time they had met and he was wearing another hand-knitted sweater: this one blue with a green mistletoe pattern. He wasn't looking at her: he was gazing intently at Rodin's two lovers. Then he dropped his gaze to meet her indignant eyes.

He smiled. "It's true. Look carefully and you'll see. She's the ardent one. He's much more removed from the moment."

Isa looked at the fleshy marble figures once again. Michael was right. There was total supplication in the S-curve of the woman's lovely back: a complete abandonment to the moment of passion. The man was turning his head from the neck and there was a hint of rigidity in the spine.

She sighed. "Well. So nice of you to point that out. Of course you've now pretty well spoiled the experience for me. Thank you very much."

"I'm sorry." His voice was contrite but there was a gleam in his eye. "Let's go look at some ships. That should be safer."

They silently threaded their way through a group of bored teenagers and a busload of neatly dressed Japanese tourists. In the Clore Gallery for the Turner Collection, they moved solemnly from canvas to canvas, not speaking, but after a while Isa had had her fill of pink-and-golden light, sails, masts, and hulls. She turned away from the pictures and walked toward the long windows that gave a glimpse of the Thames and framed the delicate bones of the outside trees.

"You don't look so hot if you don't mind my saying so." Michael had joined her at the window. He was looking at her searchingly.

She noticed the sketch pad clenched underneath his arm. Of course, now she remembered. He spent Mondays in the Tate, copying the artwork.

"I'm fine," she said. "Couldn't sleep, that's all."

"Why not?"

"No real reason."

He didn't push. Later, though, when they were sipping some lukewarm coffee in the cafeteria, he said: "It must be a little spooky living in that house all on your own. Are you okay with it?"

She watched his hands. The fingers were long and thick. He was turning a paper napkin into an intricate doily: folding and tearing the tissue paper with a skill and delicacy that was surprising in someone who gave the impression of being clumsy.

She took a deep breath. "Do you believe in ghosts?"

He smiled. "Don't tell me Alette's been floating up and down the staircase. I'd have expected something a little more classy from her."

"Well, then you won't be disappointed. She's been calling me." Isa paused. "On the phone," she added defiantly.

There was an awful silence. She looked up. She had expected to see embarrassed amusement in his eyes, but his face was stiff with shock.

Oh, God." Isa dropped her face into her hands. "You think I'm crazy."

"Explain this to me," he said at long last. "You mean the two of you actually have a conversation?"

"Well, we did the first time." Just saying the words out loud made her feel deranged.

"The *first* time? You mean this is a regular thing?"

"Twice. Only twice it's happened. The first time I didn't know she was dead. Last night's call lasted only a few moments and afterward I was scared witless and pulled the phone from the wall."

Silence again. "So what do you think?" Isa said. "Padded cell for me, right?"

"Isa. This is insane. No, not you." He stopped, took a breath.

His eyes still showed shock but not, she realized with faint surprise, complete astonishment. "Okay," he was saying. "Okay.
First things first. Tell me everything."

While she spoke, he placed his hand on hers, his fingers gripping strongly. She didn't mind. The pressure of his hand was
comforting: sane, *real*.

"So there's a definite link between the dream and the phone
call," he said after she had finished. "The one leads into the other.
From sleeping to waking. From death to life."

She looked at him gratefully. "So you believe me. You don't
think I'm demented."

"I believe you. Absolutely I believe you. Let's forget about the
phone call for a minute. Let's start with the dream you had last
night. At least lucid dreaming has been scientifically verified.
And its familiar terrain to you."

She grimaced. "Although the idea that I might be sharing a
dream with someone who's dead is not exactly reassuring. And
there's something else. Last night's dream was very different from
the lucid dreams I shared with Alette as a child. Those dreams were
wonderful dreams: joyous, magical things. Even encounters with
monsters did not feel perilous. I always knew we had the power to
think them away—or at least Alette had. And I always woke up
refreshed, feeling on top of the world. Last night's dream . . ."
She shivered, remembering the panic which had clamped itself
around her like a vise. "Last night's dream was frightening beyond
anything."

He frowned. "What exactly did you see after you took Alette's
hand?"

"Not much. All I can remember was movement. As though I
were traveling at a very high speed. As if I were imprisoned in an
out-of-control vehicle. It felt—" she hesitated—"it felt like a run-
away car."

"A car?"

"Yes."

"Alette died of a car crash," he said slowly.

"I know. I've been thinking of that as well. But I'm not sure. The feeling of panic became so strong that I let go of Alette's hand before I had a chance to focus properly on what was going on around me."

"And then?"

"Well, then I had the phone call."

"Ah, yes, the phone call."

Something in his voice made her glance up sharply.

"When the phone rings," he said, "it sounds different, right? There's something about the sound that's unusual."

She thought for a moment. "Yes. Yes, there is. It sounds sort of . . . flat, I suppose. Like it's just the tiniest bit off pitch. And I don't react well to it at all. In fact I get sick to my stomach." Her voice sharpened. "How did you know?"

He stood up and swung his satchel over his shoulder. His face seemed troubled. "Let's go."

"Go? Go where?"

"I need to show you something."

THE CABDRIVER DROPPED THEM OFF IN FRONT OF A SMALL, GOTHIC-looking stone building overlooking a large garden square. Michael pushed open the heavily studded doors. With almost a sense of disappointment Isa realized he had brought her to a library.

The place looked exactly the way she would have expected a British library to look: old—authentic old—with mullioned windows and desks with deeply carved initials in the wood. It was tiny: only one room with a mezzanine section, and it didn't take her long to realize that this was by no means your ordinary, garden-variety library.

The signs marking the various sections were handwritten in a beautiful, flowing script: GNOSTICISM; THE CATHARS; CABALISM; SHEK-INAH; HERMETIC ORDER OF THE GOLDEN DAWN; CLAIRSENTIENCE; ORDER OF THE ROSY CROSS; MARIAN APPARITIONS; TAOISM; THEOSOPHY; NUMEROLOGY, I CHING, RAPA NUI.

The only other occupant of the library, apart from the motherly-looking librarian, was a man dressed in an impeccable three-piece suit. He looked like a banker and was making notes with a Montblanc fountain pen. As she passed by the desk, Isa read the titles of the two books in front of him: *Malleus Maleficorum* and *The Book of the Dead*.

She followed Michael as he led her down an aisle marked by the signs BLACK MAGIC, WHITE MAGIC, and—Isa started—SEXUAL MAGIC.

Michael noticed her stare and grinned faintly. "Some people believe you can reach a higher level of consciousness by having sex with archangels, saints, and historical figures. Sounds like fun. Anyway, that's not it. What I want to show you is this."

He stopped in front of a glass-fronted book case and took out a thick encyclopedia-size volume. The spine was broken, and when he carried it over to the study table, a few loose pages fluttered to the ground.

He moistened the tip of his forefinger and paged rapidly through the book.

"Here," he said. "Read that."

Isa looked at the entry to which his finger was pointing. The heading stated baldly and without apology: *Telephone Calls from the Dead*.

The text was equally sober and unsensationalized:

Most phone calls from the dead take place within days of the death of the caller. The person called is usually someone with whom the caller shared an emotionally close relationship.

The call may terminate suddenly and often the connection is poor. When the phone rings it may sound abnormally flat. The reason for the call is either to impart some information that is necessary for the well-being of the recipient such as a warning of imminent peril—or a request for assistance.

Thomas Edison was working on designing a telephonic link between the living and the dead shortly before his death. In the 1940s further experiments were conducted in England and the United States to reach the deceased by making use of a "psychic" telephone. Interest in the phenomenon peaked in the 1960s when Konstantin Raudive managed to capture voices of the dead on electromagnetic tape. Experiments in the area are still being conducted by a number of modern-day parapsychologists.

Some psychiatrists and parapsychologists suggest that the phenomenon can be explained by hallucinations, which are in part the product of Psychokinesis (PK) done subconsciously by the recipient.

Isa pointed to the last sentence: "'Done subconsciously by the recipient.' So this is all my fault."

"Look, I don't know what it means," Michael said, "and maybe a shrink will tell you it's all fantasy and some kind of subconscious wish fulfillment on your part—you miss Alette, you're traumatized by her death—so you start hearing voices. I just find it mind-blowing that Alette had been extremely interested in this subject. Passionate about it, in fact. She was the one who introduced me to this place." Michael gestured at the leather-bound books behind them. "The very passage you just read, she read to me once. And she's read everything else written on the subject, I can assure you. She told me her interest in afterlife communication started in her childhood. She had this friend; a black woman . . ."

"Siena."

"Yes. As I understand it, she was the one who introduced Alette to the idea of ongoing communication between the quick and the dead."

Isa said slowly, "Regeneration and reincarnation are central concepts in traditional African religion. Siena taught us that death does not liberate you. The newly dead especially are still required to play a role in the lives of the people they care about who are still alive. They help to right wrongs; are instrumental in settling scores."

"Of course," Michael said. "I keep forgetting. You were there, too."

She said wryly, "Yes, probably lurking somewhere in the background."

She leaned back in her chair. She was feeling slightly nauseous again. "Which reminds me," she said. "Did Alette ever show you carvings of two wooden dolls—about twenty inches high—very darkly polished?"

He frowned. "I don't think so. Why, what are they?"

"They're marriage dolls. They symbolize spirit marriage partners and perfect unity between two souls. Perfect love. Alette had requested they be cremated along with her."

"I didn't know that." He sounded surprised. "I knew of course that she would prefer cremation to burial. Fire, to Alette, was a symbol of spiritual energy and a link between successive lives. She was interested in alchemy, you know, and believed, as the alchemists did, that fire is a medium of transmutation: first destroying and then regenerating." He stopped himself. "But she never told me about the marriage dolls. Why do you ask? Has it got something to do with the phone calls?"

She shook her head. "It's just something else that's been troubling me. I don't know why. There's something about it that's
not right. But no, it's got nothing to do with the phone calls."

It was quiet between them. Then he said quietly, "Why is she
calling you, Isa?"

"What do you mean?"

He didn't answer, just looked at her steadily. The green-shaded
reading lamp was throwing a pool of light over the book; over his
large hands resting on the rice-paper-thin pages. The yellow light
illuminated the soft, fair hairs on the back of his fingers.

"She wants me to do something for her."

"What?"

"I can't tell you that. But I think last night's call was because I
was thinking of not doing it: of walking away from it all."

The silence dragged on between them.

"And I think she's trying to warn me."

"Warn you?"

Isa nodded. "In that first phone call she mentioned danger. Fear.
Last night's dream was pure terror. Alette could have stopped it—
she has that power over dreams. But she didn't. It's as if she wants
to show me something."

His face was set and his voice sounded almost stern. "When
Alette first introduced me to all of this—lucid dreaming, afterlife
communication—I was fascinated. It's completely beyond my
ken, but I saw it as something positive." He paused. "I've
changed my mind since then."

"Why? Lucid dreamers themselves use words like 'euphoric'
and 'exhilarating.' And Alette believed that if you're able to control your dreams, you're on the road to fully taking charge of your
waking life as well."

"Yes? Well, think about this for a minute. If dreaming is indeed
functioning as an outlet for the pressure cooker that is our deepest,

basest emotions and desires, what's going to happen if you're able to simply bypass all those symbolic, archetypical demons? Dreaming is supposed to help you gain insight into what's troubling the unconscious, right? If you have the power to edit out anything you find threatening and uncomfortable—or, for that matter, add anything you feel like—how will you ever reach any insight? The mind is already such a cunning, cunning thing. It's programmed to be dishonest, to lie to us. Throughout our lives we train it to become even more deceitful. It's only in our dreams where the mind can't lie. Where we can't escape."

"Last night's dream certainly did not feel like an escape."

"Fine. So maybe this is a demon that needs to be confronted. But take care. This is still not an ordinary dream—it's a lucid dream. And you're linked to it through Alette. Some research on alert dreaming suggest it can be dangerous in the extreme. To exercise that kind of power can place on the mind an unbearable burden."

"I take it you're talking about insanity."

"Many of the experiences of the lucid dreamer and the schizophrenic are alike. There have been reports of lucid dreamers getting lost in their dreams, unable to find their way back; unable to distinguish between what's real and what's not. Lucid dreamers may find their dreams taking possession of them and they end up literally unable to find their own self again."

"Why don't you just come right out and tell me what it is you're trying to say to me?"

"I'm saying you should beware. And that you should think very carefully before encouraging this."

"It's not up to me, Michael. Alette is accessing *my* dreams. And *she's* the one calling. Not me."

He shook his head. "She needs a willing partner. For one thing, you can keep your phone unplugged. Just for a while. I know that sounds silly, but I'm trying to be practical here. And at least you won't be sitting around passively, scared and confused. You'll be doing something proactive to try and control the situation."

"And what about the dreams?"

"Just don't take her hand. It *is* up to you."

"Michael, this is Alette we're talking about."

"I know. And she was a good friend. But I'm worried about *you* now. I just don't think this is stuff one should mess with."

She looked away. She was suddenly immensely tired of all of this. She had an urgent need to get out of the silent, murky atmosphere of this library; to breathe in fresh air.

She glanced at her watch. "What time is it? I still need to stop by Alette's solicitor's office."

"He'll be gone by now."

Isa pushed her chair back. "No. He said he'll be working late tonight. I only need to pick up an envelope."

Outside a cold wind was blowing. The lowering sky was black blue. The grass was purple. The rustle of dried leaves in the garden square sounded like secretive, conspiratorial whispering.

Michael was looking at her with concern. "Why don't you call me when you get back and we'll get something to eat. We can talk."

"Thank you." She shook her head. "But what I need now is to allow all of this to settle in." She paused, and when she spoke again, she kept her voice deliberately light. "Actually, I was thinking about working out tonight." She gestured at the large, floppy gym bag she had been carrying around with her all day. "I found Alette's gym card. Do you think they'll let me in?"

"Oh, certainly. It's the council gym. They're pretty lax; they'll let in just about anyone if you put down your two pounds. But I have to warn you, it's not swish at all: rather Victorian. But there's a swimming pool if you're interested. And it's convenient: only five minutes from Alette's house."

As he turned to go, she put her hand out and touched his sleeve. The rough wool scratched against her fingertips. "Michael."

"Yes?"

"Thanks."

"For what?"

"For listening. And for believing me."

"Don't mention it." His eyes crinkled into a smile. For a moment they simply looked at each other. Then the smile faded and he said almost abruptly, "Alette was fascinated by death. Even when she was a little girl."

Isa nodded, didn't answer.

"Why?"

"Death didn't fascinate her." She shrugged. "Cheating death did."

SHE HADN'T EVEN TOLD MICHAEL ALL OF IT, ISA THOUGHT. AFTER his dire warnings about possession and dementia, she hadn't had the courage to mention the glimpse she'd had of Alette in the bathroom mirror. No doubt that would have freaked him out completely.

She glanced over her shoulder through the smudged back window of the cab. Something did not feel right. It was impossible to say exactly when she had first noticed this prickling, claustrophobic feeling of unease that was nudging at her. This sense of being observed. She has been aware of it ever since she had left Michael at the library. It was as though something—someone—was warning her to pay attention, to watch out. As though an invisible finger was tapping her on the shoulder. *Tap. Tap.*

The corridor leading to Mr. Darling's office was empty and with a sinking heart she saw that no light shone through the fan-shaped window above his door. She glanced at her watch. It was actually much later than she had thought. But just as she put out her hand to try the door, she heard something behind her and spun around. A man dressed in black biker's clothing, a helmet under his arm was standing to one side, quietly watching her.

"Miss de Witt—I had given up on you."

Isa apologized for being late. She blinked. Lionel Darling seemed quite different today. Gone were the brogues and expensive suit. His attire was almost a parody of the bad-biker look. The leather jacket actually had a skull-and-crossbones patch on one arm and his boots were studded with metal. His fair hair was slicked back.

As he fitted his key to the lock, he looked at her with amusement. "Don't let the clothes rattle you."

She colored. "Sorry, it's just . . ."

"I know. But solicitors don't only play golf." He smiled again and held the door wide for her. "It's a good thing I had to come back to the office. I didn't think you were coming anymore and left for home a while ago. But I forgot my wallet."

Inside the office he unlocked a steel cabinet. "If you'll just sign here."

Isa took the envelope from him gingerly.

"Our office is closed from tomorrow until well into the New Year," he said. "But I'll make arrangements to have the third letter couriered to you next week."

"You don't have to go to so much trouble. I don't mind waiting. When do you open again?"

He looked at her sternly and wagged his finger in mock disapproval. "No, that won't do. Our office is very particular."

Outside in the corridor he held out his hand. "A merry Christmas to you."

"And to you." She nodded at him and started to walk down the corridor. At the end of the passage she turned and looked back. He was still standing where she had left him, watching her. He smiled charmingly and lifted his hand in an elegant farewell salute.

She turned around and stepped through the wide doors into yet another long, empty corridor. She was very conscious of the manila envelope clutched in her one hand. It was identical to the first envelope she had received, but in the upper right-hand corner were the words *Second Envelope.*

When she finally reached the stone steps outside the building, Isa stopped. For a moment she looked at the envelope irresolutely, her finger lightly rubbing against the sealing label bearing Alette's signature. Then, with an abrupt gesture, she tore through both the label and blue waxed seal and took a quick peek inside. As before: two smaller envelopes addressed to the *FT* and the *Post.* And Alette's letter. She withdrew it halfway out the envelope:

Dear Isabelle,
   If you're reading this letter, you have decided to help me.
Thank you. Thank you so much. I knew I could count on you . . .
   Here's what we'll do next . . .

Isa's eyes skipped over the words and paragraphs, but then she slid the letter back into its sleeve. This was not the place to read it. Zipping open her gym bag, she tucked the envelope underneath her sweats.

She turned to her right, thinking it would be a shortcut to the main street, where she might be able to hail a taxi. But she miscalculated and found herself in a maze of tiny alleys. This was not a residential area. The buildings were dark and the streets so narrow that when she looked up it seemed to her as though the rooftops on both sides of the road would touch. Despite some tall, modern glass-and-steel buildings, it was an old part of London this: some of the walls on both sides of her were impregnated with the grime and sweat of centuries. A vaguely urinal smell clung to the side-walks. Large black garbage bags, streaked with a diamond glitter of raindrops, lay piled up on every corner. Apart from two other pedestrians and a silent figure crouching in a doorway, clutching at a tangle of dirty blankets, she saw no one. It was quiet here. And again she had that feeling of being watched, of being fol-lowed. *Tap. Tap.*

She was walking faster and faster. The echo of her footsteps bounced off the walls. It sounded jerky, irregular. Now she was slowing down; now she was speeding up; now she was stopping as she stood still to listen. The wind tugged loudly at a sheet of tarpaulin covering the steel skeleton of a piece of scaffolding and her heart jumped. The loose piece of gray canvas billowed and flapped.

She turned the corner. At the far end of the narrow street she could see a stream of cars passing by as a traffic light flashed green. She had found the main street. The relief was so great, she tasted salt in her mouth.

She tried to flag down a taxi, but every cab had passengers in the back or its yellow roof light switched off. It was cold. The fog had suddenly thickened, turning bright beads of light into misty halos. She was never going to get a taxi.

On the other side of the road she spotted the brightly lit blue-and-red circle marking the entrance to the tube. She crossed the street and walked down the shallow steps. After buying her ticket, she stepped onto an enormously tall escalator packed with commuters. She was squeezed in between a burly man and a teenager with a long ponytail.

Tap. Tap.

She peered over her shoulder at the long line of passengers stacked up behind her. Her eyes met the disinterested gaze of the teenager. He was listening to a Walkman, his lips making breath-less *mpa mpa* noises along with the beat.

As she stepped off the escalator, she did not follow the flow of passengers. She pressed herself against the dirty margarine-colored wall tiles, watching and waiting as the stream of commuters passed her by. No one looked at her. No one seemed interested in her.

She started to walk again down the echoing corridors. The walls were shuddering, the ground underneath her feet was vibrating, and as she rounded the corner leading to the platform, she was just in time to see the train disappearing noisily into the black tunnel.

The platform was now almost empty. At the far end stood a turbaned Sikh and a young woman wearing a jean jacket and sneakers with reflector strips on the heels. Each time she moved her feet they glinted with the gaiety of ballroom shoes. Silently the green letters on the electronic billboard spelled out that the next train would be arriving in three minutes.

On the other side of the tracks, on the wall facing her, were giant posters advertising an exhibition of Russian icons and medieval art at the National Gallery. Isa looked intently at the figures on the poster, strangely mesmerized by their soot-black faces and golden halos. One martyr, eyes turned up inside his head, was grasping a jewel-encrusted cross: from his garroted throat spewed forth a silently petrified, motionless arc of red blood.

Tap. Tap.

She started nervously, but just then the train rushed into the station with a whoosh of dirty air and clamoring noise. She got into the shadowless carriage, drawing comfort from the glaring, unflattering light. The train started moving forward and the Russian saints with their enervated eyes slid slowly past the window and disappeared.

MICHAEL WAS RIGHT. THE GYM WAS NOT SWISH. ACTUALLY, IT WAS dank and more than a little smelly. Arranged over four floors in a dark, red-brick building, it was very different from the gyms she was used to at home: large, airy places with enormous plate-glass windows and aerobics instructors with glo-bright smiles. Here you had to negotiate your way from one level to the next by narrow stairwells painted an institutional green. It was quiet: no urgent rock music or even the sound of voices. As she passed by the swimming pool on the ground floor, she heard the soft splash of water. Three swimmers, wrapped in a cocoon of quiet con-centration, were swimming in a pool sparkling with a lunar light.

There were very few people around, but that was probably because she had arrived a mere half hour before closing time, as the cashier at the till had told her, annoyed. At least she had experi-enced no problem getting in.

The dressing room was a large, cavernous space with concrete floors and row upon row of empty stalls. As she stripped, she shiv-ered slightly. The building was insufficiently heated. She placed her gym bag in one of the lockers, but took out the envelope and looked at it irresolutely. It was probably safe to leave it in the locker, but somehow she was hesitant to do so. She looked around her. Against the wall was a wooden bench. She knelt down and slid the envelope underneath the seat. It fit snugly and was invisible.

In the aerobics room, an elderly man with soft underarms was pedaling on one of the bikes. He hardly acknowledged her pres-ence. She mounted one of the treadmills and started running.

The swoosh of the treadmill and the rhythmic slap of her feet were soothing. She was starting to space out a little, her mind fill-ing with a jumble of unformed, unsorted images and sensations. The book smell in the paneled library. Michael's powerful wrists and the hair on them gold. Dark cobbled streets. A piece of tarpaulin flapping like the broken wing of a giant bat. The scent of roses everywhere and a saint bleeding. Justin's lips twisting into a smile: "The only certainty is death." Michael frowning, "Why is she calling you, Isa? Why is she calling you, Isa?"

The gym assistant's voice jerked her back to the present. "Five minutes," he shouted. As if to emphasize his point, he leaned from behind the door and flicked off one of the wall switches, plunging one half of the room into darkness.

She stepped reluctantly off the treadmill.

The running had unknotted the tension in her back. As she walked down the stairs and then into the dressing room, she was tired in mind and body. But there was no feeling of apprehension as she stood inside the open shower; the warm, soapy water sliding down her body. There was no sense of unease as she walked naked toward the other end of the room, unlocked her locker, and took out her gym bag. There was no invisible hand to nudge her into awareness. Only a sudden, inexplicable pain behind her ear; a feeling as though her eyes were breaking into pieces inside her head and the ground coming up gently to meet her.

HER FIRST SENSATION WAS THAT SHE WAS COLD. THE CEMENT FLOOR was ice on her exposed skin. Her face was pressed up against her bare arm. The skin was puckered with gooseflesh and a few stray drops of water glistened where she hadn't dried herself properly.

Slowly she pushed herself upright: her elbows wobbly. The side of her face hurt. She started walking toward the swing doors when she realized she had no clothes on.

She felt like an old woman. She pulled on her pants, her sweater. It all seemed to take a long time. Her locker stood wide open. Her gym bag was turned over, the contents spilling out.

She sorted through the items. Her scarf. A lipstick and a pen. Socks. She picked up her shoes. In the toes of her one shoe were the three twenties and a ten she had stuffed in there before she had left for the aerobics room. Her watch was pushed inside the other shoe and had also not been removed.

Nothing was missing. Nothing was missing?

Alette's letter.

She pulled the wooden bench violently toward her, her fingers scrabbling hastily underneath the seat. The side of the envelope cut into her palm. She withdrew it and turned it upside down. The two envelopes addressed to the newspapers fell out. So did Alette's letter. Everything was just as it should be.

She brought her hand to her head and when she removed it there was a tiny smudge of blood on her thumb. Whoever had coshed her had hit her hard enough to break the skin.

What should she do about this? If it had happened in South Africa, she wouldn't even dream of going to the police. Back home people get mugged as a matter of course and the police, understaffed and overworked, had far more heinous crimes to attend to. But maybe in this country you're supposed to report an incident like this? But nothing had been stolen. When her opportunistic attacker couldn't find a wallet, he had obviously not thought to search her shoes. She was okay, if you discounted the pain inside her head. If she told the person at the desk, there would be questions. Then the police. Forms to fill in, more questions to answer. She couldn't face that.

She walked into the lobby. "You're the last one out," the gym assistant said, and held the door open for her. He sounded almost accusing. Isa looked at him and then past his shoulder at the girl behind the till. "Merry Christmas," said the girl. Isa looked at her and hesitated.

"Merry Christmas," said Isa and pulled her coat tightly around her.

Dear Isabelle,

If you're reading this letter, you have decided to help me.

Thank you. Thank you so much. I'm so grateful, Isabelle. Please know I am not taking your assistance for granted. I know you so well: I know how alien the entire concept of revenge must be to you. Kind Isabelle, always ready to see the best in everybody. It's your gift. This must be very difficult for you and I'm sorry. But I need you to do this, Isabelle. Justin terrorized me—oh, subtly, cleverly, but with devastating effect. He's a thief. First he stole from me my self-respect, my sense of self-worth, and made me feel ashamed of who I am. Then he robbed me of my peace of mind. He made me despair. He made me weep. He bled the joy from my life. He deserves everything I have planned for him, believe me. And you're the one person I can count on. The only person. You, I know, will never betray me.

Here's what we'll do next. Once again the brokers will receive a call from Sophia. Once again there will be letters to send to the papers.

You never got to know Justin very well, but even so I'm sure you remember that single-minded energy of his. It was one of the things that attracted me most when we first met. Once he sets his mind to something, the idea of failure is not an option. What Justin wants, Justin gets. He wanted me: he got me. He wanted to achieve great success in his professional life and he did: first as a researcher and then as a businessman.

Most biotech companies are run by visionary but quite fanatical biochemists who believe absolutely in their product. Justin is no exception. He had been interested in the medicinal qualities of plants for a long, long time; convinced it holds the key to a cure for Alzheimer's. But research requires money. Lots of it.

Companies finance their activities from two sources: shareholder money and bank money. A tiny, one-product pharmaceutical company with no proven track record is not likely to get that much assistance from the banks—they are risk-averse providers of capital—unless there is someone in the company they can do business with who has a reputation for safe hands. And this is where Justin made his winning move.

Justin knew it would be imperative to gather around him the best managers he could possibly find. A team that would impress the banks; soothe the nerves of investors during the bad times; and in the pharmaceutical industry there are always bad times during the development process.

Gabriel Perette is Temple Sullivan's finance director. He commands enormous respect in the City. For many years he managed the financial affairs of Sidicis—a very successful technology group—and in the process, he also made a pile of money for himself. At the age of fifty, he decided to call it a day. Two years later Justin managed to talk Perette out of his early retirement and into joining Temple Sullivan. This was a coup: the smartest move Justin ever made. For the past ten years Gabriel Perette has been steering Temple Sullivan with great skill through some very choppy financial waters.

Louise Perette, Gabriel's wife, is a very close friend of mine. Even after my divorce from Justin, we kept in touch. You know the kind of thing I'm talking about: matinée movies, lunches for the girls, visits to the hairdresser's. A few months ago she moved to France after telling me that she and Gabriel were having marital problems. She also told me that she had presented him with an ultimatum: resign from Temple Sullivan or lose his wife. Gabriel is a sweetheart. He made the right choice.

Louise is no friend of Justin's. She's never forgiven him for persuading Gabriel to come out of retirement and she blames him for the tensions in her marriage. And so, when Gabriel finally made his decision, she sent me a bottle of champagne accompanied by a copy of his letter of resignation. She knows I own a lot of Temple Sullivan shares and wanted to prepare me for the possible impact the news of her husband's resignation might have on the market. She was taking a risk, of course. If caught, she would have been accused of assisting in insider trading. But she is a very loyal friend.

I have made two more copies of this letter and they are included in the envelopes you will be sending to the Financial Times and the London Post. Gabriel's letter is signed but undated; he has agreed to let Justin decide when the right time would be to go public with the news of his resignation.

Louise says Justin had indicated that he would like to release a statement soon after the next annual report. This is a smart decision. The annual report this year promises to be a poem: the balance sheet will be a thing of beauty and the reports on the company's operations will reveal that the market's expectations for the product are well justified. No doubt Justin's letter to the shareholders will make the most of the highlights of the past year and his predictions of even better things to come will leave investors with that warm glow. It will be the perfect time to announce the bad news that Perette will be leaving the company.

But we won't allow Justin the luxury of waiting that long.

Timing is everything in life, don't you agree, Isabelle? If news of Perette's resignation follows hard on the heels of news that the company is experiencing sourcing problems with regard to Taumex, the effect is likely to be quite dramatic. There could even be speculation that the reason given for Perette's resignation—his wanting to spend more time with his family—is a smoke screen, and that he is leaving because of the problem in Madagascar. Furthermore, in his resignation letter he stipulates that he may wish to sell his share options soon after his resignation takes effect. This could easily be perceived as lack of faith: as though he wants to dump his shares because he is nervous about the company's prospects. Investor confidence will take a knock, believe me. And Justin will have a nasty little problem on his hands.

Isa folded the letter carefully; the stiff paper crackling under-neath her fingers. She was curled up in the armchair in Alette's bedroom, and had wrapped herself in one of Alette's cashmere throws. Maybe it was delayed shock after her experience in the gym, but she couldn't seem to get warm. Next to her on the table stood a glass of whiskey and a bottle of painkilling tablets. It was probably not at all the wise thing to do, but the pills and the alco-hol had taken care of her headache very nicely.

But she was still feeling shivery and it was difficult to focus on the contents of the letter in her lap. And she couldn't shake this nagging feeling at the back of her mind that she might have missed something about her experience earlier tonight. She remembered the sense of unease that had dogged her as she had left Lionel Darling's office and the feeling that she was being observed. Maybe it hadn't been a random mugging. Maybe her attacker hadn't been searching for loose cash. Maybe he had had a very spe-cific goal in mind: the envelope.

And maybe she was letting her imagination run riot. The only person who could possibly be interested in the contents of the enve-lope was Justin. But he knew nothing about her arrangement with Alette. Or had she inadvertently let something slip that aroused his suspicions? She had had quite a lot of wine to drink during their dinner together. Perhaps he had decided to keep an eye on her and was following her when he saw her collect the envelope.

No. This was getting more farfetched by the minute. And what-ever else Justin may be, she had no reason to believe he was a vio-lent man. Obsessive, yes. But violent?

For a moment she wondered if she should have the locks on the front door changed. That's the kind of precaution one should take after a mugging. Except in this case her keys had not been stolen. So it would be overkill. And it was probably going to cost a for-tune to get someone out so close to Christmas.

She sighed and shoved the letter back into its envelope. Getting up from her chair, she carefully removed a few books from the top shelf. The first envelope Alette had sent her peeked out from behind the row of books. Isa placed the second envelope with the other letter and slid the books back into place. Now there was no sign that something was hidden behind them.

As she settled back into the chair, stretching out her hand toward the glass of whisky, her elbow knocked over one of the many photographs propped up on the table.

It was a picture of herself in a glamorous dress with an eye-catching shawl wrapped casually around her middle. Prom night. The shawl had not originally been part of the ensemble. But that night she had had an accident: clumsily spilling nail polish onto the ivory-colored skirt. She had been devastated until Alette had taken this beautiful antique shawl from her closet and had draped it skillfully around her waist to hide the stain. She remembered the shawl well; Alette had saved up for months to put together enough money to buy it.

Slowly Isa placed the picture in an upright position back on the table. She owed Alette so much. But she had deep reservations about Alette's plan. Destroying the most important thing in some-one's life was a harsh, maybe even unforgivable thing to do. Justin deserved to be punished, but could anything he had done deserve retribution this severe?

Isa looked up at the row of books sheltering Alette's letters. Throughout her life she had been able to depend on Alette. And now Alette was depending on her. How could she refuse her? Despite her misgivings, she must do what Alette asked of her. She supposed she might draw reassurance from the fact that the first set of instructions had had no effect whatsoever on the company's health. As a matter of fact, the Sunday supplement of one of yes-terday's papers had showcased a glowing article on Justin and

Taumex. It featured a full-page, posed photograph of Justin appear-ing sternly competent—eyes looking straight into the camera. Nothing, she thought, could shake the composure of a man with eyes that cool.

So maybe Gabriel Perette was an ace financial director. But the resignation of one man couldn't do that much harm, surely. The news of his resignation won't be enough to dent Temple Sullivan's armor: "the tiny titan of pharmaceutical companies," as the article had stated with fine alliterative flourish. What's more, Alette had bargained on rumors about potential supply problems to prepare the ground, but no one had paid any attention to that rumor. So really, there would be little harm done if she agreed to Alette's demands once more. And if the company did suffer slightly as a result, which seemed unlikely, well—Justin had it coming. Any possible anxiety her actions might bring him wouldn't even begin to compare with the trauma he had inflicted on Alette. If she sent out those letters, made those calls, she would be able to face the day with the knowledge that she had not betrayed Alette.

Isa looked at the telephone. It was still unplugged: the cord sprawling across the carpet like a sleepy snake.

And maybe, after this, sleep would come to her deep and dreamless.

TEN

The beating of thy pulse . . .
Is just the tolling of thy Passing Bell.
> —"My Midnight Meditation,"
> Henry King (1592–1669)

THE ROOM WAS DARK, BUT THE DARKNESS WAS NOT IMPENETRABLE. Even though the light in the room was turned off, the curtain in the front window was open and the room was bathed in the faint light of the lampposts outside. He was able to see without any trouble.

She was wearing Alette's nightdress. He recognized the delicate embroidery around the collar, the lilac ribbons and ruffled sleeves. He was standing so close to the bed, he could hear her breathing.

He placed his hand against his forehead. He could feel the onset of a migraine: throbbing pain spreading through his skull, the beginning of an aura painting the objects in his vision with a sickly hue. This always happened to him when he became deeply upset. Anger. Such anger. It was choking him, leaving him light-headed.

How dare she? The dress was not hers; was not hers to wear. That nightdress belonged to Alette. No one else had the right. He felt like smashing his fist into her face. Feeling her cheekbone shatter against his knuckles, her face simply caving in underneath the weight of his hand. The scream of pain. Her lips sagging with shock.

He took a deep breath. Calm. The thing here was to stay calm. He looked down at his hands and willed his fingers to unclench themselves.

She was breathing so very softly: the rise and fall of her chest almost unnoticeable. Her arms were flung to the side in a curious gesture of yearning. One slim leg was uncovered, the other twisted tight in the bedclothes. For such a tall woman she was surprisingly fragile looking.

He had noticed this about her earlier tonight as well, in the locker room as he had stood over her, rummaging through her bag while she lay motionless on the cold cement floor. She had reminded him of that bird—the dead bird—gripped in the frozen embrace of the pond. He had been walking in the park last week when he had spotted it, its head completely submerged by opalescent ice but one wing sticking up crazily. Isa seemed like that bird. The same thin, delicate bone structure. The same defenselessness.

On the bedside table stood a vial of tablets and next to it an empty glass. He picked it up and brought it to his nose. Scotch. So that explained this deep, deep sleep.

Cautiously he moved through the room. There was no sign of the envelope. He had already looked in the kitchen and in the living room. It bothered him that he wasn't able to find it. Earlier tonight, in the gym, he had thought it would be easy to lay his hands on it. He knew she had it on her. And he knew the letter troubled her. That much was clear from her reaction as she had sneaked a peek at its contents shortly after collecting it. Careful not to be spotted, he had watched her as she stood outside the building, the wind almost whipping the page from her hand. After reading for only a few seconds she had shoved the letter into her bag with a kind of hopeless vehemence. Maybe he was wrong: maybe there was an entirely innocent reason for all of this. Maybe. But something was off-kilter. He knew it.

He sat down in the deep, wing-backed armchair. How many times had he wanted to do just this. To sit in this chair, in this room, as though he had the right to do so. As he leaned back into the shadowed recess, he felt the softness of cashmere against his cheek: Alette's throw. He smiled in the darkness. Pulling the throw close, he wrapped it around him.

A slight sound from the bed stilled his movements. Isa had turned onto her back. For a few moments she lay motionless.

Suddenly she was sitting up.

He tensed. He was hardly breathing. Slowly she swung first one leg and then the other over the edge of the bed. She yawned.

Would she see him? Would she turn on the bedside light? He'd have no choice. He would have to do what has to be done. His fists slowly tightened into knots.

She reached out her hand, but not for the light switch. She picked up the empty glass.

With a slightly uncertain gait she walked past him, glass in hand. She passed by so close. If he reached out his hand he could touch the lace on her sleeve. And still she doesn't see him; was oblivious to his presence.

He heard her walk into the en suite bathroom behind him and then water running from a tap as she filled the glass. Now would be the time to leave. But he did not want to go just yet . . .

He was still sitting in the chair when she returned to bed, placing the glass carefully on the bedside table. He was still sitting in the chair, long after she had fallen asleep again: her breath slow and even. He was watching her from the shadows and it felt so right.

ELEVEN

Loe where a wounded heart, with bleeding eye conspire;
Is she a flaming fountaine, or a weeping fire?
                              "The Weeper,"
                              Richard Crashaw (1612–1649)

DAPHNE CAMPBELL WAS EXCITED. SHE BURST INTO MARTIN
Penfield's office; in her enthusiasm almost knocking over his fake
Christmas tree with its cheesy-looking red and yellow lights.

"This story is bizarre," she said.

Martin Penfield was a small man with a permanently saturnine
expression. He had the reputation of being one of the most exact-
ing editors in the newspaper business. He smiled and his thin lips
drew away from startlingly pink gums. "You're drooling," he
said. "I like that. What's up?"

Daphne sprayed open a sheaf of papers on his desk and pointed
to a black-and-white photograph of a sorry-looking, scrubby palm.

"*Palmetto angelicus*," she said dramatically.

"Indeed. So what?"

Daphne didn't answer. She picked out another photograph, this time a glossily colored print of a lavender-pink blossom and placed it next to the black-and-white photograph.

"*Catharanthus roseus.*"

He moved his shoulders irritably. "Are we playing twenty questions? What are you trying to tell me?"

"These two plants together are responsible for Temple Sullivan's little miracle."

Penfield folded his arms across his chest and raised his brows.

"*Catharanthus roseus* is a prime source of vincristine and vin-blastine—"

"For Christ's sake, Daphne. Stop showing off and speak English."

She took a deep breath. "Okay. *Catharanthus roseus* belongs to the periwinkle family and was originally native to Madagascar. Its medicinal value has been known for a long time: vincristine and vinblastine are, among other things, used in the treatment of childhood leukemia and Hodgkin's disease. The medicinal value of *Palmetto angelicus*, found exclusively in Madagascar, was dis-covered by Temple Sullivan scientists. It is the source for a new compound called XM-14. Together with the vincristine and vin-blastine found in *Catharanthus roseus*, it is used in Taumex for the treatment of Alzheimer's. For some reason, the combination is able to reverse the acetylcholine deficiency in the brain and to stop the formation of the protein tangles and plaques that lead to catastrophic tissue loss."

"That's nice. So what's that got to do with anything?"

"XM-14 is found in the heart of *Palmetto angelicus*. In order to get to it, you have to kill the tree's stem."

She paused. When he didn't respond she said impatiently, "Don't you get it? Every time you harvest the tree, you destroy it. Even with these trees as common as weeds out there in Madagascar, how long do you think it will take them to run out of trees?"

"So they plant new ones."

"Right." She nodded. "They're trying. Are they ever. But there's a wrinkle; it's not working too well." She started to giggle. "And the reason for it is completely off-the-wall."

"What is it?"

"In order for the seed to germinate, it had to have passed through the digestive system of a certain type of animal, an animal found only in Madagascar: the white-eared paradise lemur."

He stared at her. "Excuse me. Are we talking about monkey shit here?"

She nodded. "You've got it. And here's the point. The paradise lemur is about to be placed on the endangered-species list. Like its cousin the indri, there aren't too many of them around anymore. So you see: no monkey poop, no palms, no XM-14, no Taumex. Big problems for Temple Sullivan."

"Well, now," he said slowly. "I have a present for you." Penfield reached over to the other side of his desk and pulled out an envelope from underneath a paperweight shaped like four brass monkeys: see no evil, hear no evil, speak no evil, do no evil. "The motto I do not live by," as he was fond of saying.

"This arrived here this morning."

Daphne drew out the sheaf of papers. "Oh, wow."

"Yes. Sophia strikes again."

Daphne slid the pages back into the envelope and said slowly, "Merry, Merry Christmas, Mr. Temple."

IsA UNPLUGGED THE SILVER STOPPER FROM THE PERFUME BOTTLE AND held it to her nose. The scent of it was heavy: attar of roses blended with some or other exotic spice. Alette had it made up especially at a tiny perfume shop in the West End.

The heady scent in this bottle was like nothing Isa would ordinarily pick for herself. She usually opted for neutral, fresh, eaux de cologne with light, citrusy overtones. But maybe it was time to be a little more adventurous. She hesitated for a moment and then drew the stopper lightly across her wrists.

She turned around and opened the door to Alette's closet. A bright green scarf draped across a hanger and squashed in between a navy suit and a red jacket caught her eye. Green was Alette's color, of course, never hers. Green made her skin look sallow, her eyes murky.

But not today. As she folded the scarf around her neck, the emerald hue seemed absolutely suited to her complexion. She stroked the soft chenille and it was the same sensuous feeling as pushing your fingers through a cat's fur.

Picking up Alette's book on alchemy, she headed toward the wide windowsill, where a lovely ray of sunshine was warming the air. She had never shared Alette's passion for mysticism, and only a few days ago she would have found a book like this totally uninteresting. But it wasn't only her taste in colors and perfume that was changing, it seemed. For the past two days she had been reading this book, fascinated by the abstruse arguments and knotty language.

True power will always demand control. In the dark ages, magicians could mold, shape, and alchemically transmute reality, as if a tractable, pliant substance. By focusing their energy on an objective steadfastly, without wavering, they have within them the power to manipulate—power over people, events, even coincidence itself—and power to shape reality to conform to their wishes. Predictable and inevitable will be the actions of those against whom they pit their will.

But there are those who make a stand. Initiates themselves, they do not allow manipulation of the self. Such a man or woman presents a challenge and temptation to the magician that cannot be withstood. But herein lies the seed of the magician's downfall. In order to manipulate those who challenge them, magicians need to step out of their protective zone, thereby forfeiting control and setting into motion events that may destroy them. The energy they unleash becomes a free force, eluding their grasp, ultimately turning on them with destructive vigor.

The front doorbell rang. Isa lowered the book and peered out the window, but she was unable to see who was at the front door. She frowned and for a moment considered ignoring the bell. But then the bell rang once again, long and uninterrupted, and she got up from her seat reluctantly.

It was Michael. He peered at her through wisps of untidy tow-colored hair. In his hand he held a clear glass pitcher with a custardy liquid inside. Steam was rising from the top.

He recognized the green scarf around her neck immediately: she could see it in his eyes. There was a brief, awkward silence.

Then he smiled. "Eggnog." He lifted the pitcher by way of explanation and pushed past her into the house.

He walked without hesitation into the kitchen and took two mugs from the cupboard. As he handed her one of the mugs, he looked her up and down. "What happened to your face?"

She touched her cheekbone self-consciously. "At the gym . . . I slipped."

His hand brushed gently against her face. "You should be more careful. That must have hurt."

"I'm okay." She took a sip of the eggnog and her cheeks puckered from the excessive sweetness. "Good Lord. How much sugar do you have in here?"

"Tons," he said without hesitation. "And whipping cream and whiskey. Good, huh?"

She nodded, took another sip. He was already pouring himself a second cup. She noticed again the awkwardness of his gestures. She found herself constantly holding her breath that his elbow or wrist wouldn't knock something over in that tiny kitchen. But there was something engaging and rather pleasantly masculine about a man this large. The heavy shoulders, the large hands, even the slightly crumpled boxer's nose were tremendously appealing. Still, he did not have the kind of dark glamour of a man like Justin, and could certainly never be labeled exciting.

"I saw you through the window this morning, but when I called, you didn't answer your phone?" His voice ended in a question mark.

"I've unplugged the phone." She couldn't help feeling slightly ridiculous owning up to it, and she felt herself coloring.

But he said immediately, "Good."

She nodded. "I only connect the phone now when I need to make a call." Like when she was calling brokers. Telling them about the resignation of a legendary finance director. Geissinger had hung up on her. One of the other brokers she had called had threatened to report her. He didn't know who she was, but all the same the threat had left her unnerved.

"So you still expect Alette to call you again."

"Well, I did what she wanted me to do. Maybe she won't call again."

His mouth twisted into a half smile. "So now you only have to be careful what you dream of."

She returned his smile weakly. "Or just never go to sleep."

It was quiet between them. He was looking around, his gaze taking in the open laptop computer on the dining table; the creased copies of *Investor's Chronicle* and *Scrip*—the trade journal for the pharmaceutical industry.

She said, suddenly abrupt: "If you owned stock in a company, and you heard that a key director was resigning, would that worry you?"

"You're asking the wrong bloke. I don't have much of an investment portfolio." He shrugged. "It depends, I suppose."

"But it's not going to make you dump your stock, now is it?"

"Again, it depends. When news leaked that Bill Gates was getting married, Microsoft's price headed down. Investors were worried that marital bliss would keep him from concentrating exclusively on his job." Michael grinned. "Of course, it was a mere hiccup. Still, it shows you how sensitive the market is. Why?"

"No reason." But she was beginning to feel uneasy.

"Are you okay, Isa? Are you in money trouble?"

"No. Nothing like that."

"Well, good, then. What I really came over to ask you was whether you'd like to have dinner with me tomorrow night. Maybe go to the movies and see something mindless and gory."

"I'd love to, Michael. But I'm meeting Justin tomorrow. He still has some of Alette's stuff and I'd like to have it back."

"I don't like this. I don't trust that man."

"I'm only meeting him for a drink. It won't take long."

"I tell you, he's dangerous. He was obsessed with Alette and it was frightening the life out of her."

"I'm not Alette. So I should be safe. And anyway, Justin may be deluded, but that's far from being violent."

Michael frowned. "It makes me crazy sometimes to think he had made Alette's life such a misery—and got away with it without suffering any consequences. If I believed in revenge I would have done something really evil to him by now."

"You don't believe in revenge?"

He shook his head. "Revenge shackles you to the past; it stops you from living in the present. Revenge is an attempt to rewrite what has gone before. It sucks away your energy and in the end you have no reserves left over for living your life today."

Isa swallowed. "Revenge can also be an act of self-empowerment."

"No. It's not self-empowering, it's self-defeating. Trying to change prior events is obsession. If something bothers you that deeply, you should deal with it decisively. As it says in the Bible: If your foot causes you to stumble, chop it off. If your eye makes you falter, pluck it out." He thought for a second and frowned. "Of course, then you'll be a half-blind cripple. Anyway, you get my meaning. Don't look back; don't let it fester."

He suddenly smiled. "As for Temple, much better to just pop him one. I did offer my services to Alette once, but she declined."

"Sir Galahad."

"That's me. Now stop looking so serious. Here, have some more." Against her protestations he refilled her mug with the now tepid liquid.

"It's a hundred thousand calories in one sip, this."

"You can afford it. You're too thin as it is."

"You can never be too thin . . ."

"Or too rich; yes, I know. I don't believe that."

She opened the front door for him and watched him walk toward the garden gate with that peculiar slouching gait of his. As he pulled the tiny gate closed behind him, he looked back to where she was watching him from the doorway.

"When you go to Temple's place tomorrow, be careful." His voice was suddenly somber. "I mean it."

"SON OF A BITCH."

Robert Geissinger spoke out loud. He stared at the newspaper, which he had propped up on the steering wheel of his car. On the front page of the *Financial Times,* just above the fold, was a two-column article headed by the words PERETTE STEPS DOWN, and below this, in slightly smaller letters, *Concerns over Potential Bottleneck in Supply of Temple Sullivan Drug.*

Behind Geissinger a taxi driver hooted impatiently as the traffic light turned from red to green. Geissinger threw the paper onto the passenger seat and let out the clutch too quickly. The car jumped forward.

Only yesterday he had received another call from the woman who called herself Sophia. He had been short with her. Actually, he had hung up on her, convinced she was a nutter. He had not believed her when she had told him Perette was about to resign. But there it was—he glanced at the paper next to him—black on white; or rather pink If it was in the Bible it had to be right. And what's more, it looks as if he should have paid more attention to her the first time around. Supply problems. Shit.

His mind started racing. Whom could he call to get more info on what's happening here? Rick Rhys, possibly. He had a contact at Temple Sullivan. And he should call Jensen first thing. Jensen was a very influential shareholder in the company.

He smiled grimly. Wouldn't it be nice if he could call Sophia and ask her what else she had up her sleeve? But the lady had been coy about who she really was. And frankly, at the time he hadn't been that interested. He tried to recall her exact words as she had spoken to him on the phone yesterday. It wasn't the first time he wished his firm—like a growing number of firms these days—taped all incoming calls. It made things so much simpler when disputes arose over what was said and when. Or when you wanted to check out what a woman with a strange accent had whispered into your ear.

It was going to be pandemonium today. Jittery investors. Inquiries, lots of inquiries. And orders.

Orders to sell.

ISA WAS IN SHOCK. SHE WAS SITTING ON THE SOFA IN ALETTE'S LIVING room. Scattered untidily on the floor around her were the financial pages of every newspaper, local and American, she had been able to lay her hands on. The headlines of the *FT* and the *Wall Street Journal* stared up at her accusingly: TEMPLE IN CENTER OF STORM OVER CORPORATE STRATEGY; TEMPLE SULLIVAN'S ENGINE GOES INTO REVERSE. She picked up a page listing the stock tables. Temple Sullivan's trading symbols were easy to pick out. The stock particulars were blackly underlined. The unusually large volume of shares traded the previous day was evidence of a stampede. The closing price in the chart was in boldface and next to it was typed a tiny minus. Temple Sullivan stock had lost forty percent of its value.

On the flickering television screen at the other end of the room, a panel of experts were discussing the previous day's financial news.

A ferrety-faced man with orange hair was speaking. He punched out his words with great intensity. "It seems a mite coincidental to me that Gabriel Perette would be resigning at exactly the time that news broke that Temple Sullivan may soon have sourcing problems with regard to XM-14."

"Well, to be fair"—the moderator's voice was weighty— "Perette did indicate that the decision had been made quite some time ago. He seemed sincere when he stated that he wanted to spend more time with his family. Daphne"—he turned to the pert-faced brunette sitting next to him—"your paper broke the story. Do you know more about whether Perette's decision to step down is tied to the Madagascar problem?"

"I can't reveal my sources, but I think it would be safe to speculate that there is a tie-in. As Tom said"—she nodded at the carrot-haired man—"the timing is suspicious. Although, it should be remembered that Perette's resignation letter was undated. Who knows?"

"And what about the supply problem?"

"Well, that's much more serious. The burn isn't on yet: the

supply is still more than adequate. But Justin Temple admitted that there could be sourcing problems ahead. If that's the case, then the time will come when factories will be handling insufficient volume. Temple says they're dealing with the problem but he'll have to deal with it pretty quickly if he wants to gain back investor confidence."

"What are his options?"

She shrugged. "I suppose the company can counter by putting up the price—"

"Absolutely not." The orange-haired man was leaning forward. He seemed to vibrate with nervous energy. "We're not talking about a drug for the rich here: it's not a drug to grow hair or eliminate wrinkles. Taumex is a drug for Everyman. This situation could, potentially, be quite catastrophic. Hospital budgets blown. Maybe even—" He stopped as though the implications were too dismal to articulate.

"And maybe we should put the brakes on." The last member of the panel, a chubby man with a prominent Adam's apple, spoke quietly. "Justin Temple has managed to weather some very tough times. Let's give him the opportunity to sort this out."

"That brings me to my next question," the moderator said. "Why did investors panic to such an extent? Temple has shown himself to be an excellent CEO. If he says he'll come up with a solution, why don't investors believe him?"

The chubby man folded his hands comfortably over his paunch. "I think after the British Biotech controversy, investors are a lot more wary when it comes to pharmaceutical companies. Investors have a love-hate relationship with biotechs. On the one hand, they stand to make a lot of money if things work out, because very few consumer-product makers have a growing demand-driven market the way pharmaceutical companies do. The West's population is graying: in the U.S. alone, baby boomers are turning fifty at the rate of one every eight seconds. They want drugs to improve their quality of life: so investors can make a lot of money if they back the right horse. But more often than not, they get burned. Usually the expectations do not live up to the results. And this makes biotech investors more nervous than most."

"So what is your prognosis for Temple Sullivan?"

There was a short silence. The chubby man said slowly, "Unless Justin Temple can do immediate damage control and show clearly and concisely how he's going to tackle the sourcing problems, I see difficult days ahead. He's going to have to post a current trading statement to the exchange and the shareholders, anyway."

"Tom?"

Carrot Top spoke with his usual intensity, his eyes blinking rapidly. "If he can't woo investors back, he's going to run into funding problems at some point. Maybe even find himself in breach of banking agreements. And if it can be shown that the directors have deliberately misled the investors on the sourcing issue, they could be open to personal prosecution. In the U.S. that could lay the groundwork for a variety of class actions against the company and its officials and advisers. Also, I can guarantee you—"

Isa clicked the remote control. She didn't want to hear any more. She sat looking at the blank television screen, feeling stunned.

It was quiet in the room. So quiet that the ticking of the charming, old-fashioned clock on the mantelpiece seemed very loud. A ray of pale sunshine fell across the rich colors of the Turkish carpet.

She placed her hand on the sofa to push herself to her feet. Her hand pressed down on the newspaper next to her. Through the pages she felt something hard; the outline of a book.

It was the book on alchemy. As she picked it up by the corner, it fell open. It fell open as though some one had marked the place especially for her, Isa, to read. And indeed, Alette had shaded the paragraph with pencil, underlining words, bracketing sentences:

Sophia: Woman as anima (the soul of man) and his guide of the spirit. Sophia, the divine virgin, originally found in "primordial man." George Gichtel and Jakob Böhme, the seventeenth-century mystics, taught that Sophia abandoned man and that he is lost without her. She forsook him and he cannot be saved unless he finds her once more.

TWELVE

When bodies join and victory hovers
'Twixt the equall fluttering lovers
This is the game: make stakes my Dear.
                    —"To the State of Love, or the
                        Senses Festival,"
                        John Cleveland (1613–1658)

ISA PLACED HER FINGER ON THE BUZZER. AFTER A FEW SECONDS THE speaker above her head crackled. Justin's voice sounded tinny.

"It's me. Isa."

"Fourth floor, second door."

The heavy, black, iron-grilled door clicked loudly and the lock sprang open. She entered and the door shut behind her.

The wood paneling in the entrance hall was dark and beautiful. The floor in the lobby was carpeted in crimson, as was the elevator. She got inside and pushed the button for the fourth floor. Next to every button was a brass plaque listing the names of the residents who called this exclusive block of flats in Cadogan Square their home.

The whine of the elevator was loud. She looked at herself in the ceiling-to-floor mirror. She had Alette's green scarf wrapped around her neck, like a banner of courage. But her eyes were staring, her pupils dilated.

She was actually going ahead with it. She had felt compelled to keep her appointment with Justin. She shivered. She was discovering a side to her own character with which she was less than comfortable. There was something exhilarating, a kind of perverse fascination, about the idea of sitting opposite Justin tonight; knowing what she knew and knowing what she had done, while he remained oblivious to the undercurrents of their situation. She was ashamed of it, but she was filled with a sick curiosity to see how he was handling the ill wind she had set loose in his life.

The door on the fourth floor was slightly open. She knocked hesitantly. He didn't answer, but she could hear his voice. It sounded as though he was talking on the phone.

She pushed the door wider and stepped into the room. The room was dark, the only light source a red fire burning in an enormous hearth. It gave off enough of a glow for her to see that the room was large, with high ceilings and beautiful cornicing. A bright strip of light fell through a door opening off to the left. Justin's voice came from inside.

She hovered just outside the threshold. Justin was standing with his back half-turned; the telephone receiver wedged between his chin and neck. In his hands he held a sheet of paper. On the table in front of him stood a glass half-filled with amber liquid.

"I tell you, the leak came from that pisser Fromm. No, Sara I trust implicitly. She's been with me for fifteen years."

Silence, then he started talking again, irritably. "How the hell should I know where he got Perette's letter from? Not from Perette, that's for damn sure." He listened; responded vehemently, "It's no use telling me I should have let Fromm go gently. We're talking about months ago. And why should I give that weasel a golden handshake? He's a fucking incompetent. He was lucky I allowed him to resign; he deserved to be fired."

Isa started to move away from the door, but just then Justin turned and saw her. He placed his hand over the receiver. "Fix yourself a drink," he said. "The box with Alette's things is on the desk over there." He motioned with his head to somewhere behind her. "I'll be right with you."

She nodded and walked back into the living room. She flicked the switch on the wall and a subdued light beamed from the wall sconces. The light showed a sofa, leather club chairs, and an exquisite antique tallboy. The color scheme was heavy: chocolate brown, reds, and gold. Above the fireplace hung an oil painting of a man in eighteenth-century dress. On the opposite wall was a mounted Peruvian tarantula: its eight legs splayed out in eerie, beautiful symmetry.

A walnut desk stood in one of the bay windows. The lovely slab of wood was highly polished but pitted: the marks of a long-ago wormwood infestation. On top of the desk stood a cardboard box. She opened it.

There wasn't that much inside. A few books; a pair of evening velvet gloves with a beaded, black fringe; old theater programs bound together with a pink ribbon; a canceled passport—Alette looking stern with her hair drawn back from her face—and a shoe box.

The shoe box was filled with a jumble of photographs. They seemed to be mostly pictures of Alette taken during a tour of Europe. Alette, sunglasses on top of her head, at the Trevi fountain; posing in front of a colorful poster of Las Ventas; propping up the Tower of Pisa. Alette sunbathing in a stunning black swimsuit, behind her a glimpse of the Croisette. In all the photographs she looked young—almost adolescent young—and heartbreakingly carefree and happy. The pictures were date-stamped and with a small shock Isa realized that they were taken shortly after Alette's wedding. The person on the other side of the camera must have been Justin.

At the bottom of the box was a slim pile of letters bound together with an elastic band. Without removing the band, Isa extricated a page from one of the envelopes and unfolded it. The handwriting was sloping, the characters seemed almost languid looking: long, lazy loops to the *l*s and *g*s. It was a handwriting so familiar to her: Alette's.

> *Dear Justin,*
>
> *We have to talk. We cannot go on like this.*

"Not that." Justin's voice right behind her made her jump. His hand swooped down and removed the letters from her unresisting grasp.

"Sorry. But these are private. I don't know how they came to be mixed up with the other stuff." He opened the desk drawer, placed the letters inside, and shut it firmly. Then he turned to face her.

His eyes were shot through with red veins. A five o'clock shadow darkened his jaw. He was still dressed in his office clothes—a charcoal, pin-striped suit—but he had removed his tie and the top two buttons of his shirt were undone. The collar seemed limp.

"So"—he nodded his head at the box—"see anything you want?"

"The photographs, and maybe the books."

"They're yours." He turned away from her and walked over to the drink cabinet. "What can I get you?"

"Sherry will be fine."

While he took down two glinting glasses from the shelf, she inspected the large oil painting above the fireplace.

He handed her a glass of pale sherry. His eyes followed her gaze. "You like it?"

She stared at the face in the painting; the arrogant eyes. She had noticed earlier that they followed you around no matter where you were in the room.

"Who is he?"

Justin shrugged. "One of my ancestors."

"He's arresting. In a sort of Byronesque way." She looked at the painting and then back at him. What a strong resemblance between the face in the canvas and the face in front of her. Once you looked past the stiff cravat, rounded chin, and effeminate mouth, the likeness was uncanny. She had only just noticed it.

"You think so? By all accounts he was an ill-tempered old bastard, and I seem to recall something about a pretty kitchen wench and cards and drinking. All very shocking. Anyway, cheers." He put the whiskey glass to his mouth and drained it in two deep swallows. "To the end of a rotten day."

She didn't know how to respond. "Cheers," she said hardly.

He walked back to the cabinet and refilled his glass. He didn't rejoin her in front of the fireplace. Instead he watched her over the rim of his glass.

The silence between them was becoming uncomfortable. She looked around her, desperately trying to think of something to say. Her eye fell on a large, potted shrub which stood in the second bay window.

"I recognize that plant there," she said. "*Justicia capensis*. Did you know that the Zulus in South Africa call it the businessman's plant?"

"Certainly. Alette told me that when she gave it to me. She told me it would bring me luck." His mouth twisted. "I'm not much of a gardener but Alette was so clever with plants, wasn't she?"

The tone of his voice made her feel ill at ease. And she certainly wasn't about to discuss Alette with him now. Turning away from the shrub, she pointed to the wall. "What are those?"

Behind him, fixed to the wall like paintings, were two boxes with what looked like X rays mounted on top of each box. The boxes themselves, however, were beautifully made and framed in gold leaf as though they were displaying works of art.

He reached out his hand and flicked a switch on the wall. Both boxes suddenly lit up.

They were brain scans. She stared. They actually did look like art, she thought: the radiant blue-white fluorescent outline of the brains, that mesmerizing dark *X* in the center of the whitish brain matter.

"This is a healthy brain." He pointed to the scan on the right. "And this one here on the left is an Alzheimer brain. These are the parts of the brain no longer functioning because of the pathology. See . . . this blackness . . . that's fluid bathing the brain."

She stared at the useless, fluid-filled spaces with sick fascination.

"Is this upsetting you?"

With difficulty she tore her gaze away from those glowing scans. "These people must feel so alone. So isolated."

"Remember, we can now help them."

"Yes."

She looked back at the image of the healthy brain: receptacle of all experiences; generator of dreams.

She was almost sure Alette had never told him of their shared dreams. For just a moment she hesitated. "Have you ever heard of lucid dreaming?"

"Of course. Very sexy subject these days."

"You sound skeptical."

He flipped the switch on the wall to the off position and the radiant scans turned a dull gray. "It's not my field. I'm a hardware

man, not a psychologist. Although I can't deny that lucid dreaming has been replicated in laboratory conditions. The Lucidity
Institute in California has developed all kinds of devices—the
DreamLight, the NovaDreamer and so on—which give flashing
light and sound cues when a person is dreaming, and help induce
lucid dreaming."

"And these things really work?"

"Oh, certainly. They're basically microcomputers which process
signal data from the dreamer's eye and body movements. They use
algorithms to deliver cues to the dreamer at the most opportune
moments to stimulate lucid dreaming. All very interesting, I suppose, but personally I think dreams—any dreams—are little more
than haphazard junk produced by the brain stem as it tests the brain
circuits for cognition and memory retention. Sort of like running a
biological maintenance check—like tuning a car."

"What a romantic image."

He shrugged. "When I started out I worked as a lab assistant.
Saw a great many brains floating on pieces of string inside white
plastic buckets. Not a lot of stardust around when you're slicing
into them: it's like slicing into a giant mushroom." He grinned at
her expression. "Sorry."

"So I don't suppose you believe in life after death, or even near-
death experiences—"

"I never said that."

She glanced up, surprised.

"After a person's heart stops beating, the brain can still show
activity for up to half an hour." The bantering tone had left his
voice. "Sometimes, I can't help thinking that there's something in
there—something imprisoned inside its cage of dead flesh, which
is desperately hanging on to life . . . frenziedly trying to find a
way out. Something that is still capable of feeling the strong emotions: love, happiness, hate."

"Hate?"

"It's the strongest emotion there is. Someone—I can't remember who—called it the 'luxurious' emotion, only to be spent on the one we love."

Despite the heat from the flames in the hearth, she felt suddenly cold. She placed her sherry glass on the table. "I should go."

"Don't go yet," he said pleasantly. "We haven't really talked." He was walking slowly toward her and she felt herself involuntarily moving backward. The edge of the walnut desk pressed into the back of her thighs.

"Alette was right, you know. Isabelle suits you better. Isabelle is the name of princesses and beautiful ladies locked up in towers, pining for their knights in shining armor. Isa is too . . . severe." He leaned forward and briefly touched the scarf around her neck. He was so close she smelled the sweetish tang of whiskey on his breath.

She flinched but said tartly, "These days it's the knights who are in distress. And the damsels who don the shining armor."

He gave a short laugh. "You're probably right." He took a sip of his drink, looked at her appraisingly. "I don't remember you as being this caustic."

"You don't remember me at all."

"That's not true. And Alette spoke of you so often, I feel as though I know you." He paused and smiled deliberately. "Rather well."

"Alette talked about me?"

"Oh yes. She envied you."

"I doubt that."

"Why do you find it surprising?"

Isa shrugged. "I have nothing she could have wanted."

"Oh, I don't know 'Isabelle never plays games,' Alette used to say. 'She doesn't need to.'"

"I don't understand that."

"I think you do."

She tried to move away from him, but he stepped gently to the side, blocking her. It was done so carelessly, she wasn't sure if it was on purpose. He spoke again. "If you had to sum up your relationship with Alette in one sentence, what would it be?"

"Alette wanted what was best for me."

"Are you sure?" He spoke quietly, his eyes never leaving her face.

"Of course."

"Alette was interested in one kind of relationship only: a relationship based on control."

"What a deeply stupid thing to say." She could hear the anger staining her words.

"Think, Isa. Think back on the kind of relationships Alette sustained in her life. They were all relationships in which she manipulated and enticed. She seduced the people in her life to become psychologically dependent on her, while she tried to keep her autonomy absolutely. Every relationship became a game of power chess. And she couldn't bear to lose. She couldn't bear it. The goal to have the upper hand at all times consumed her."

"That's not true."

"Oh, yes it is. And you know it, too. She was relentless. And she insisted that those who love her constantly prove their feelings, their undying affection." He looked past her, his eyes blank. "Tests. She'd set me tests to prove my devotion."

In the hollow beneath his eye was a pale blue vein. It stretched all the way to his outer eyelid. "You remember that ring I took from the house? The 'poesy ring'?"

She nodded. Her throat felt dry.

"My mother gave me that ring. I should give it to my daughter one day, she said. My mother is not a particularly demonstrative person, so this ring was special to me. Alette insisted I get rid of it. It's as though she needed me to prove how much I cared for her. When I refused, she nagged at me till I gave it to her as a gift. She never wore it, but after the divorce she refused to give it back."

He returned his gaze to her face. "But you're the same, aren't you, Isa? Isabelle? You and your Eric. Let me guess: his absence was as important to you as his presence. You welcomed it, because you knew it ensured that every time he saw you he looked at you with fresh eyes."

His hand suddenly on her arm, fingers gripping tightly. "Did you like it? Did you like it that he constantly schemed to be with you and rushed to your side with all the hungry excitement of a brand-new lover? Year after year coming to you with the same breathless passion?"

As if mesmerized she watched his mouth: his lips, the way they moved. A tiny speck of saliva clung to the lower lip. His fingertips were hot through the thin fabric of her blouse. So close, he seemed overwhelmingly vital and alive: his energy a tangible thing. A flush was creeping down her body, slowly, slowly. She suddenly felt like weeping. Her throat was tight, her eyes starting to prick.

She wouldn't give him the satisfaction.

She placed her one hand against his chest and pushed. Hard.

He looked surprised, gave a step backward. She balled both her fists and struck him with all her strength in the hollow between his collarbone and his shoulder. He gave a grunt of pain.

"Get out of my way." Her voice shook. She swung around and grabbed at her coat. "Get out of my way."

At the door she looked back. He was standing where she had left him, arms crossed over his chest. She couldn't read the expression in his eyes.

She slammed the door behind her and started to walk down the long empty hallway toward the elevator. She tried to moderate her stride, but she was walking so quickly now that at times she was almost skipping. The heels of her shoes clicked loudly against the tiles: a silly, fluttering, frightened sound.

BY THE TIME SHE REACHED THE HOUSE, SHE WAS CALMER, BUT HER hand was still shaking as she tried to fit the key to the lock. She had been badly spooked: as much by Justin as by her own reaction to his presence and his words. For the first time in a very, very long time, the blood was flowing strongly through her veins and all her senses were alive, as though they had been forcefully rubbed the wrong way. The insidious sense of lethargy and the brooding unease that had become her constant companions since Eric's death were gone. Along with simple, outright fear, she had found the situation with Justin tonight exciting . . . tantalizing even. What the hell was wrong with her?

"Isa."

She turned around with a small scream.

"Hey, it's only me." Michael bent over to pick up the keys she had dropped.

The sight of his bulky figure was a relief. She tried to speak, but the tension of the evening was suddenly too much.

"What's wrong?" He placed his arm gently around her shoulder. All of his gestures were always gentle, she thought. Almost hesitant, not wanting to hurt. In her mind, unbidden, came the memory of strong fingers pressing into the soft flesh of her underarm. *Did you like it? Year after year . . . the same breathless passion?*

"I'm sorry. I'm just tired. I'm okay now, thanks."

"How did things go with Temple? Did you get the stuff?"

Isa thought of the cardboard box on the walnut table. So much for that. No way was she going to return to that place.

She made a slight, negative motion with her head. "There wasn't really anything I wanted after all."

"Good. So you won't be seeing him again."

"No."

"That makes me feel a whole lot better." He smiled. "The rea-son I came over is to let you know that I'll be away for the next few days. I'm spending the holidays with my family and I don't really need to go back to work before the second week in January. But my mum's house is just over the bridge in Putney, so I want you to promise me you'll call me if you need me." He took out a scrap of paper from his pocket. "This is the telephone number."

"Thanks, Michael. You're being very nice."

"Are you sure you'll be okay?"

"I'll be fine, really. Don't worry so much." Although, she real-ized with slight surprise, she did suddenly feel just a little uncer-tain, a little abandoned. She'd better get a grip. She couldn't depend on Michael all the time to hold her hand for her. "I'm fine," she stated again firmly.

"I have a great idea. Why don't you spend Christmas with us? It won't be a big party: only my mum and my sister. And my brat of a nephew. Last year he threw up all over us, but if you come I'll make sure he behaves."

"I wouldn't dream of intruding. Christmas is for family."

"You wouldn't be intruding. We'd love to have you. And my sister's a spectacular cook."

"No." She shook her head. "But thanks very much anyway."

"Well, then," he said reluctantly, "promise me that if you get nervous about anything—anything at all—that you'll call me."

"I will."

"Oh," he said just as he was about to turn away from her. "I almost forgot. This is for you. Merry Christmas."

From his carryall he took a cardboard tube the kind that would hold a small poster—and handed it to her.

She looked at him. "May I?"

"Please."

Opening the plastic top, she withdrew a white, rolled-up piece of rag paper and unfolded it.

She looked at it in surprise. It was a pen-and-charcoal sketch of herself. He had signed his name to it. She supposed it was a flattering likeness—the bones of her face delicately drawn—but did she really look so sad? Were her eyes really that shadowed?

He was watching her anxiously, one large hand brushing through the tow-colored hair with a nervous gesture. "Do you like it?"

"Thank you. I shall cherish it."

He grinned, relieved. "It's looking for trouble, drawing a picture of a woman. You can either be accused of insincere flattery or the likeness isn't flattering enough. But you have such an interesting face, I couldn't resist."

She felt herself blushing. "Oh . . . well, thank you."

"Now, are you sure you're going to be okay?"

"Positive, thanks."

"All right then. But if you need me, you call me. Promise?"

She held up her hand, palm turned outward. "Promise."

THIRTEEN

We can dye by it, if not live by love.

—"The Canonization,"
John Donne (1572–1631)

SHE WAS DEAD. WHY, THEN, DID HE FEEL AS THOUGH SHE WAS STILL around, watching him, her eyes crinkling with amusement? Why did he feel as though she was dogging his footsteps? He heard her voice in the echo of every other woman's voice; her silvery laughter reached his ear as he walked down the street. Only yesterday he had sat behind a woman in the train, a woman with upswept hair and a lovely neck. She was reading a paperback, her head bowed. Almost he had reached out and touched her. There was something of Alette in the unconscious grace of her posture. It made him long to draw his finger down the nape of her neck, right there where a few strands of hair had escaped from bondage. Silky skin; the sense of her blood pulsing just beneath the pad of his finger: the idea of it had left him short of breath. But then she had turned her head and glanced at him, and he saw that her face was common and coarse and no light shone from her eyes.

He couldn't understand what was happening. After Alette's

death he had felt newly invigorated. But now his brain felt heavy in his skull, his arms and legs were stone.

He missed her; of course he missed her—it was only to be expected. His demon angel. She was solace. She was pain. Joy and grinding humiliation. She inspired a sick fidelity, a strange devotion.

Tired, so tired. His thoughts were murky, as though the blood pumping through his brain was foul and oxygen-deprived.

How was he going to cope?

THIRD ENVELOPE

FOURTEEN

Riddles lie here; or in a word,
Here lies Blood; and let it lie.

> —"Epitaph on the Earl of
> Strafford,"
> John Cleveland (1613–1658)

JUSTIN WAS COPING. THE STOCK WAS RALLYING; UP ANOTHER FIFTY-
five pence. He had embarked on some serious damage control and
there was every indication that his salvage mission could well be
successful.

He had gained the support of Donne Asset Management, the single biggest shareholder in his company. He had issued a twenty-
two page rebuttal of allegations that investors were misled by not
being informed earlier of a potential sourcing problem. The circu-
lar, crucially, also set out in great detail a plan on how to cope
with this problem. The financial pages and City analysts had been
virtually unanimous in their approval.

This morning Isa had switched on the television set and had
watched a solemn-faced analyst with a flamboyant tie discuss with
great seriousness the steps Temple Sullivan was taking to ensure

an adequate supply of lemur droppings. It seemed the company had made arrangements with a number of zoos worldwide to feed palm seeds to their paradise lemurs and to collect the precious manure afterward for processing. The company had also managed to work out a deal with the authorities in Madagascar to sponsor the development of two new lemur sanctuaries, as well as special measures to bolster the breeding of paradise lemurs in the existing national park of Perinet. All these measures, investors were assured, had already been in the pipeline; but up till now the authorities in Madagascar had balked at the idea of taking land away from the Sakalava people on the island of Nosy Be. Fear that the drug might have to be rationed, however, had caused world-wide pressure and concern, forcing the authorities to give way. Temple Sullivan had also agreed to sweeten the deal by assisting the government with land recompensation claims and investing heavily in adult education programs on the island.

Justin was managing. He was riding the tiger. She couldn't deny feeling some relief, but she also felt flat, let down. Cheated.

THE AISLES IN SAINSBURY'S WERE CROWDED WITH LAST-MINUTE Christmas shoppers: pensioners looking for bargains, irritable mothers and their hyperactive toddlers, fathers who looked as though they were praying for deliverance. A rap version of "Rudolph the Red-Nosed Reindeer" pulsed from hidden speakers and Isa could feel the onset of a headache.

With difficulty she maneuvered her trolley past a display of reduced Chrismas crackers and party hats and parked it next to the cat-food section. She needed to get some milk but it would be eas-ier to cut through the crowd at the refrigerated compartment with-out the trolley.

As she returned from her quest, two milk cartons clutched in her hands, she immediately noticed the tall man standing next to her trolley. A tall man in a dark suit, a tan raincoat draped over one arm. Lionel Darling.

He was staring at the contents in her cart as though they held some special significance. When she came up to him, he turned slowly toward her and smiled, unsurprised. "Well, hello."

Somehow his presence in that overbright shop seemed unreal. Compared with the desperate faces of the shoppers around him, he seemed cool and unencumbered. In his hand he held a single red rose wrapped in transparent plastic with a gold ribbon tied at the end.

"This is unexpected." She placed the cartons in the trolley and turned to face him.

He gestured to the flower in his hand. "Last-minute shopping."

"Indeed." She stared at the rose and wondered why someone would brave a store filled with manic shoppers in order to buy a single flower.

"Well." She smiled at him and gently started pushing her trolley away. "It was nice seeing you."

"And you." But he didn't leave her side, instead falling in behind her as she entered the line at the checkout counter, pushing her trolley behind that of a large, red-faced man who coughed wetly.

She glanced at Lionel Darling. "You're welcome to go ahead of me."

"That's quite all right. I'm in no hurry."

"Do you live around here?"

"Not too far away." His gaze took in the frenzied scene around him. "'Tis the season to be jolly.'"

"You don't like Christmas?"

"I never have, come to think of it."

"Not even as a child?"

He lifted a lazy eyebrow. "My parents are of the fire-and-brimstone generation. They never believed in jingle bells, jingle bells. They saw this time of the year as the perfect opportunity to impress on me the more fundamental aspects of heaven and hell." With an abruptness that was startling, he suddenly dropped his voice to a stagy whisper: 'Be sober, be vigilant; because your adversary the devil, as a roaring lion, walketh about, seeking whom he may devour.' One Peter 5:8," he added in a normal voice.

She stared at him, slightly taken aback. Before she could think of how to respond, he continued, and now the mocking tone had left his voice. "My parents have a very simple perception of the world. Evil breathes fire on the one side of the divide, the virtu- ous cower together on the other side. And ne'er the twain shall meet. Gray areas do not exist."

She looked at him dubiously. This was becoming a decidedly odd conversation. Exchanging views on matters of theology in a checkout line. Somehow the environment of canned foods and frozen turkeys made the discussion seem even more surreal.

"I suppose it could be comforting to a child to have the lines drawn so clearly?" She was becoming a little alarmed by the grim- ness of his expression.

But then he flashed a smile at her and the bantering tone returned to his voice. "Well, you know what Samuel Butler said when he offered an apology for the devil: 'it must be remembered that we have only heard one side of the case. God has written all the books.'"

She returned his smile, relieved at the change in tone. "And Mark Twain said that even if it would be indiscreet to pay Satan reverence, we can at least respect his talents."

"Just so." He looked at her approvingly and then glanced at his watch. "You know, I may take you up on your offer after all. Would you mind if I slip in ahead of you?" He placed the rose del- icately on the conveyor belt and took a beautifully tooled leather wallet from inside his pocket. As he removed from it a ten-pound note, he noticed her eyes on the wallet.

"From your native country, actually." He tapped his finger against the tiny bumps on the leather surface that are so typical of ostrich skin.

"I thought it might be. Did you buy it here?"

He didn't answer but busied himself with paying the weary-looking woman behind the till. Carefully picking up the rose, he turned around and held out his hand. "I enjoyed our conversation." He smiled charmingly and squeezed her hand. "I'll see you soon."

Soon? There was only one envelope left and he had said he would courier it to her. But before she could ask him what he meant, he had moved away from her.

With one final, airy wave, he turned around and walked with long, sure strides toward the exit. He held the rose in front of him like a symbol. His fair hair shone like a halo underneath the bright lights.

CHRISTMAS DAY. QUIET STREETS AND THE SOUND OF CHURCH BELLS in the air. The sky overcast with the promise of snow. Isa stood by the window and looked out to where the stained-glass panels of the church sparkled darkly.

She had come to associate Christmas with loneliness and longing. She never saw Eric over Christmas. This was family time: going to church with his wife and children, entertaining parents and in-laws. Presents under the tree and Santa.

But there had always been the knowledge that come the New Year, there would be a knock on the door and he'd be waiting to grab her into his arms, holding her so tightly she could hardly breathe; holding on to her as though he would never again let her go. And they'd make love and talk and share with each other their resolutions for the New Year.

She turned away from the window. No resolutions this year.

She descended the staircase and entered the kitchen. She had, foolishly, bought an enormous turkey yesterday, which she would now have to prepare and eat all by herself.

Alette's kitchen was small but well equipped. Alette had liked to cook. She relished the flavors and the smells of good food. "Every scent captures an emotion," she'd say, chopping herbs with stunning precision. "Cinnamon is remembrance. Paprika is desire. Basil is contentment. Garlic is pure, earthy, uncomplicated happiness."

After lunch Isa went for a chilly walk and then took a long, hot bath, using some of Alette's sandalwood oil. She dressed herself in Alette's nightdress. It had become almost a rite now. As she closed the drapes in her bedroom, she looked up at the corner window of the apartment block opposite. The window was uncurtained but dark. Michael was still away. Strange how quickly she had become dependent on seeing a light in his window.

Boxing Day she stayed in front of the TV watching *It's a Wonderful Life* and *The Philadelphia Story*. But the next day was spent in the library to which Michael had brought her two weeks earlier. She was the only person using the library, and after a while even the dumpy librarian had disappeared—where to, she did not know. As the long hours ticked away, time became suspended. Outside, restless clouds were whirling across the sky with great speed and the wind shook the branches of the trees. But in here the air was still and so quiet, she could almost sense the blood pumping through her every vein.

She sat all by herself at the very end of a long, polished refectory table. She had opened every book at the correct page and had placed the books next to each other. They stretched the length of the table, looking like white, broken-winged birds.

There was an amazing amount of literature on the topic.

Everything from pseudo-scholarly journals extensively footnoted, to floaty, New Agey prose, to stark, sober firsthand reports. The firsthand reports were what she was really interested in. She had expected a kind of breathless "I was touched by the light" tone to these accounts, but in every case the report was completely devoid of sensationalism and in most cases the people writing, or being interviewed, sounded almost unwilling to share in their experience.

Many mentioned that when they had received the telephone call, they had not realized the person they were speaking to had died. In almost every case frustration was expressed at the poor quality of the connection. If more than one phone call was received, the quality of the connection in the later phone calls was sometimes markedly poorer than the first, as though time was taking its toll. Some reports stated that the conversations consisted of one phrase being repeated over and over again by the caller. There were even reports of phone calls not being received, but being placed, to the dead. The caller, not knowing that the person he or she had called was dead, would conduct a normal conversation and only discover afterward what had happened.

The person who was contacted was the only one able to hear the deceased's voice, even though someone else in the house might also be able to hear the phone ring. Often the ringing of the phone produced a physical reaction: nausea, headache, colored auras.

One denominator was common in all cases: the person who was contacted had shared an exceptionally close relationship with the deceased. And emotional bonding was not the only requirement. Caller and receiver were more often than not genetically linked: blood relatives. What disturbed Isa was that many recipients seemed to believe that they were in some way responsible for the contacts. Even though she wanted the calls to stop, one woman said, she recognized that there was something inside her which invited these calls.

Only one book mentioned a possible link between lucid dream-ing and phone calls from the dead. The book dealt with the topic of lucid dreaming as such and on the first page was an eye-catch-ing, colorful illustration from an illuminated Iranian manuscript dating from the year 1550. *Seven Sleepers* read the caption. The painting depicted seven sleeping Sufi masters sharing a collective dream as part of a meditative practice. Isa looked closely at the exquisitely drawn figures: seven, sweet-faced men in turbans hud-dling together, in some instances hugging each other; their eyes closed, their minds wandering together through the same fantastic landscape. She suddenly felt an immense sense of kinship with those tiny figures from the past. "Yes," she felt like saying. "I've been where you've been. I know what you know."

Near the end of the chapter, buried in a footnote, she came upon the following:

Lucid dreaming has been loosely linked to the mysterious phenomenon of phone calls from the dead. Access for these calls can no doubt be gained in more than one way, but one possible route may be through telepathic, lucid dreaming. This theory proposes that those who are able to control their dreams, thereby building a bridge between the sleeping and the waking worlds, may also have it in their power to find a way to link the worlds of the living and the dead. To walk in full consciousness through your own inner psychic labyrinth is a stupendous achievement and may serve as a dress rehearsal for exploring the realms of the dead.

In the Vigyan Bhairava Tantra the seventh sutra contains the instruction that the lucid dreamer should utilize his third eye and with tenuous breath "reach the heart at the instant of sleep and seek direction over dreams and over death itself." Over death itself. Isa stared at the words for a long time.

She suddenly realized how weary she was and how stiff from sitting in one position for so long. She was becoming light-headed from too much reading. She'd finish this chapter and then pack it in. Glancing back at the book, she turned the page over.

She felt her breath catch. There, stuck in the deep fold of the book, was a postcard and she recognized her own handwriting. The words were unexceptional, a kind of "wish you were here" message. She couldn't even remember where she had sent it from.

She turned the card over in her hand and looked at the picture. A view of a turbulent ocean: white spray and a vast sky. Now she remembered. Betty's Bay. She had spent ten days there supervising the initial work on a glorious holiday home. And for some reason she had felt compelled to write to Alette, to let her know that she would have liked to have her company.

A ray of startlingly bright light fell through one of the mullioned windows, drawing a golden line across the open pages of the book in front of her and onto the dark wood of the table. She suddenly had a picture of Alette sitting at this exact spot, paging through these same pages, inhaling the same dusty, throat-catching smell of unused books and then marking these pages for future reference with a postcard she was carrying with her. A postcard that had been sent to her from thousands of miles away by someone who was missing her.

The translucent beam falling through the window was fading. Only a moment before, it had pierced the gloom of the narrow aisle stretching ahead of her, shining off the faded titles on the spines of the stiff-backed volumes on the bottom shelf. But a cloud was moving in front of the sun, and as she watched, the worn, gilt lettering on the books receded back into shadow.

She was suddenly cold. She slipped the postcard into her handbag and shrugged into her coat. As she closed the books on the table one by one, a thought stuck in her mind. Alette had always seemed so self-sufficient. For the first time Isa wondered whether Alette had felt herself alone; lonely.

THE NEXT MORNING, AT TEN O'CLOCK SHARP, THE DOORBELL RANG and she opened the door to find a smiling Lionel Darling on her doorstep. Today he was dressed in a rugged canvas jacket and corduroy trousers.

"I told you I would see you soon. This is for you." He handed her the manila envelope and a form to sign.

"I didn't expect you to deliver this yourself," she said, signing the slip of paper. "I'm sorry for the trouble."

"Not at all. It was on my way. We're taking the children to the Trocadero."

She looked past his shoulder to where a car was parked outside the garden gate. A slightly harassed-looking brunette was in the passenger seat. Two small boys stared grimly at Isa through the back window.

She handed the form to Mr. Darling. Every time she saw him he was in a different role. Solicitor, biker, shopper, family man. It was disconcerting, somehow.

He was peering past her into the entrance hall. "I never asked you," he said. "Was everything in order on the day you arrived?"

"Thank you, yes."

He turned away from the door—rather reluctantly, she thought. "Well, this is the last envelope. But don't hesitate to let me know if there is still any way in which I can assist you."

"Thank you."

At the garden gate he stopped and looked around the winter-bleak garden. "I love roses." He stretched out his hand and brushed it against the naked stem of one of the rosebushes lining the outer wall. "This garden will be lovely in summer."

She nodded.

"A pity you won't see it."

She glanced at him and he smiled. "I assume you'll be back in South Africa by then."

"Oh, yes. Yes, I suppose I will be." But truth to be told, the thought of returning to Durban hadn't crossed her mind in days. Just after her arrival she had been convinced she would never be able to call this home. That had changed, she realized. I recognize it as my place.

She shook her head sharply. What was she thinking? This was Alette's home, not hers.

A demonic howl came from the car, where the two boys were engaged in an act of sibling savagery. The brunette was making futile gestures across the back of her seat.

Mr. Darling sighed. "Domestic bliss. Well . . . I should go." He held out his hand, suddenly formal. "Let me know if there's anything more I can do for you. My office won't open until next week but you can always leave a message on the machine. I'll keep in touch."

He got in behind the wheel and she watched as he calmed his fractious children with what seemed like no more than a single word. As the car moved away from the curb, Isa turned around and walked slowly back to the house, the envelope in her hand. An envelope sealed with dark blue wax that crackled as she slid her finger underneath the flap.

Dear Isabelle,

This will be my last letter to you.

With luck Justin will be knee-deep in lawyers by this time, with more problems on his plate than he can handle. It is time for the final blow.

Dearest Isabelle. I am forever in your debt. Love, friendship, and loyalty are the most important things there are, and you've

come through for me. I cannot begin to express my gratitude.
This is not easy for you, I know that. And maybe by this time
you think I'm insane. But never forget that Justin stole from me
that part of me that makes me who I am. His ultimate aim was
to turn me into a willing victim, and for a while he succeeded.
No more.

Now, let me tell you a story.

Just before the outbreak of the war in Yugoslavia in 1991, a
certain Jakob Jurić was employed as a senior researcher at the
Zagreb Institute for Immunology. Professor Jurić's specialty was
medicinal plants and their use in ailments of the central nervous
system. He also had a special interest in Alzheimer's.

In August 1991, he was scheduled to deliver a seminar at a
scientific symposium in Belgrade. The topic of the paper was the
potential of vincristine and vinblastine in combination with essence
of Palmetto angelicus to slow the progression of Alzheimer's.
This was still just a hypothesis on the part of the professor. No real
trials had yet been conducted. As is the custom, he sent his paper
to the organizers of the conference ahead of time. The paper was
received and date-stamped by the organizers on May 10, 1991.
Keep this date in mind Isabelle; it's important.

On 25 June, Croatia and Slovenia declared their independence
and war broke out. The organizers of the conference were Serbs.
They canceled their invitation to Professor Jurić and they did not
publish his paper along with the other conference papers. A month
later Professor Jurić was killed by sniper fire.

End of story, right? Not quite.

On May 12, 1991, a certain Justin Temple filed for a patent for
the development of a compound that would come to be known as
Taumex. Remember, the professor's paper was date-stamped to
have been received on May 10. In other words, Justin filed for a
patent two days later. When he filed for the patent, Justin did not

know about Professor Jurić's research. He had never even heard of Professor Jurić.

Let's move our story forward. It is now several years down the road. Taumex has just finished the first clinical trials. The way is open for human testing. After a lot of hard work and many difficulties, Justin is in the home stretch. The market is showing real interest in the drug for the first time.

I remember that day so well, Isabelle. Justin came home and his eyes were desperate. I had never seen him looking so helpless. Somehow he had gotten hold of Professor Jurić's paper; the one that had never been published.

In order for a patent to be valid, there must be no prior art. To put it very simply, it means that if you want to file for a patent, you have to give assurances that no one else has come up with the same idea ahead of you. Even though the professor had not filed for a patent himself, his paper had effectively wrecked Justin's—or anyone's chances, for that matter—for an exclusive patent. Any nonsecret, public use qualifies as prior use. The professor's paper was never formally published, but it still qualifies as prior art.

If this becomes public knowledge, Temple Sullivan's patent for Taumex will become invalid. Any other pharmaceutical company will have the right to manufacture the drug. It will become a free-for-all; the compound would no longer be Temple Sullivan's exclusive property. You can imagine what that would mean to the company.

Justin was weeping that day. "Two days," he kept saying. "Only two days." Two days only: but what a difference that can make.

To make a long story short, Justin decided to keep the whole thing quiet. "It's not as though I'm stealing from the professor," he said. "I developed this without his assistance, and what's more, he never had to go through the agony of getting the drug approved. And after all, he's dead. No one gets hurt."

*Shortly afterward I asked for a divorce. When Justin threatened
to play rough, I told him I would not hesitate to reveal what I
knew about the patent. Justin's company is the most important
thing in his life: even more important than his hate for me. So he
let me go and he also gave me a very generous alimony settlement.*

*What Justin didn't realize was that I had made copies of the
article. You will find those copies, along with a translation, in this
envelope.*

*By now you know the drill. Call the brokers, contact the papers.
And then you can go home.*

It will be over.

Isa opened the laptop computer and accessed the file in which
Alette stored the addresses and phone numbers of her clients.

Alette had often spoken of one of her clients, the wife of a retired
investment banker. "She's one of the 'ladies who lunch,'" Alette
had said, "and has probably never done a stroke of work her entire
life, but she belongs to that generation of women who is extremely
accomplished in the art of conversation and who has turned entertaining into an art form. I adore her company. Her husband's a real
sweetheart and also a killer investment counselor." More to the
point, Alette had mentioned that the husband had been a patent
attorney before turning to investment banking. "A good thing he
switched careers," Alette had said. "Because he has given me some
excellent financial advice over the years. I trust him implicitly."

Tunbridge, that was the name. Isa moved the cursor slowly
down the list of names. And here it was: *Mr. and Mrs. Henry
Tunbridge, 44 Eaton Crescent, Belgravia.*

She picked up the phone and started to dial. The phone was
answered by a young, fresh voice who promised to call her grand-
father to the phone immediately.

Isa waited. She could hear the sound of a radio playing and children's laughter in the background. A voice said, "Danny, will you stop that," and then there was the noise of someone closing a door and picking up the phone.

"Tunbridge." The voice was thin, with the high-pitched intonation of the elderly.

"Mr. Tunbridge, you don't know me, but I'm a relative of Alette Temple's. My name is Isa de Witt."

"Oh yes, I believe she mentioned you. I was so sorry to hear what happened. A tragedy. Is there anything I can help you with?"

She took a deep breath. "As a matter of fact, there is. I was wondering if we could meet."

"Well . . ." He paused. "I was actually on my way out to lunch. I have lunch at the Savoy Grill every Monday afternoon. Would you care to join me?"

"I promise I won't take up much of your time."

"Not at all," he said courteously. "I look forward to seeing you."

The driveway of the Savoy hotel was jam-packed with black taxicabs. A steady stream of dark-suited men, their faces red from the cold, pushed through the revolving door and turned immediately left to enter the restaurant.

Henry Tunbridge had not yet arrived. But the maître d' confirmed that they had his reservation. "His usual table" was the way he put it.

Rather than wait at the bar, Isa decided to go directly to the table. She was escorted to one of the dark green corner banquettes and given a glass of mineral water and a menu.

The chef obviously did not believe in lean cuisine. The fare ranged from the hearty—kidney pie with sweetbreads; bangers and mash—to the decadent: chicken breast stuffed with langoustines; sweet pepper salsa with smoked eel and quail's eggs.

She looked around her. The room was large, with impressive

paneling: yew wood at a guess. The clientele was overwhelmingly male and had that unmistakable look of the banker and the businessman. She was one of only three women in the room.

A thin, tall, elderly man dressed in a beautifully cut suit approached her table and held out his hand. "Henry Tunbridge. How do you do."

She shook his hand and watched as he carefully maneuvered himself into his seat. He moved with some difficulty.

"I hope you'll enjoy the food here," he said. "The plats du jour are always good; and anything that needs to be carved or flambéed." He nodded a greeting to a diner at one of the adjacent tables. "Another regular," he said to Isa. "I'm afraid we rather consider this dining room to be our own private club."

They placed their orders with a waiter who waited on them with a kind of chilly warmth. Tunbridge turned toward her and fixed his gaze on her face.

"Again, I'm so sorry about Mrs. Temple. She was a remarkable and charming lady. She was my guest at this restaurant more than once."

"You gave her investment advice."

He nodded. "Yes, although she had a remarkable head for business herself. Very shrewd indeed." He smiled. "My wife was convinced Mrs. Temple's special talents assisted her in this regard."

"I take it you did not share that belief."

"I do not presume to scoff, you know. More things in heaven and earth and all that. Certainly, it was uncanny the way Mrs. Temple seemed to know—intuit—things that were about to happen. She also had an amazing insight into what motivated people. My wife compared it to a beam of light illuminating dark corners of the mind. And she was a wonderful listener." He nodded almost to himself. "Yes, she listened with her heart." He touched his hand briefly to his chest.

His eyes switched back to her. "Now, how can I be of service?"

"Mr. Tunbridge, I seem to recall Alette telling me that you have a background in patents."

"Yes. In my youth I practiced as a patent attorney. But it was not a life that appealed to me. So I switched to investment banking. Why?"

"I would like to present you with a problem. But I'm speaking hypothetically, of course."

"Of course." Pale, old, wise eyes looked at her with a tinge of amusement.

"Suppose—" she stopped.

"Why don't you just tell me," he said kindly. "I promise you I can be very discreet. Now, let's say you have a hypothetical friend with a hypothetical problem. What is it all about?"

While she talked, he kept his eyes focused on a spot just behind her shoulder. She was grateful. It made it easier for her to speak. She did not tell him anything about her arrangement with Alette; she simply implied that she had a friend who was the CEO of a company and who might have encountered a patent problem.

When she stopped talking, he looked back at her. His face showed no emotion. "Patents are complicated," he said. "The operating bits of a patent all go into the making of a claim and the whole thing can become very involved. But from what you tell me, I would say the CEO of your hypothetical company would face severe difficulties if this information came out." He thought for a moment. "You see, here in the U.K., up to 1977, one only had to prove local novelty when filing a patent. The reason for this can be traced back to the original Statute of Monopolies as long ago as 1623, when it was considered just as meritorious for an explorer to bring a new idea home from abroad as to invent it himself. So if all of what you told me had happened before 1977, your CEO would have been in the clear. At least in the U.K. However, in response to a European directive, the rule changed. Instead of only local novelty, a criterion of absolute novelty was adopted. What kind of product does the company manufacture?"

She didn't want to mention the word "drug." That would be a dead giveaway. Tunbridge must have sensed her discomfort because he shrugged and said, "Not that it matters that much. One thing is certain though. When your CEO discovered that prior art existed, he should have notified the patent office. Of course, after that he could then just as well have closed up shop."

"What would happen, exactly?"

"His claim will be invalidated almost immediately. That doesn't mean he won't be allowed to continue manufacturing the product, but any of his competitors will have the right to jump in and manufacture it as well. At first he'll still have the upper hand: he does, after all, have everything set up already; factories, distribution. But if his company is small, he'll eventually lose out to bigger competitors. It will only be a matter of time. Slow death."

She swallowed. "Will there be any way in which he can get out of this jam if prior art is discovered? Any way at all in which he can keep the patent exclusive?"

"No." Tunbridge's voice was cold and emphatic. "This man is facing disaster. There is no way out."

FIFTEEN

*Love toucht her **Heart**, and lo it beates*
High, and burnes with such brave Heates,
*Such **Thirsts** to dye, as dares drink up,*
*A thousand cold **Deaths** in one cup.*

> —"Hymn to Sainte Teresa,"
> Richard Crashaw (1612–1649)

SHE COULDN'T DO IT.

She couldn't go through with it. Her conversation with Henry Tunbridge had made that clear to her. The situation was mad, completely insane. Alette could not expect this of her. It was not fair of Alette to place her in this position. For the first time Isa felt anger.

The sound of the doorbell made her walk quickly toward the front door. It could be Michael. Maybe he had decided to return early.

At first all she saw was an enormous bunch of pink-and-crimson-spotted tiger lilies. Then he lowered the arrangement so he could look her in the face.

"Peace?"

She stared at him. Justin's eyes were tired but calm.

"I don't know how to apologize enough," he said. "The other night I behaved like a dangerous lunatic. Please forgive me. I must have scared you to death."

In her mind came the memory of that night: his voice, lazy and dangerous. The feel of his hand on her arm. His body so close.

She felt her face grow warm. Scared? Yes, she supposed fear was part of it.

"The last thing I ever wanted to do was mess with your memories of Alette. All I can say in my defense is that I had had a really bad day. Although that's no excuse for taking it out on you. It was hardly your fault."

She flinched and her eyes slid away from his.

"Say something, will you? Please."

She hesitated. Then she held out her arms and took the flowers from him. "I should put these in water."

He followed her as she walked into the kitchen and watched as she placed the flowers into the kitchen sink and turned on the tap.

"I had no idea what your favorite flower is," he said. "I asked the lady at the shop what would be a good flower if you needed to apologize for being an idiot. She suggested roses, but I hate roses." He caught her glance. "Always have," he went on hurriedly, "ever since I was a boy. Oh, God, I've put my foot in it again, haven't I?"

She couldn't help smiling. "These are lovely, thank you."

"I have my car here," he said. "And a picnic basket. I was hoping I could persuade you to have brunch with me."

"Picnic? It's freezing out there."

"So wrap up tight. It'll be fun."

She started to shake her head but he said, "Come on, Isa; take a chance."

She looked at him doubtfully.

"Please?" He took a step toward her.

His pupils were ringed with blue and he had tiny yellow flecks embedded in the iris. As she watched, the pupils suddenly dilated. The eyes were a direct extension of the brain, she thought irrelevantly. Windows to the soul? As a scientist he'd probably disagree.

She looked away and sighed. "Let me get my gloves and hat."

Outside the sky was ice blue and cloudless; the air crisp and very cold.

He lifted the check cloth from the basket. "Pâté, chicken croquettes, hot lobster bisque"—he lifted a thermos flask—"crème brulée, and of course champagne. It's been a good week. We need to celebrate."

"You prepared this yourself?"

He smiled. "I can't lie to you. No. Harrods Food Halls."

He had brought along a travel rug as well, but in the end, after an uncomfortable fifteen minutes under a tree in Regent's Park, he agreed sadly that it was indeed too cold to sit outside, and they ended up back in his car, balancing paper plates on their laps and steaming mugs of soup on the dashboard.

He shoveled the debris of their meal unceremoniously into the basket and placed it on the backseat. "Now," he said firmly, "I'm going to show you London. I'm sure you haven't seen anything since you've arrived."

First stop was the British Museum. They gazed solemnly at massive granite figures in the Egyptian Sculpture Gallery, walked through halls filled with ancient artifacts and precious stones. An hour later they ended their visit in the Medieval Room staring at the Lycurgus cup: a single block of green glass depicting the agonized face of a Thracian king imprisoned by the deadly tendrils of a vine.

He took her to a tiny shop just around the corner from the

museum that was filled with old English silver, reams of silk, and woven rugs of dazzling beauty. He insisted on buying her a gift: a deeply dyed Indian scarf, which he tied around her neck himself after first removing Alette's green chenille one.

They visited a gallery that was home to the largest number of newspaper cartoons she had ever seen under one roof, and there was a cartoon of him on the wall: nose lengthened, mouth twisted into an evil sneer, riding a snorting bull, whip in hand.

They stopped off at a large warehouse where plaster casts of museum pieces were made. The place had the feel of a cathedral: quiet, serene, with wonderful light streaming through the enormous skylights. Stacked on wooden shelves were row upon row of off-white casts. The foot of a Greek athlete, with strong ankle and long second toe. Saints and gods and languid ladies. The bust of an angel staring at the world with naked eyes. Underneath their feet the floor was covered in white plaster-of-paris dust, and as they walked, they left their footprints behind them.

They had green tea and exquisite, sweet dumplings at the grimy counter of a tiny take-out place in Soho. He took her to the office of a friend of his who had a balcony with a view and they watched as the lights in the Square Mile turned to pricks of gold against the lavender sky. They ended the day in an extremely noisy Lebanese restaurant that "serves the best kibbeh in the realm" and shared a table with a pack of handsome, dark-eyed teenagers.

His moods changed swiftly. He could be boyish: his gestures quicksilver, his voice enthusiastic. In repose, his face seemed restrained, although the sense of leashed-in energy never left him.

He had a habit of jumping from one topic to the next with dizzying speed. He liked Nina Simone, just like her. He liked urban photography, just like her. He disliked art-house films. He certainly did not believe in psychic powers—this with a sidelong glance—but he confessed to reading his horoscope while waiting at the dentist's. Cricket was his favorite game and he sometimes watched sumo wrestling on late-night TV.

He laughed at her expression. "So now you know the worst about me. But it's actually a very spiritual sport. First the clay in the ring has to be blessed by a Shinto priest: there's this whole ritual. Of course if a woman should then touch the clay, it becomes impure and they have to repeat the entire ritual once again. Fascinating, don't you think?"

She pulled a face. "Awesome."

It was a charmed day. She felt happy. Even the memories of Alette that crossed her mind with amazing infrequence seemed to have little power to disturb. Oddly enough, the person who kept intruding into her thoughts was Michael: his gentleness, the slow smile and awkward gestures. She sensed that a relationship with him could develop if she wanted it—allowed it. But though she felt so comfortable around him, she believed that inside of her was no spark of tension that might ignite into heat.

She looked across at Justin. He was staring down, his dark lashes crescents against his cheekbone. Such a twisted, complicated thing: sexual desire. Why, oh why does it have to be touched by that wing brush of darkness before it feels so alive?

He suddenly looked up and straight into her eyes.

"I'm having a good time," she said.

He smiled and his eyes were very blue.

SEVEN DAYS WERE ALL IT TOOK, THEN. SEVEN DAYS DURING WHICH the lights seemed brighter, the cold more intense, and an added lilt sounded in the voices around her. Seven days in which the world turned starkly beautiful: a cold yellow tint burnishing the sky; the black limbs of the trees slim and vulnerable. Seven days only: not long at all to lose something as prized as the heart.

"I've lost my heart," we say, as though forces beyond our control have snatched from us a treasured object. How strange, Isa thought, this idea that we do not profit, but lose; that we are not enriched, but become the poorer for falling in love. Because surely, we gain. We gain back our sense of wonder. We close our hand around a blessing: the ability to look at the world with fresh eyes and to savor that sense of awe we have deemed lost to child-hood forever.

What once would have passed her by, barely tugging at her thoughts, now lay claim to her attention with a fierce insistence. The thin curve of a baby's eyelid. The explosive grace of a startled cat. Two men arguing with their hands; their expansive gestures unintentionally elegant. A trapped fly with silky, trembling wings. Frosty mornings and Justin's breath a ghostly flower blooming from his mouth.

He touched her hand and her heart leapt. He smiled at her and she felt such joy. She had been so lonely. She hadn't realized how lonely. Even when Eric was still alive, loneliness had been a dark presence hovering at her elbow: her most constant and assiduous escort. When Eric was around the lights came on, the music played. But then he'd leave and she'd be back in limbo—wait-ing—with loneliness stepping forward once more to claim her.

With Justin it was different. She did not feel as though loneli-ness was still in the room, watching them from the shadows. Being with Justin was like looking into the sun—an experience so fierce, it allowed no room for any other sensation. He made her feel vibrant, beautiful, and young. And every morning she woke up drunk with anticipation.

The days were blurring together in her mind, a string of dis-jointed, heightened images and sensations. Jogging in the park, with Justin looking back at her over his shoulder, shouting encouragement, his hair silky with sweat and curling blackly against his neck. Reading the newspapers together and knowing without looking that he was watching her. Taking a drive into the country: long swirls of early-morning fog rising from the side of the road and inside the car the heady smell of leather and the singular fragrance of his skin. The caress of soft wool as he tucks a travel rug around her knees, his hand lingering against her thigh. Feeling cosseted; feeling desired.

Too easy, she'd think. Too easy by far this headlong slide from total distrust into total surrender. She knew she was being reckless. She knew she was being irresponsible. How could she so simply and easily set aside everything she knew about him? But in a way it was part of the miracle, as though she had pushed her fingers into the dank hollow of a dead tree, and upon extracting her hand had found within it not the spider she had expected, but a butterfly of many colors.

London was recovering from its Christmas hangover and the streets were empty. They went for long walks and they talked for hours. He spoke about himself, his work, his childhood. A privileged childhood—growing up in the country, nannies, exclusive boarding schools—but also, it seemed to her, a lonely one. He described vividly and with enthusiasm the house in which he grew up and where his mother still lived. A sprawling house on the north coast of Devon, it was built of granite and Delabole slate and had been in his family for eight generations. He described pockmarked flagstones, leaded windows, and giant fireplaces. Tapestried sofas and chairs with hollows where the dogs had left their imprint. A fine Jacobean staircase, installed by a Victorian ancestor who had admired the period. And on every wall and in every room framed and matted prints of dried flowers. His mother's handiwork: she would dry and arrange them herself. Even the books in the library bore evidence of this craft: their pages stained with purple and yellow smears of petals crushed between the covers.

"When I was little," Justin said, "if I promised to be really quiet, my mother would allow me to watch her while she worked. Ever since, I always think of her with these delicate, dead flowers in her hands." He shrugged. "It has all stopped now. For the past few years she's had very bad arthritis."

"And your father?"

"He died several years ago. We were never close. Actually, growing up, I didn't see all that much of him. During the week he lived in his town house in London and only came home over the weekends. He and my mother did not have a happy marriage." Justin's voice was without emotion. "Everyone, my mother included, knew he spent his time with other women when in London." He shrugged again. "Anyway, when he was old and tired he had to come home. He was too frail to visit London anymore. So I suppose in the end my mother had her revenge. He never liked the house, the wildness of the countryside. That part of the coast is precipitous, you know, and in winter it's always wreathed in mist. It must have been a very special kind of hell for him to have had to return to it and be dependent on my mother."

Isa shivered. It was more the way he had told the tale of his parents' failed marriage, than the events themselves, that was distressing. His voice had sounded disturbingly flat and there was a curiously detached, almost dead expression in his eyes. It made her feel afraid.

"I'm sorry," she said.

He flicked his fingers against her cheek. "Don't look so sad. It's all water under the bridge now. And there was never any hope of their relationship ever working out. It was fake from the beginning. He faked love and she faked passion." He leaned forward so that their eyes were level. "I hate fakery," he said. "I detest counterfeit emotions. You probably won't understand. You're so very, very sweet. I can't imagine you ever pretending or being manipulative. With you it's what you see is what you get, isn't that right, Isa?"

His face was only inches from hers. There was something in his eyes that was hard to fathom. It left her feeling cold, a little uncertain. And suddenly the sense of her own duplicity was overwhelming. What would he say if he knew the truth? What would he do if he knew that theirs was a relationship rooted in a poisonous mix of lies and revenge? She was such a coward. She should tell him the truth now. Make a clean breast of it. But she couldn't move. Couldn't speak.

He smiled. With a quick movement he got up and pulled her to her feet. He lowered his head and soft as a moth's wing she felt his lips brush against her hair.

ALTHOUGH THE TENSION BETWEEN THEM WAS UNMISTAKABLE, THEY were not lovers. In fact, the relationship was chaste in the extreme: they had never even kissed. She sensed that he had decided she was not to be crowded and was willing to take his cue from her. But sometimes, unexpectedly, she'd catch an expression in his eyes that took her breath. And every night, hugging her pillow to her like some lovesick teenager, she would fantasize.

But still she hesitated.

So far she hadn't had the courage to demand of Justin that he talk to her about his relationship with Alette. She had raised the subject only once, but his expression had been so forbidding and the coolness of his manner so unwelcome that she did not dare mention it again.

She told herself that this was a reasonable response on his part. Of course he would not want to rake through painful memories. She also told herself that he had changed: that he was no longer the tyrannical man who had married Alette. Alette had been badly scarred by the marriage and she might have misconstrued Justin's subsequent actions to reconcile. Maybe she had been so trauma-tized by her unhappy marriage that she couldn't accept the fact that Justin was deeply repentant. Flowers, greeting cards, cham-pagne: none of it sounded truly sinister. Alette had been unable to bring herself to forgive Justin. But everyone deserves a second chance. People do change.

Still, at night when Isa was all alone, aware of her every heart-beat, her every breath, she would turn and sigh, and deep inside of her would pulse the knowledge that she must beware. But she was drawn to him. And the lure he held for her was, after all, not that difficult to explain. The desire to play with fire is an old, old temptation.

There was really only one reason she was still holding back. Guilt. For now her sense of guilt was more insistent than her desire. Consummating her relationship with Justin would open the door wide on the feelings of shame she experienced whenever she thought of Alette. Despite her attempts to rationalize the situa-tion, Isa knew she was letting her cousin down. Disloyalty, betrayal: these were dark, treacherous emotions. She had no wish to face up to any of these feelings now. That was for later. That was for much later. Her relationship with Justin was still so frag-ile, so murky and unknowable. It was imperative to draw the boundaries tight and keep Alette on the outside. So even though she wanted him, desired him, was so intensely aware of his light-est, most casual touch, Isa held back. And every day she'd find Justin's eyes on her; watching, waiting.

The house, which once had started to feel like home, was becoming an alien place. Isa tried to spend as little time there as she could. Alette's presence was almost tangible: every object a reminder, every picture a reproach. Each night, after saying good-bye to Justin, Isa locked the door behind her and walked up the three flights of stairs, her eyes on her feet, her hands not touching

the balustrade or the shiny walls. The house felt sad and melancholy, and though she turned up the heat, she could not dispel the
chill that hovered in the corners and settled about the furniture.
Whenever she left the house to be with Justin, it was with a sense
of escape.

Tonight he had taken her dancing. The dance floor was small
and crowded and the music very loud. The DJ was sticking to the
classics: Dire Straits, Van Morrison, lots of Springsteen:

Now you play the loving woman
I'll play the faithful man
But just don't look too close
Into the palm of my hand . . .

Justin's hand pressed into her lower back. She looked up at his
half-averted profile. His features were accentuated by the colored
lights in the ceiling: the lower lip full, the strong sweep of the jaw
unrelenting. The dramatic lighting wiped years off his face, blot-
ting out the tiny wrinkles around his eyes, the shadows at the corner of his mouth.

He glanced down at her and caught her eye. He smiled and she
felt a sudden rush of emotion. Surely she was entitled to a little
happiness? Surely the past should not be allowed to intrude on the
present? If there was even the slightest chance that things could
work out between them, she should grab the opportunity with
greedy hands. So maybe she was being rash and imprudent. She
might even come to regret her actions. But who wanted to be wise
if it meant denying emotions that were so lavish, so giddily extravagant?

For a brief moment Eric's face was before her; but then, with
only slight regret, she felt it slide from her mind. For the first time
she could look back on her relationship with Eric with a clarity

and an honesty that had not been possible before. She had loved him passionately and with all her heart, but she had never allowed herself to acknowledge the claustrophobia that was inherent in their relationship. For twelve years their life together had played itself out within the walls of her apartment. They had rarely gone out, had never received the affirmation from others that they were a couple. And then, the need to always be the perfect companion: always welcoming, always loving. A subtle tyranny that—a silken noose around her neck. Because if she was crabby or short of temper, he might simply not return after his next goodbye. She had to ensure that the hours they spent together were as perfect as pearls on a string. No wonder Alette had been so derisive, so critical. Alette would never have allowed herself to buy into the wishful lie that it is better to love the wrong person than not to love at all. But why was she thinking about Alette now?

> So when you look at me
> You better look hard and look twice
> Is that me baby
> Or just a brilliant disguise

"Hey, you." Justin had placed his mouth against her ear. "Come back. Where are you?"

She looked up into his smiling eyes and suddenly color, light, and music were contracting into a single, pure pinpoint of excitement. "I'm right here," she said. "I'm not going anywhere."

He smiled again and once more his hand tightened possessively against her back. "Good," he said. "Because you're not going anywhere without me."

IT WAS LATE BY THE TIME THEY LEFT THE CLUB. THEY SPOKE VERY little on the way back, but the darkness in the car was intimate and warm. She suddenly, furiously, did not want this night to end.

She glanced over at him. His face, intermittently highlighted by the glare of uncoming headlights, seemed eerily calm. His body was completely relaxed. She looked at his hands on the steering wheel: *touch*. She looked at his mouth and tasted: *kiss*. He turned his head and their eyes met. Without saying anything he turned his attention once more to the road. But he was smiling quietly, as if in secret. And deep within her stirred an almost painful antici-pation.

By now it had become almost a routine. Every night he waited in the car until after she had unlocked the front door before driv-ing off. He never got out. But tonight he carefully parked the car at the side of the road. As she reached for the catch of her door, he opened the door on his side and stepped out. And again she felt that sense of nervous exhilaration, almost fear, fluttering in the pit of her stomach.

She had left the outside light on and as they walked through the front garden their shadows stretched ahead of them, long and spi-dery. They weren't touching—he was walking slightly behind and to the side—but she could feel his eyes on her. She inserted the key in the lock with a hand that was sticky with sweat. By the time they stepped into the lobby, her heart was drumming in her throat and her face felt flushed. Any second now he was going to pull her in his arms and then . . .

He reached for her, his movements slow and unhurried. For a moment he just held her against him and she buried her face deep into his shoulder, inhaling his scent, listening to the beat of his heart. And now his hands were in her hair and he was kissing her forehead, tilting her face up to his and brushing his lips against her eyelids, her cheeks. His breath became a delicious trickle of warmth against the side of her mouth.

His hand slipped underneath her sweater, his palm hot against her skin. But even as she arched her back slightly and opened her mouth to him, she felt the hair at the back of her neck rise.

The phone was ringing.

His grip tightened. "Leave it."

Against her skin was the cold prick of sweat. A wave of nausea washed over her. Justin's mouth on hers felt smothering. The phone kept ringing. On and on it went, an off-key, atonal sound. Stop, she thought. Please stop. But the ringing was getting louder, the sound bouncing off the walls now, ricocheting within her head. The sound was a warning—utterly compelling—and she could not ignore it.

She tried to pull away from Justin, but his hold was firm. "No," he said, and his mouth searched for hers once more. "Don't answer that."

She placed both her hands against his chest and twisted from his grasp. "Let go."

He stepped away immediately. For just a second she saw a flicker in his eyes but the next moment his face was still. "I'm sorry," he said, and gestured with his hand toward the kitchen, where the phone was still ringing. "Please."

She turned and walked away from him, stiff as a wooden doll. The phone was on the far side of the kitchen, sitting on the edge of the dresser like a squat, malevolent frog. With a tremendous effort of will, she managed not to touch it, although her brain was screaming at her to lift the receiver. Bending down swiftly, she pulled the cord from the wall.

For a few moments she stayed where she was, eyes closed, her heart jerking erratically inside her chest. She had reconnected this particular instrument only yesterday after Justin had complained that he could never get her to answer his calls. She had been reluctant to do so, but she didn't want him to think she was suffering from some kind of phobia. And there was no possible way to tell him the truth. He would think her deranged. For just a moment she felt like laughing hysterically. What if she went back to him now and told him she had just hung up on his dead ex-wife?

Slowly she got to her feet. Now that the noise had stopped, her breathing was becoming more regular, her heart gradually calming itself. But as she stepped back into the hall, her breath stalled in her throat with an audible gasp. For a moment her mind stopped working

Justin was standing next to the console table that flanked the one wall. On the table was a bamboo tray and in it a large, manila envelope. Underneath it, she knew, would be two smaller letter-sized envelopes fastened to a sheet of paper. Alette's third letter.

How could she have been so careless? How could she have been so utterly stupid? After her meeting with Tunbridge, she had simply dropped Alette's letter and the letters addressed to the newspaper editors into the tray. She had meant to stow them with the two other envelopes, but had never gotten around to it. The letters were of no importance to her any longer. And aside from that very first visit when he had invited her to have a picnic, Justin had never followed her into the house.

But now she was going to pay for her carelessness.

Absentmindedly he picked up the large fawn-colored envelope. He was staring at the handwriting. Between his brows was a faint frown.

She had to distract him before he noticed the smaller envelopes addressed to the newspapers and the letter that was clipped to them. They were now in plain view. All he needed to do was look down at the tray and he'd see them. Even from where she was standing, she could make out the first lines of Alette's letter: *This will be my last letter to you. With luck Justin will be knee-deep in lawyers by this time . . .*

"Justin."

He glanced at her, the manila envelope still in his hand.

"Would you mind if we called it a night?" She knew her voice sounded high-pitched and strange. She tried desperately not to look at the table.

With a careless gesture he flipped the envelope back in the tray, keeping his eyes on her.

"Is something wrong?" Taking a step toward her, he gently tried to draw her into his embrace. Involuntarily she stiffened her back and shoulders, resisting the pressure of his arm.

He let his hands fall by his side. "What's wrong?"

"Nothing. I'm just really tired."

"Tired," he repeated, his voice completely uninflected.

She couldn't meet his gaze. The silence ran on for several heart-beats. This time when he spoke, there was a tightness behind the words. "Well, if you're tired, of course I won't keep you."

"Wait. Please."

He looked at her over his shoulder, his hand on the doorknob. His mouth was a thin line in his face and his eyes were bright.

She was handling this badly. He must think she was behaving like the worst kind of tease. And now her eyes were filling with tears. Wonderful. Puffy eyes and a red nose; how attractive. The tears ran down inside her nose and she sniffed dismally.

He took a handkerchief from his pocket. "Here."

"I'm sorry," she said, her tongue sluggish in her mouth. She dabbed the handkerchief at her face.

"No. I should have known better. But I really thought . . ." He paused and she saw something come and go in his face. But then he blinked and the expression in his eyes went blank. "I've never liked this house," he said suddenly.

She waited wordlessly. "Don't look so stricken." His voice was abrupt and dry. "It's all right. Really. I'll pick you up tomor-row evening as we planned. Okay?"

"Thank you," she said hardly. "Again . . . I'm sorry."

He shrugged and made a gesture with his hand: a gesture at once dismissive and weary. "It doesn't matter. At least I know where I stand now."

ISA REACHED FOR THE TOP SHELF. AS SHE CAREFULLY REMOVED A FEW books, the first two envelopes Alette had sent her peeked out from behind a thick, green-backed volume. Isa placed the third manila envelope with the others and replaced the books. She should have done this days ago. The real question, of course, was why she was keeping these letters. She wasn't ever going to send them. They should be burned. Maybe tomorrow that's just what she'd do.

She sat down on the side of the bed, sick at heart. She remembered the shuttered expression on Justin's face and felt like weeping. Closing her eyes, she experienced again the warmth of his arms around her, the coolness of his lips. And then the ringing of the phone. The stomach-clutching nausea, the cold sweat. The sense of imminent peril. The perception that she had been caught in an action that was dark and perverse . . . incestuous almost. One moment she had been swept away, and the next moment it had been like looking onto darkness.

She wished she could go to sleep, but her mind kept reliving the evening over and over again. For a moment she considered calling Michael. It would be good to hear his voice. If she could just talk to him for a little, she'd feel better. And he had made her promise to call him if she needed him. But it was already so late. And what would she tell him? She certainly couldn't tell him about Justin, he would be aghast. Why it was so important to her that Michael continued to think well of her, she couldn't explain. She only knew she didn't want to lose his respect. So she should probably wait until he returned and try to explain to him face-to-face. And she couldn't tell him about the phone call either. He'd be so alarmed, no doubt he'd drive over immediately and that would not be fair to him or his family. No, she was just going to have to get through this by herself.

She walked to the bookcase. Maybe something escapist and forgettable would help her fall asleep. On the bottom shelf she found a paperback crime novel. It was not the kind of book Alette would normally read, and as Isa opened the cover, she saw the initials J.T. written on the flyleaf. J.T. Justin Temple?

The novel was slickly written, even though it trod familiar paths. A serial killer, mutilated women, a spunky, self-deprecating woman detective, herself a potential victim. The details of the murders drawn with excruciating care: sliced-off fingers, eyeballs impaled on toothpicks, toilet plungers shoved into female orifices. Sexual sadism, misogynist fantasies. "Serial killers are always a good bet," an editor friend once told her. "And viruses." Not the casual cruelty of relationships gone wrong; the ferocity of soured emotions or the subtle savagery of careless words.

But the book was addictive and held her attention. She read on until the early-morning hours. After she had turned off the light, she fell immediately into a deep, dreamless sleep. When she woke up, it was as though someone had flicked a switch. One moment she was dead to the world, the next moment she was wide-awake, her senses stretched to full alert.

For a few moments she lay quietly, trying to pinpoint what it was that had triggered an alarm bell within her. She turned her head slowly to one side on the pillow and her eyes wandered through the room, taking in the dark shape of the writing desk by the window, the loom of the bookshelves, the black, strangely unwieldy outline of the wing-backed armchair . . .

She eased back the covers and groped for her robe. Silently she walked out onto the landing and stopped to listen. And then she heard it—a tiny sound. It seemed to come from somewhere in the house below her. She held her breath, straining to identify what it was she had heard, and for a few moments it was quiet. But then she heard it again: a sound that was unfamiliar, alien.

It was probably nothing. It could be coming from outside. No need for the apprehension, which was turning her stomach to acid. Silently she chided herself for her jitteriness. So much for her professed indifference to the scenes of carnage she had read earlier tonight. Obviously the deranged violence in the book had spattered her unconscious and was now playing skittles with her nerves.

Beneath her bare feet the carpet felt soft as velvet. She started down the stairs, one hand barely touching the balustrade. Her robe brushed the stair runners with a sibilant swish and she stopped to pull the hem upward.

The large, double doors leading to the living room gaped wide open. In the pure, moon glow, the spacious room with its exquisite furnishings was an illustration from a dark fairy tale. A magic place this—caught in a spell—waiting for a sleeping princess to bring it back to life: to restore color to the rugs, the drapes, the large lacquered screen with its exuberant pattern of birds and foliage.

On the mantelpiece the gilt frame capturing the large studio picture of Alette winked at her. It seemed to have fallen over. She picked it up and turned it around in her hand.

It took her a heartbeat to realize that the photograph inside the frame was gone. In her hand she held nothing more than a flat, black square. The gaping emptiness was a shock.

She was still staring, stupefied, at the empty frame when she heard it again. A thin shiver of sound.

Not in this room.

She replaced the frame on the mantelpiece and walked out the double doors. At the bend in the staircase her eyes fell on the two carved masks that Alette had brought with her from Africa. The top one had its lips flattened into a fastidious sneer. The bottom one stared solemnly at the world with round eyes. For the first time she found them sinister, and as she continued down the stairs, she imagined them staring after her. One expression malevolent. The other unnervingly vacant.

A silvery tinkle. Much closer now. The kitchen.

The blood was rushing in her ears. She was sweating.

Switch on the light. Intruders are scared away by signs of activity. But she couldn't bring herself to flip on the light switch in the hall. If she did so, the moment of confrontation would inevitably be upon her.

Confrontation with what?

She leaned against the half-open door leading to the kitchen and stepped inside. A freezing wind gusted through an open window immediately facing her and the door behind her slammed shut.

She whirled around, her hand uplifted as if to ward off danger. But there was no one there. It was only the wind.

She turned her attention to the window. Inside the opening to the window hung five, swaying wind chimes. The wind pushed through again. The chimes responded with an icy tremor.

She tugged the window closed and the billowing lace curtain collapsed against her hand. Bunching the chimes together, she fastened them with the thin, silver restraining chain. How had the chain come undone? More to the point, how did this window come to be open?

Perhaps she could persuade herself that the chain had slipped off by itself. She peered at it closely. An enlarged link at the end of the chain fitted firmly around a small hook at the other end. She brushed her hand against it. The chain held fast. Still, it wasn't impossible. Maybe link and hook hadn't connected properly. Yes. Definitely possible. As for the window—well, she must have opened it herself. But earlier tonight, when she had been in the kitchen, she had not been aware of a draft. Considering, though, that she had been scared out of her wits at the time, and intent only on silencing the phone, her memory was probably not reliable. She looked at the window again. There was no way for an intruder to get in through those burglar bars.

In the hallway she tested the front door. It was locked solid and, even more reassuring, the keys were in the tray on top of the console table,

Her confidence returned and stayed with her as she walked up the stairs and paused inside the wide doors of the living room. She switched on the lights and the room seemed cozy now. No more chilly shadows. But then she looked toward the mantelpiece.

A flawless smile. The hair swept back in a mass of curls. Alette's amused eyes looking straight at her.

The photograph was back in its frame.

SIXTEEN

. . . *our very sorrowes weepe,*
That joyes so ripe, so little keepe.

> —"To *Amarantha,* That she
> would dishevell her haire,"
> *Richard Lovelace (1618—1657)*

TRAFALGAR SQUARE WAS PACKED WITH TOURISTS ENJOYING THE windfall of a mild evening in January. It was surprisingly warm and the sky was a deep, soft midnight blue. The road was busy: cars and buses congealed into a seemingly never-ending stream of traffic. Justin swore lightly under his breath and glanced at Isa. "Sorry about this, I should have taken a different route."

"Are we in a hurry?"

"I made a reservation—"

He swore again and stepped on the brakes as a girl with a pom-pom hat and a black mini crossed the road directly in front of the car. Justin jabbed his hand at the horn. Without missing a stride, the girl flashed an impudent smile and blew him a kiss. Isa watched her as she disappeared into the crowd, the red pom-pom a brave splash of color moving farther and farther away.

She looked back at Justin. "I'm sure they'll keep the table for us."

He sighed. "If not, we'll have to settle for McDonald's. All the restaurants will be booked solid by now."

It was another thirty-five minutes before they arrived at the restaurant, but their table had indeed been kept for them. It was the kind of place Justin liked; small and intimate, with pretty tablecloths, soft lighting, and attentive waiters. A serious menu with serious prices. The gloss of wealth without the vulgarity of excess.

He had ordered a bottle of champagne and she smiled and nodded at this attempt at festivity. He was making it easy for her. He was behaving as though nothing was wrong, as though last night's aborted embrace had never happened. He was keeping up a light flow of conversation; safely banal, amusing at times. But underneath the quiet tone of his voice lurked something that had not been there before.

She wasn't feeling particularly well herself. After her broken night she had spent most of the day sleeping—or rather, oversleeping. She had woken up late in the afternoon with her mind clogged and sluggish, a faint headache nagging behind her eyes. As for wind chimes, open windows, and missing photographs— maybe she had imagined most of it. She had, after all, been half-asleep at the time. There was a rational explanation, she was sure. And if she repeated this to herself often enough, she might even start to believe it.

The waiter had poured too much champagne in their glasses and some of the silver liquid splashed over the rim. Isa watched a tiny translucent drop travel down the side of Justin's glass; down, down until it reached the tablecloth, where it spread in an ever-widening stain, much too large for such a tiny drop of moisture.

"What are we drinking to?" she asked.

"Well, this is a bit late in the day, but maybe we should toast our New Year's resolutions."

"I don't have any."

"You should. It's expected."

She looked at him and thought silently: *If I could make things right again.*

"Come on," he quizzed. "Surely you can come up with something."

"I don't have high aspirations. To be happy, that's enough for me. I know it sounds bland—"

"It's not bland. It's hugely ambitious. I'm not even sure it's not verging on hubris." He clinked his glass against hers. "But I'll second it. Be brave and challenge the gods—why not?"

"And yours?"

"Oh"—he paused—"not to take anything for granted. That'll do." His voice held the same detached inflection she remembered from the previous evening, as though he was talking about something supremely uninteresting. *At least I know where I stand now.* How quickly things had changed. Only yesterday there had been a connection between them that felt true; now he was a friendly stranger.

The food was excellent and on the surface everything seemed fine. They made pleasant conversation, but it grated on her. Too much between them remained unsaid and the weight of those unspoken words was almost palpable. "Don't you understand," she felt like saying. "I did not turn from you. I did not reject you. But Alette was there with us. Surely you felt her presence?"

It was still early by the time they left. As they walked to the car, she felt a sense of bleakness stealing over her. All she wanted to do now was to get to bed and sleep for a hundred years.

He opened the door of the car for her and said, "Are you in a hurry to get home? There's something I'd like to show you."

"What?"

"A special place. I'll take you there." He did not say any more, and they did not speak during the drive. They drove for what seemed like a long time. She was starting to feel apprehensive. When he finally parked the car in an almost empty car park, she did not exactly know where they were. It was dark here, and deserted. But in front of her was the Thames and on the other side a panorama of cool, glamorous light. She recognized the tower at Canary Wharf, an immensely tall finger of glittering glass. And there, looking like a toy, was the Docklands Light Railway.

They carefully negotiated a series of steps leading downward. Around them the darkness was soaked through with the smell of the river. An intense smell: a smell of rotting leaves and the tang of salt. The water seemed black as pitch; the smears of light streaking across its dark surface transitory and ephemeral.

"Isn't it beautiful?" He was staring at the water as if mesmerized.

She didn't answer. There was something sinister about a large body of water at night. As children, she and Alette had often slipped out after their bedtime. Sometimes they had visited the river that curled through the farm like an enormous brown snake. Alette loved the water, but Isa had sensed something ancient and primal and not very friendly lurking in its warm, loamy depths. During the day the river awed and overwhelmed. At night it became something that defied comprehension. Something beyond imagining. It had always left her feeling deeply uneasy. She had the same sense of disquiet now as the cold wavelets of the Thames slopped against the pebbles at her feet.

She hugged herself as if cold and looked around her. They were alone. There was no one else on this stretch of pebbled embankment and no light shone from the few barges moored close by.

Justin was standing with his back toward her, his shoulders

hunched slightly forward. His eyes were fixed on the huge column of the Canary Wharf Tower.

"Did you know," he said suddenly, "that migrating birds run
the risk of smashing themselves to death against skyscrapers?"

The remark was so inexplicable, she had no idea how to
respond.

He nodded as if to himself. "It always happens at night. And
then the next day you find these dead and dying birds at the foot
of tall buildings. Most of the birds die from the force of the impact.
Those who survive are usually horribly maimed, with broken
beaks and bloody feathers. I lived in Toronto for a while and during the migrating season there would be volunteers searching the
streets every morning for these mangled birds."

He paused again. "But you know what's the most amazing
thing about it? The birds never fly into dark, unlit buildings.
Never. You'd think that would be the reason, right? That somehow they can't see these structures at night. Not so. It's the tall, lit
buildings that are hazardous. The birds fly straight at them,
smashing themselves to pieces against those yellow windows."

"Like moths burning up in a flame." Her voice sounded strange
to her ears.

"Yes," he said. "Like that."

"Justin."

He kept his eyes on the far side of the stretch of water.

"Look at me."

He turned on his heels, facing her now, but in the darkness she
saw only the whites of his eyes, not the expression.

"Tell me about Alette."

Just saying Alette's name out loud felt daring, as though she
was tempting fate.

For a few moments it was silent between them. Then he said
simply, "What do you want to know?"

"Tell me why it didn't work out."

She thought at first he wasn't going to answer her. The silence ran on and on.

"Do you know what first attracted me to Alette?" He sounded almost surprised. "Her walk. She had this way of walking as though she didn't give a damn. She looked so free, so unfettered . . ." He paused and it was quiet again.

He balled his hands and pushed them into his pockets. "It went wrong between us because the pact didn't work out."

"What pact?"

"The pact you make when you fall in love. You know how when you're first attracted to someone, you always present only a certain side of yourself? The best part of you, your most attractive qualities? It's like this game we all play."

"Of course."

"Well, inevitably things move on, and you're getting ready to hand over your trust as well as your heart. Point of no return. The time for complete honesty. At this stage you have to put every-thing on the table and show who you really are. All the flaws, the insecurities. If you don't . . . if you persist in faking it, you violate the pact."

"But if you love someone, you love them regardless."

He turned away from her and stretched out his hand as though he might actually be able to touch that distant column of glass and light.

"I thought so, too," he said, "but I was wrong."

His voice was filled with such sadness, it tore at her heart. She walked over to him and placed her arms around him from behind, hugging him close.

"I don't want to talk about her anymore," he said, his voice muffled.

"Then we won't," she said. "We won't talk about her."

They stood like that for a long time. It seemed to her as though the darkness around them had deepened. The heavy smell of the river was in her nose and inside the narrow confines of her ribs she felt the sad beating of bruised and bloodied wings.

When he finally turned around to face her, she placed her hand on his cheek and found it wet with tears.

"Come home with me," he said.

SEVENTEEN

My Love is of a birth as rare . . .
It was begotten by despair
Upon Impossibility.

—"The Definition of Love,"
Andrew Marvell (1621–1678)

HE STOPPED THE CAR AT THE GARDEN SQUARE OPPOSITE HIS apartment and turned the key. For a while they didn't say anything; just sat there listening to the cooling engine.

He turned to face her. "If you've changed your mind, I'll understand."

She hesitated. This, after all, was not the way it was supposed to be. Where was the joy, the breathlessness? The heart-racing excitement? Melancholy and passion were not meant to be bedfellows.

"At least come up for a drink. Please. I just want to be close."

Still she hesitated, she was feeling apprehensive now. But then she looked into his eyes. They left her with no defenses. Last night she had squandered the moment. She shouldn't do so again.

Inside his living room, he took her coat. His fingers brushed against her neck. "Sherry, right?"

"Thank you, yes."

The light winked off the rims of the glasses; drew sparks from the diamond facets of the cut-glass decanter. The sherry dripped into the glass with an oily whisper.

She said, suddenly desperate, "Justin, maybe I should go after all."

"I want you to stay with me." His voice was almost a sigh.

She didn't answer.

Her hand hung limply by her side. He picked it up and brought it to his cheek, his eyes never leaving her face. Then he turned his head sideways and his hot breath was on her wrist. He moved his lips against the palm of her hand, pressed his mouth on the swell of the fleshy mound at the base of her thumb.

"Stay with me."

Softly his finger pressed against her lower lip, forcing her to slacken her mouth. He brought his face close to hers. His eyelashes were dark and long.

He kissed her. His tongue was exploring her mouth gently: a self-assured intruder prying, probing, insisting that she give way.

She felt her lips soften.

His breathing became sharp and shallow. Then her hand was in his and he was pulling her toward a closed door. As he placed his hand on the doorknob, she felt herself holding back.

"Don't be afraid." He pushed her gently into the room ahead of him.

She had a confused impression of a low, wide bed; a room decorated in shades of flannel gray. But her eyes were held by the reflection in the long, full-length mirror facing her. A reflection of a woman with tangled hair and bruised mouth. A woman with irresolute eyes.

She tucked her hands behind her back. The woman in the reflection ducked her head and her hands moved behind her back in a timorous gesture. Now she was moving backward, as though trying to escape.

He was standing a few paces behind her, his face unreadable. He made no move to touch her. The message was clear: If she wanted to leave, he was not going to stop her.

She gave a last look at the woman with the uncertain eyes and turned her back on that diffident figure. She walked up to him and pressed her body against his. Reaching up to take his face in her hands, she pulled it strongly and deliberately toward her.

THROUGH HER MIND RACED WISPS OF A DREAM, A MEMORY OF another life. She was back on the farm and it was dark. Black night and bright stars. She was swimming in the murky water of the dam by the steel windmill. She was naked and the cold water lapped at her thighs and breasts and caused her nerve ends to leap and crackle. She dipped her head underneath the water and forced her body down, down until her feet touched the bottom and she recoiled at the slippery feel of slime. Her hands and arms started rowing upward again, she was blinded by water and her chest hurt, but as her head broke the surface she laughed exultantly with panic and exhilaration.

He was drawing his finger down her body, down the inside of her arm, her armpit. It hovered at her breast, the curve of her hip. He lowered his head and flicked his tongue all the way down the length of her, touching the hollow at her throat, lingering at the back of her knees, the soft arch of her foot.

She started trembling and the shiver that gripped her made her tighten her hands, made her pull her shoulders forward as though she felt a chill. His mouth pressed against her stomach, lingered in the damp fold of her thigh. And the chill turned to heat and every vein inside her was touched by fire; every sinew in her body burned.

The crushing pressure of his weight. His lips hot as a flame against her mouth. His hips rocking against hers: waves, water, drowning. Her skin dewed by his sweat. She placed her hands on the small of his back and pressed him against her. She wanted him close, she wanted to feel the sharp, knobbly angles of his hip-bones, the muscles moving like thin snakes underneath his skin.

She opened her eyes. His face loomed above her; he was watch-ing her. Then his eyelids closed painfully as though he was shield-ing himself from her gaze. His head drooped. He placed the palm of his hand over her eyes and it became dark.

THE SCENT WOKE HER UP. A HEAVY, INTENSELY SWEET SCENT. THE powerful perfume of crushed roses.

For a moment she lay completely still, but even as her brain rec-ognized the fragrance, it was already dissipating, evading her.

From somewhere far away came the scream of a siren. Light from the street lamp outside filtered into the room and caused shad-ows to curdle in the corners of the ceiling.

She turned her head. Justin was sleeping soundly: his breath slow and even. He was lying on his stomach, his pillow gathered against him in a kind of flaccid embrace.

She swung her legs over the edge of the bed and walked noise-lessly through the door and down the passage until she reached the living room. The embers of the fire were still alive: a sullen, dark, orange glow. Her eyes fell on the oil painting above the mantel-piece, on that figure dressed in purple velvet and lace; on the arro-gant, proud face with the narrow nose and dark eyes.

It was stifling in here. She needed fresh air. Opening the win-dow, she breathed in deeply. She suddenly noticed the cardboard box with Alette's things, which was still on the walnut table in the window, just as it had been on that night almost three weeks ago when she had visited him here for the first time. A lifetime ago.

She pulled the box toward her. Everything was still there. Her hand touched the front of the table, the sharp edge of the metal knob of the drawer. Instinctively, without thinking, she pulled at the knob and the drawer slid open in her hand.

The letters Justin had taken from her that night were still inside. The letters from Alette he hadn't wanted her to read. She remembered how he had snatched them from her hand.

She looked up. The eyes above the fireplace were watching her. They seemed amused.

She picked up the letters. They were still fastened together with a rubber band. Quietly, without any haste, she walked to the couch and opened her purse. She slid the letters into the inside pocket. Afterward she would look back on this moment and realize she had felt no shame in doing so.

"Hey."

She turned around quickly.

He was standing inside the door, his dark hair tousled.

"I miss you, come back to bed." He held out his hand.

She followed him back down the passage and into the room. He had switched on the bedside lamp. It cast a warm glow over the sheets. Warm. Inviting. Why, then, was she feeling chilled? In the air was the merest suggestion of a sweet-smelling scent.

She got into the bed next to him and he pulled up the bedclothes so they covered her bare shoulders.

"You shouldn't leave me like that," he said. "I woke up and your side of the bed was cold."

She noticed for the first time the framed print on the wall. It was an odd choice for a bedroom. It was an old-fashioned doomsday scene: moldy skeletons rising from the putrid earth, angels with vacant faces and flowing hair blowing on trumpets; muscular demons with strong teeth and eyeballs of a pure, pure white. One of the angels, unlike her sisters, was staring out of the frame with yellow eyes, a smile on her lips. She had red hair swirling around her hips.

Justin switched off the lamp, plunging the room into darkness. He yawned and put his arm around her, drawing her close. She tried to relax in his hold, but even as her thoughts grew cloudy, something was hammering away at her brain. Just before she slid into sleep Isa wondered how it was that the artist had included Alette in his picture.

WHEN SHE WOKE UP AGAIN, SHE WAS MOMENTARILY CONFUSED AS TO where she was. She turned her head sharply.

The bed next to her was empty. On top of the crumpled pillow was a note.

> *Isa,*
>
> *Can't bring myself to wake you. Have to leave early for a meeting. Will call you this evening. Stay close to the phone.*
>
> *Thank you. Thank you for last night.*

She crumpled the note between her fingers. The paper bit into her skin, and against the palm of her hand a paper cut oozed blood. She brought the hand up to her mouth. Her lips felt dry.

She took a shower in a bathroom gleaming with chrome and polished granite. Standing quietly underneath the stream of warm water, she tried to think back on the night before. But she couldn't get her mind to focus. The entire experience seemed insubstantial. All she seemed to remember was an interplay of texture and light and shadow. Skin, satin, dark hollows, moon drops on the pillows.

Stepping out of the stall, she walked with wet feet toward the towel rack. One of the towels felt damp, and as she dried herself in front of the mirror, she noticed a tiny fleck of wet shaving cream inside the washbasin.

The place felt eerily empty without him. She entered the living room and the sunlight falling through the sash windows seemed stale and sharp. There was dust on the windowsill.

She felt ill at ease alone in his apartment, but as she shrugged into her coat, she realized that she also did not want to return to Alette's house. If only she didn't have to go back to those quiet rooms, those smiling pictures.

Inside the taxi she found that she was tensing her arms and legs as if by doing so she could postpone the moment of arrival. And when Alette's house finally came into view, it was as though— for just a second—a cog had slipped her brain and she did not recognize the place. It was suddenly not a house of bricks and mortar anymore, but the line drawing of a child. Walls aslant, windows uneven, door out of proportion to the rest of the house.

She paid the driver and got out of the car. Then she turned around and pushed open the garden gate. Taking a deep breath, she started walking toward the front door.

EIGHTEEN

Your very shaddow is the glasse
Wher my defects I finde.
—"Song,"
Sidney Godolphin (1610—1643)

IT STARTED THE MOMENT SHE ENTERED: A FEELING OF UTTER DREAD, which closed itself around her heart like a fist. The air inside the house seemed thick and heavy, but cold. So very cold.

As she walked up the stairs, the feeling of trepidation grew. There was a huge weight pressing on her chest, keeping her from breathing deeply. Halfway up the stairs she stopped and placed her hand against her breast. Her heart was actually racing.

She entered Alette's bedroom and dropped her handbag onto the bed. What was happening to her? She felt hot and feverish. Every object around her seemed terrifyingly sharp-edged, as though by merely touching the rim of that Chinese vase, she would find her finger red with blood. And she was restless, she was so restless.

She left the room and started walking through the house, aim-lessly opening and closing closets and drawers. As she moved from one floor to the other, entering and exiting rooms, the minutes ticked away, became hours. And still she could find no peace. Why was she feeling so agitated, and at the same time so sorrowful? Why this sick feeling that her heart was beating out of step?

She wanted nothing more than to escape, to walk out the front door and find new air to breathe, but she found herself completely incapable of doing so. It was not possible for her to leave. She did not deserve it. She was a prisoner, marooned in this sad place; this prison built with the sharp stakes of deceit and betrayal. Guilt. Terrible, terrible guilt. How could she have betrayed Alette?

Images started racing through her mind with frantic speed. Alette in her pale nightdress, standing next to her bed, a finger to her lips. Alette, her hands two white moths darting across the keys of Aunt Lettie's upright piano. Alette in her wedding dress of whitest lace. Alette who was here in the house with her now. She could feel her presence. She knew with certain dread that if she were to turn around right now, she would find Alette immediately behind her, her eyes reproachful. And she would ask a question and expect her, Isa, to have the answer. But she would have no answer to give. For how does one justify the betrayal of friendship?

"I love him." She spoke out loud. But of course, these were words that carried no weight, words that were worthless, and so they made no sound.

If she could only find a place to rest, but every room in the house was hostile. She finally ended up sitting in a corner of the bathroom, her arms around her knees, her back pressed up against the tiled wall. She glanced at her watch and a minute later looked at it again and two hours had passed—time sucked away—and her not able to account for it. She saw her face in the mirror and it was the strangest feeling. She had stepped out of her body and was looking from the outside back at herself, at this person she hardly knew. Who was this hunched-over figure with the strained and watchful face, this woman who was listening to the *drip-drip* of the tap with fearful fascination? It was as though she was watching herself turn into something else, someone else . . .

She had to leave this room. She pushed herself upward and out the door. The sun was streaming through the window and onto the landing, throwing thick yellow blobs against the wall. She started to walk down the stairs, holding on to the balustrade, but then she stopped. There was something wrong with her shadow. Her shadow was sharply drawn and dark against the sun-washed wall, but it was too slight and not nearly tall enough to belong to her. She felt the panic rise in her throat. She placed her hand on her stomach as though that would quiet the nausea that threatened to overwhelm her.

The doorbell rang sharply—the sound slicing like a scream through the still air. It jerked her out of her panic and she blinked like a sleepwalker who had just been awakened. The bell rang again.

She almost ran down the stairs and at the door her hands worked feverishly to open the lock.

Michael was staring at her. "My God. You look terrible. Are you all right?"

She nodded, she couldn't speak.

"Can I come in?"

"Yes, yes." She clutched at his hand, almost dragging him inside.

She was breathing easier now. His hand in hers was warm and comforting. The largeness of him, the immediacy of his presence, filled the tiny hall and was immensely reassuring.

He looked at her searchingly as she simply stood there. He gestured at the stairs. "Shall we go into the living room?"

"Of course," she said. "Let's go into the living room."

"You sure you're all right?" he asked again as he settled down in one of the big chintz-covered armchairs.

She hugged herself. "I'm sorry it's so cold in here. There must be something wrong with the heating."

He shrugged. "Feels fine to me." He reached behind him to position one of the throw cushions at his back. "I came to look for you last night." He looked at her inquiringly.

"Last night?"

"Yes. I got back last night and stopped by to ask you to have dinner with me. I was worried about how you survived the holidays. Christmas and New Year's Eve blues and all that. And you're far from home." He smiled his slow smile, but there was puzzled concern in his eyes.

She didn't even want to mention Justin's name. She did not want the expression in Michael's eyes to change to disappointment. Somehow it was vitally important to her that he not lose faith in her, that he continue to hold her in high regard.

"I went out. With a friend."

He lifted his eyebrows, surprised. "I didn't know you knew anyone here."

"Well . . ." She stopped, uncertain how to continue.

He stared at her. "No."

"Michael—"

"You saw that man again. Why?"

She didn't answer. He leaned forward in his chair. "Why, Isa?"

"Because I wanted to." She got out of her chair and walked to the window. She sat down on the wide sill and leaned her forehead against a pane of glass. The smoothness of it was cool against her skin. There was a layer of dust against the window and in it she could see her own faint, distorted reflection.

When she looked back at Michael, his face showed utter disbelief. "You've been with him, haven't you."

She dropped her gaze, didn't answer. The silence dragged on and on until she felt like snapping her fingers to break the tension.

When he spoke again his voice sounded stunned. "What's wrong with you? You know what kind of man he is. You know what he did to Alette."

She brushed her hand across her eyes. "So he loved her. Okay, maybe he went too far and refused to accept that it was over between them. He didn't want to lose her. It doesn't make him a criminal."

"For Christ's sake. He would not leave her in peace for one minute. He undermined her self-confidence to such a degree that after a while she wouldn't leave the house. She was becoming almost reclusive, convinced that he was always waiting: watching her. I would come in here and find her weeping. And the worst of it was, she felt ashamed and humiliated."

Isa turned her head away. She didn't want to listen to any of this. She wanted the door on the past shut tight. Over. Done with. If the past couldn't be altered, at least it should not be allowed to intrude on the present. What she and Justin had together was separate from what he had shared with Alette. Maybe Justin had made mistakes, but you do not have to repeat your mistakes. In her mind came the memory of Justin's hands on her body, his lips in the hollow of her throat. She wished she could hear his voice right now. He had said he would call. He had promised her he would call tonight.

Michael spoke in the same disbelieving voice. "You must know how he made her life a misery. Alette must have told you about it while she was alive."

Isa said dully, "Not while she was alive."

"What?"

"Wait here." She mounted the stairs and entered the bedroom. She removed the books on the top shelf and took out the envelopes. She hesitated for a moment and then folded the third envelope in half and slid it into the inside pocket of her jacket. On her return downstairs she handed Michael only the first two of Alette's letters.

She sat down on the windowsill again, her feet neatly tucked in beneath her, her hands folded primly in her lap. She looked out the window and everything appeared strangely lifeless, as though someone had pulled a plug on it all.

"My God." There was a line running down from his nose to his chin she had not noticed before. "Why didn't you tell me about this?" He glanced back at the page in his hands. "Alette talks about three envelopes."

She managed to look him in the eye. "She never gave the solicitor the third one."

"Pity."

"I thought you didn't believe in revenge."

"I don't. But now that he's moved on to you, I'm beginning to have second thoughts." His lips tightened. "You have to stop seeing him."

Her throat was thick with tears. "I won't. I love him."

"Listen to me." He was stooping over her and shaking her, his fingers grabbing her arms painfully. "You don't love him: you hardly know him. And what about Alette?"

"This is about Justin and me. Alette has nothing to do with it."

He stepped away from her and there was such pity in his eyes she couldn't bear it.

"Alette has everything to do with this. He doesn't care for you. Why do you think he took you to his bed?"

She waited. She knew what was coming and she was breathing shallowly.

"It was to get back at her. This man is sick. It's his way of getting back at Alette for having rejected him."

"No," she shouted at him. "You're wrong."

"I'm not wrong." His face seemed tired. "And tell me, when were you planning on telling him about these?" He gestured at the letters. "Do you really think he'll want to be with you after knowing what you've done?"

She made no reply. She was standing next to the dark water of the Thames, her eyes blinded by light. *If you love someone, you love them regardless.*

I thought so, too, but I was wrong.

"If he ever finds out what you've been doing, who knows how he'll react? I would not want you to be alone with him."

"He's not a violent man."

"How do you know?" Michael sounded thoroughly exasperated. "I want to ask you something, but I don't want you to take it the wrong way."

"What is it?"

"Are you sure you're really attracted to him? You're not just doing this to prove something?"

"Prove what?"

"That Alette is not the only one who can have him. That you're up to it as well."

For a moment she just looked at him.

He spoke again, his voice low. "I understand, believe me. You felt flattered and—"

"Flattered?"

The tone of her voice stopped him in his tracks. "Well, not flattered exactly . . ."

"Oh? Then what exactly?" She was suddenly so angry, she was shaking. "Tell me. Come on, Michael. Let's hear it. I should be flattered that Justin has actually noticed someone as insignificant as myself? I mean, compared to Alette I'm nothing, right? That's what you're saying."

"Isa, stop it. That's not what I'm saying at all."

"Please leave."

"I'm sorry." He took a step toward her, his eyes miserable. "I'm so sorry. That was unforgivable. Don't you understand, I care for you, and—"

She did not give him a chance to finish. "You know nothing about my relationship with Justin. Or Alette, for that matter. Nothing."

"Isa—"

"Just leave. Please."

He gave a defeated sigh. At the door he looked back at her. "He's dangerous. I know it. I know he's dangerous. I'm afraid for you. Please, please be careful."

She closed her eyes.

She heard his heavy footsteps as he walked down the stairs. The sound of the front door slamming. Then silence.

She brought her fist up to her mouth. Her eyes were streaming.

She was on her own now.

A HEAVY GUST OF WIND SHOOK THE WINDOW AND ISA STARTED, suddenly awake again. She was fighting sleep, waiting for Justin's call. As she had done so many times during the past few hours, she leaned forward once more to check that she had indeed reconnected the phone to the wall.

Outside it was pitch-black. She glanced at her watch: it was already after eleven. The window frames rattled again and the wind threw a spray of raindrops against the glass pane.

She pulled her legs up underneath her on the chair and hugged herself. The envelope in the inside pocket of her jacket crackled. Alette's third letter and the two letters for the editors. For some reason she needed to feel them against her: next to her skin, close to her heart.

Her throat felt swollen. Her eyes ached. Her entire body hurt from weeping. But after hours of thinking, she was now able to be honest with herself. Michael was right. Why would Justin be interested in her? Shy, mousy Isa with her raw nails and uncertain mouth. Not to be compared with the woman he had really loved. A woman who walked with a sure stride, a walk that said, "I don't give a damn." A woman who was free and independent. Not like her, Isa, who was afraid of everything.

When he called her tonight she would tell him it was over. She couldn't tell him face-to-face. And first thing tomorrow she'll make arrangements to go back to South Africa. She would never return.

The idea that she might never see Justin again was so distress-ing, it made her breath leave her body with a desperate, burning sob and for a few seconds she sat quietly, breathing painfully.

Slowly she let her eyes move through the room; from the jewel colors of the rug, to the accordion folds of the books on the shelves, to the long sweep of the swagged drapes, where the glow of the lamp was too weak to reach and the shadows clotted thickly. In the far corner of the room she saw a figure with a defeated slump to its shoulders. She knew it was her own reflection, captured within the elaborately curlicued frame of the tall standing mirror.

The minutes ticked away one by one by one. Tick following tock following tick. She was beginning to feel drowsy once more, so very sleepy. Her head was enormous on her neck. Though she tried, she could not keep her eyelids from sagging.

Blackness.

Blackness and Alette standing next to her bed; placing her fin-ger against her lips. "Shh. Don't wake Mother. You've had a bad dream."

Blackness as Justin's hand moves over her face; his fingers mask-ing her eyes. The rubbery feel of his thighs and buttocks. His lips sucking the breath from her mouth.

Black crystal reflecting no light: an unblinking eye filled with venom. Sinuous slither and ripple of scales. "Isabelle, I'm scared."

Two blackly colored wooden marriage dolls burning to a fine white dust. Michael's voice: "He's dangerous. I'm afraid for you."

And suddenly—black shadows and a white hand emerging from the gloom: *Take my hand.*

No. Her own hands were clenched into fists. She did not want to take the hand. In her mind came an echo of the terror she had felt the last time she had touched those pale, outstretched fingers: the prickly sense of horror crawling over her body like a million, multiplying insects; the loud beating of her heart. No, she would not take the hand again.

With a movement as swift as a snake's the hand snatched at her. She looked down to see her wrist encircled by Alette's hand: the skin on her wrist white where the fingers gripped. She tried to pull free, but was unable to do so. She placed her other hand on top of Alette's in an attempt to prize away those viselike fingers. But scarcely had her hand touched Alette's when the surface of her dream stretched and rippled like a sinewy, organic piece of tissue and the next moment she was hurtling forward, forward, and the speed of it took her breath. The speedometer needle rising. Headlights burning into the fog. Trees spinning blackly past the window. The sound of a distressed engine. Terror. Blinding, choking terror.

The phone rang; the sound ripping through her dream. Her eyes flew open and her body jerked so violently that her arm fell off the armrest of the chair.

Justin?

But then she knew. Behind her eyes she could feel the trembling of nausea and the sound of the phone was strange, flat; curiously off-key. She placed her hand on the receiver and as she did so the slight figure in the mirror opposite her stretched out one hand to the phone while using the other to tuck the strands of long, red hair behind her ear.

"No." Isa's voice was a scream. She placed her hands over her ears to try to block from her mind the sick, atonal sound. She closed her eyes to shut out the image of the red-haired woman looking at her from the mirror. And then she was running down the stairs, grasping at the front door lock, and running, running through the front garden. She was barefoot and she shuddered at the cold, slippery feel of flagstones under her soles. She didn't stop running until she reached the sidewalk on the far side of the street.

She waited, her eyes fixed on the lighted square of Alette's living-room window. She could see the edge of a bookcase, the fall of a drape. The phone was still ringing. Even from here she could hear its continuous, drawn-out, monotonous peal.

Then it stopped.

Still she waited. The wind had died down and it was very quiet. Raindrops dripped off the branches. From somewhere farther along the street came the soft rushing sound of an overflowing gutter.

Her face was wet with tears. She turned around and started walking. When she reached the main street there were people and traffic. A woman looked at Isa's bare feet and giggled nervously. The man at her side placed his arm protectively around her waist.

Now she was standing outside the post office in front of the outside post box. She took the folded manila envelope from inside her jacket and withdrew the two stamped, smaller envelopes from within. She glanced at the addresses written in black: *Martin Penfield: London Post. Dan Harrison: Financial Times.*

Will there be any way in which he can get out? No. This man is facing disaster. There is no way out.

She placed her hand inside the black maw of the post box, still gripping the letters in her fingers.

He doesn't care for you. Why do you think he took you to his bed?

She opened her fingers. The letters left her hand and fell to the bottom with a soft plop.

NINETEEN

And every where **Erynnis** *raignes* . . .
　　　—"An Ode,"
　　　　Sir Richard Fanshawe
　　　　(1608–1666)

IT WAS A SLOW NEWS DAY, BUT EVEN SO MARTIN PENFIELD'S STOMACH was acting up. He opened the drawer of his desk, his fingers searching for his antacid tablets. He knew what it was, of course. Christmas and New Year's were murder on his digestive system. Every year he made a promise to pace himself at the dinner table, and every year his resolve vanished in the face of tortellini, cappelletti di Romagna, polastro in Tecia, and slabs of tiramisu. His mother-in-law was Italian and cooked like there was no tomorrow. He was going to pay the price for days to come.

He belched just as the door to his office opened and looked up irritably, but it was only the mail boy with the day's second batch of mail.

Before even opening it, Penfield knew what it was he held in his hands. There was no mistaking the handwriting on the envelope; the strong yet delicate penmanship, that deliciously extrava-

234

gant loop to the *P* of Penfield. Another missive from his mysterious lady. Although it could be a man, he supposed. He looked closely at the handwriting once more. No, it was a woman, no doubt about it.

For just a moment he sat quietly, tugging at his upper lip. There was something very odd going on here. And though he had never considered himself squeamish, there was a relentlessness in this systematic dismantling of Temple's business that was quite disturbing. Impressive, but disturbing. He wondered what the poor bastard had done to her.

Still, he was not going to look a gift horse in the mouth and so far the information they had received from their anonymous source had been spot-on. He turned the letter around and speared the flap of the envelope with the hideous chrome letter opener he had received as a Christmas gift from his secretary.

The letter was much longer than the previous letters she had sent him, and it took a while before the full implication of what he was reading sank in. For a moment he sat perfectly still. Then, with a sudden movement, he picked up the receiver and spoke to his secretary.

"Gail, find Daphne for me and call John Page in legal. Tell him I need him in my office right away."

Penfield slammed the receiver back in its cradle. He almost felt like rubbing his hands. It was going to be a hectic day after all.

TWENTY

The Pestilence of Love does heat.
>—"Dialogue between the Soul
>and Body,"
>*Andrew Marvell (1621—1678)*

THERE WAS A CRACK IN THE CEILING. A TINY CRACK, BUT IT SPREAD right across the entire expanse of white before disappearing into the egg-and-dart cornicing. It bothered her; this crack. It irritated her subconscious.

Isa stared at the ceiling. As she had done an hour before. As she had done yesterday, and the day before that. And the day before that.

Since mailing the letters to the newspapers she had stayed indoors. She had unplugged the phones, closed the curtains. Twice someone had rung the doorbell and then hammered at the door. She hadn't even gone to the trouble to look out the window to see who it was. Justin; Michael: she did not care. As far as she was concerned, she might just stay in the house forever. Since mailing those letters, the house no longer felt strange or hostile. It was as though she had done what was expected of her and now the house was ready to accept her back again.

In all this time she had been outside only once. Late last night she had felt ravenously, mouth-drippingly hungry and there was nothing in the kitchen to eat. She had walked to the all-night Europa store five blocks away; blindly picking cheese straws and milk and a box of cereal from the shelves. As she left the store her eyes had been caught by an *Evening Standard* poster trumpeting the day's headline news event: MELTDOWN: NEW CRISIS FOR TEMPLE SUL-LIVAN.

Such a tiny crack—thin as thread—hardly noticeable in that perfectly decorated ceiling, but somehow managing to spoil the entire effect. It reminded her of something else, but what? A perfect facade, marred by something tiny, offbeat, hinting that all was not as it appeared to be. For days now something has been scratching at the back of her mind: mental poison ivy.

She pulled the cover blanket closer around her body, and as she did so, she noticed again the chain of blue bruises around her wrist. The imprint of the thumb was particularly strong. Isa touched her wrist gingerly. She thought of a shining white hand darting at her from dreamshadows. She thought of a reflection in the mirror of a woman with long red hair and delicate bones. She thought of Michael's warning: *Lucid dreamers may find their dreams taking possession of them and they end up literally unable to find their own self again.*

Possession. The word carried with it a whiff of exorcism: clergymen dressed in swishing black robes, doleful chants, violent rites. Was that what it was? Was she becoming possessed by Alette? Crazy lady, she thought. Crazy lady, that's me, to even consider such a thing. But her eyes returned once more to the delicate imprint of bruises around her wrist.

Turning her head sideways, her gaze moved on to the pictures on the nightstand next to the bed. She looked into the slitted eyes of Siena. She was gripped by an intense longing for the old woman. She needed her wisdom. But Siena was dead; almost fifteen years now. Ashes to ashes; dust to dust. Just like Alette.

Isa picked up the photograph and pressed it to her heart. This picture used to rest on the nightstand in Alette's bedroom in South Africa, right beside the two wooden carvings Siena had given Alette as a gift. Isa hadn't seen those two marriage dolls in years—Alette had given the carvings to Justin as a wedding gift—but she could still remember exactly the way they looked. The male figure was slender, almost adolescent looking, whereas the female figure was that of a mature woman: wide-hipped, with pendulous breasts and heavy thighs. They were carved from stinkwood: a black, very hard wood, not really suitable for carving. Maybe that explained why the expressions on the faces of the dolls were so enigmatic and strangely twinlike: the eyeballs large and protruding; the lips a straight line except at the ends, where the corners curled upward only slightly, as though the two dolls were smiling over a secret known to them alone. The dolls were old. Oils from the palms of other, unknown owners many years in the past had bestowed on them a fine sheen.

Isa had been jealous of this gift, she remembered that well. And she had once asked Alette if she could keep one of the dolls in her own bedroom. But Alette, usually so generous, had refused. "These two dolls must never be parted. They are spirit marriage partners. If you part one from the other, the union would be forever broken. As long as they are together, love endures. Love is still alive."

Love is still alive.

Isa sat bolt upright. As if wiping a clean cloth over a dirty window, allowing the light to pour in, she suddenly knew. She knew what it was that had been nudging her mind: tugging at her unconscious so insistently. Looking back, she realized it had bothered her ever since Mr. Darling had told her about the specific instructions Alette had left for her cremation. Alette had stipulated that the marriage dolls be cremated along with her own remains and Isa had sensed that something about it was peculiar. She had even asked Michael about it; hoping that he could still the nagging feeling within her.

Alette had given these idols to Justin as a wedding present. Presumably, after such a disastrous marriage, the idols would have lost their meaning for Alette. Why, then, would she want to take them with her? Why take with her these symbols of perfect unity? They were tokens of the enduring love a woman experiences only once in her life for a man: her true mate in death as well as life. The person she would most want to be with for all eternity. Not the person who had made her life a nightmare.

Isa threw the blanket off her. On the Regency writing desk below the window stood her purse. She opened it and pushed her hand into the zippered side bag. Her fingers closed around the letters she had taken from the walnut table in Justin's living room. She had completely forgotten about them. She slipped the rubber band off and pulled a sheet of pink notepaper from one of the jagged-edged envelopes.

> *Dear Justin,*
>
> *We have to talk. We cannot go on like this.*
>
> *You've changed your phone number again. And again it is unlisted. Why? Why can't you just talk to me? Why do you insist on shutting me out of your life? You know you will not succeed in doing so. We are linked you and I—not just in this life, but also in the next.*
>
> *Last night I stood in the square and looked up at your window, hoping to see your shadow on the blind. I stood there for hours. The light was on but there was no movement. And then, without warning, the light went off and I was left staring at darkness and my heart ached for you so.*

I long for things to be the way they used to be; your arms around me, my body touching yours. Your lips seducing me, and in your eyes images of what you were, what you will become.

Before I met you, I had searched, but I could not connect with any man. It's my fault, I thought. I have sabotaged my own chances by giving too freely of myself. I have indulged myself too much, with too many lovers, too many times. Maybe those who have known but one lover only are the ones destined to feel intensely and strongly: their love undiluted by memories of other loves and other moments of passion. By sharing myself with so many, maybe I had tranquilized my senses and blunted my capacity to feel completely.

But then I met you. And now I can say that I have known many men but only one love. You are my life. Don't take away my life. Don't leave me lonely.

I suck the oxygen from the air, you say. I am too needy. My love smothers you. My jealousy wearies you. I'm sorry. I'm so sorry. Tell me what to do and I will do it. All I ask is that you allow me back into your life. Open the door, just a little. Please.

The word "please" was written in blue: a different pen, clearly, from the black one that had been used to write the rest of the letter. It seemed indescribably poignant; as though Alette had mulled over what she had written and then, much later, had added that one, last, impassioned plea as a desperate afterthought.

Most of the other letters were written in the same vein.

Love and death go hand in hand. By loving utterly, we experience the same obliteration of the self as when we face death's embrace. I have always realized this, I suppose, and have shied away from loving so extravagantly. Then you came. And I gave myself to you with no attempt to save myself from losing myself. But you rejected me.

One letter consisted of threats of the most obscene nature. Isa could not believe what she was reading. The handwriting was Alette's, but the words were alien. This could not be Alette: so fastidious; so careful of investing herself emotionally; it could not be Alette who wrote these shrewish sentences that were acid with hate and spite.

Some letters were piteous. On a lined piece of paper, which looked as though it had been ripped from a scrapbook, Alette had written:

> *Dear Justin. May I ask you three questions only:*
> *Why don't you love me?*
> *Have you ever loved me?*
> *What can I do to make you love me?*
> *Please answer.*
> *Thanking you in advance,*
> *your former wife*
> *Alette Temple.*

The letters had been written over a period of three years. The last letter was dated three months before Alette's death. Around the time Alette had visited Mr. Darling, Isa thought. Around the time Alette had drawn up her will, had sold her shares in Temple Sullivan. The letter consisted of one sentence only: *Do not make me give up on you.*

Stiff as a mechanical puppet, Isa folded the letters with exaggerated precision along the original creases. She pushed the letters away from her to the far side of the table. The table was dusty and the letters left a shiny mark. She really should clean the place up. Alette would have been disgusted at the way she had let the house go: dust collecting in the corners, the bed unmade, an airless smell in the rooms. On the table stood the glass vase with the lilies that

Justin had given her. The petals had long since browned and the long stems were slimy. Earlier she had noticed a dank smell coming from the green water.

Michael had told her Alette had been terrorized by Justin: that she had been his captive. She *had* been his captive, but not in the sense Michael had thought. Alette had deceived Michael. Just as she had deceived her, Isa.

The most frightening thing was that Alette had clearly convinced herself that she, not Justin, was the victim here. *The mind is already such a cunning, cunning thing. It's programmed to be dishonest, to lie to us. Throughout our lives we train it to become even more deceitful.*

Where had she heard that? Oh yes, Michael. He did seem to have the handle on everything.

How surprising that she should feel so calm. She had been duped into playing a destructive game, the rules written by a deeply distressed woman. But she wasn't hysterical. She wasn't weeping. Even though she herself had destroyed her chance at happiness. Even though she herself had destroyed Justin.

She had destroyed Justin.

Her breath caught in her throat. And for a moment it felt as though a switch in her head had been flipped, depriving her of all sensation: not a sound to hear; nothing to see; no feeling in her hands; her lips cold. Deaf, blind, mute Isa.

She had destroyed Justin.

TWENTY-ONE

Bold Lover, never, never canst thou kiss,
Though winning near the goal—yet, do not grieve;
She cannot fade, though thou hast not thy bliss,
For ever wilt thou love, and she be fair!
—"Ode on a Grecian Urn,"
John Keats (1795–1821)

THE FIRST TIME HE HAD SEEN HER SHE WAS DOING YOGA AND SHE WAS naked. He was looking through his telescope, cursing the city glow that reflected off the night sky, wishing he could be in the country instead, when somehow the scope was knocked off balance; and there she was.

She was in the house on the other side of the road, but she seemed close enough that he could reach out and touch the hollow in her throat. The room she was in was lit by candles only and her throat and neck were ice cream in the sepia light. She was so close, he could see beads of sweat on her collarbone; he could lick them off: the taste was in his mouth even as he watched.

And she knew it. She knew he was watching. Stretching, fold-

243

ing her limbs—white flesh and dark shadows—she smiled. And then she had looked over her shoulder straight at him.

She had allowed him to watch her every night, but she never allowed him to touch her. They became companions. Companions of the soul and spirit—far more erotic than companions of the flesh could ever be. Denial, he came to realize, was the most sensual thing in the world. "It's like that picture on a Grecian urn," she said, "the nymph just out of reach of the satyr's grasp: a mad pursuit that never ends, an ardor that never cools." She smiled gently. "In chivalric love, the knight may at times share a bed with his lady, but she would still be forbidden to him. If their love were to be consummated, his passion would wither. I know. That's what happened with him."

Him. Justin Temple. Her voice sometimes sad when she spoke about him, sometimes angry and shrill. He darkened their lives. If it hadn't been for that man's shadow, he and Alette could have been happy. They were soul mates, the two of them. They had so much in common.

They shared a passion for roses. Alette with her straw hat and her rebellious red hair thrust underneath it. Alette with the scissors in her hands cutting back the tough, prickly stalks. You shouldn't cut them back so hard, he told her. You have to be cruel to be kind, she replied in return. She had accompanied him to his mother's house; tackling the soulless, formal garden in Putney with its straight garden paths and hemmed-in squares of grass and turning it into a riot of jubilant color and heady scent. His mother had not been grateful. She had stared at the flowers, her mouth stiff. She had found the wildness, the wanton lushness of it all, overwhelming.

They shared a love for poetry, although Alette loved poems that sang of dappled light and full-throated nightingales. Wordsworth. Keats. The poets his mother had dismissed. Their wistful melan-

choly did not appeal to one who preferred the work of men who
wrote of death with unsentimental wit.

Roses, poetry. And they had shared another passion: a fascination for what lies beyond this life; the mystery and fire of what
cannot be seen and hardly comprehended. So many times they had
talked about the tenuous, shimmering link that yoke together the
quick and the dead. So many times had they sat shoulder to shoulder, paging through books that smelled of must and disuse, whispering together, sharing notes. He was in awe of her gift. When
Isa first told him of Alette's calls, his first emotion had been exhilaration. After his initial reaction of delight, he had felt apprehension. What would Alette tell Isa? Why was she calling?

Temple did not like roses. He was scornful of Alette's gift and
critical of her ideas, the things she was passionate about. He did
not understand her; did not deserve her. But he was the one Alette
loved, even though she continued to take into her life a string of
lovers who could never satisfy her. "I hate him, Michael." Her
face flushed and her eyes tearful. "I love him so." He had tried to
cure her of her obsession, had begged her not to throw herself at
this man. But her fixation with Temple was out of control. She
was losing her dignity: stalking Temple, intercepting his mail.
When a gossip columnist reported that Temple was seriously dating another woman, Alette had sent the woman a package in the
post. Before sending it off, Alette had shown him the contents:
pale, strawberry colored strands of pubic hair. Coarse to the
touch. Unmistakable in its message.

Toward the end she had become almost a recluse. Sitting in her
chair, wrapped in her throw, watching the phone constantly; hoping for a call from Temple. It was painful to watch, but he could
also feel the anger building up inside of him. That last day he had
begged her not to follow Temple to the country. Did she have no
shame? She was humiliating herself. Her life was becoming irrele-

vant. She was turning into a ghost. A malevolent ghost. She talked about revenge constantly. It was simply the other side of obsession: the midnight side.

He had never believed in revenge. Revenge was not self-empowering, it was self-defeating: a cold fire, a necrosis of the soul. Alette seemed incapable of grasping this truth.

That was when he had started plotting her death. Only death could cure her of the sickness. His love for her was that strong. He would willingly deprive himself of her presence to save her soul from the spreading rot. It was up to him to help her. Obsession is an open wound. Revenge keeps it festering. Uncompromising action was what was called for. Soft hands make stinking wounds, as his mother is fond of saying, and she's right. A break has to be clean and final. Absolute. With no possibility of a comeback.

No possibility of a comeback?

He should have known. The other day, in her house, while he was reading those letters Isa had handed him, Alette was leaning over his shoulder. Her hand rested lightly on his arm. He smelled her perfume. Against his cheek he felt her breath.

TWENTY-TWO

Until sweet Isabella's untouch'd cheek
Fell sick within the rose's just domain.

> —"Isabella, or The pot of Basil,"
> John Keats (1795–1821)

THE ROOM SMELLED FRESH. DESPITE THE RAIN, ISA HAD KEPT THE
windows open the entire day, only closing them a half hour before
she knew he was due to arrive. She had dusted, had bought fresh
flowers. The fire was burning in the hearth. Alette's jewel box of
a room has been restored to its original comfortable luxury.

As though any of this would make a difference. She bit down
on her lip. Her jaw muscles were aching from tension. Her mouth
was filled with the taste of self-loathing. She tried to speak, but
her voice made no sound. At the third attempt, she managed to
utter the words she has been practicing all afternoon.

"I love you. Please forgive me."

The words sounded inane. They could never convey what she
wanted him to know.

Justin was staring at her as though he had never seen her
before. His eyes seemed puzzled, as though he was trying to

247

recall something, but something that was too unimportant, too trivial for his memory to retain. A chance encounter; a vaguely familiar face.

She had told him everything; starting with the telephone call from Mr. Darling. She hadn't tried to excuse herself. After all, what could she say? Alette made me do it? She had asked him to sit down in Alette's living room and had given him the letters, watching as he read the blueprint that outlined Temple Sullivan's destruction. His expression had not changed. But now he was looking so tired: small and shrunken within himself. Suddenly old.

"Justin . . ."

The expression in his eyes made her stop.

"Do you know what you've cost me?"

He stood up; his hands hung nervelessly by his sides.

"Twelve years. Twelve years of risk and backbreaking work. Twelve years of dreaming and wanting success so badly I could not sleep at night. When I found out about the professor, I thought it was over. But I didn't steal from him, and the man was dead. I had perfected something that I knew was worthwhile; that could make a difference."

She could not speak, could not face him any longer. She kept her eyes on the clock on the mantelpiece. It had stopped: the hands stuck at ten past two.

"And now it's gone."

He sounded disbelieving. "Gone," he said again, but this time there was something in his voice that made her look at him swiftly.

His hands tightened into fists. "You bitch."

She got up quickly and stood behind the chair, keeping it as a barrier between them.

"Did you enjoy fucking me, Isa? Lying in my arms knowing what you'd done? Did it give you a buzz? A sense of power?"

She watched in shock as a vein swelled blue above his eyebrow. Before she could react, he had crossed the room and kicked the chair in front of her to one side.

He grabbed her by the arm and shook her so hard that her head flopped back and forth, back and forth. He lifted his hand and she thought he was going to hit her.

But he was weeping, his face glistening and his mouth distressingly slack. He turned away from her. He stretched his arm out wide and brushed it across the mantelpiece. The clock and the large, framed photograph of Alette crashed to the floor.

"I will never forgive you."

He spoke with his eyes fixed on the floor; fixed on the image of that beautiful face with the flawless smile. She didn't know if he was speaking to Alette or to her.

It hardly mattered.

TWENTY-THREE

Darkling I listen; and for many a time
I have been half in love with easeful Death,
Call'd him soft names in many a muséd rhyme,
To take into the air my quiet breath;
Now more than ever seems it rich to die.
                    —"Ode to a Nightingale,"
                    John Keats (1795–1821)

HE HAD BEEN WAITING PATIENTLY: MIDNIGHT HAD COME AND GONE and then the first, early-morning hours. And still there was light in the room on the top floor of the house on the opposite side of the street, forcing him to wait at his darkened window. But patience was his one particular virtue. He was always willing to wait for the good things that come to those who have the strength to bide their time.

For the past few hours he had merely sat quietly: his eyes fixed on that square pane of glass on the other side of the road. The last time he had been in the house, he had also waited a long time for her to go to sleep. He smiled when he thought of his last visit. She had been totally spooked by the wind chimes and by the photograph. Initially he had removed the picture of Alette to keep for himself. But as he watched Isa from behind the laquered screen in the living room, the opportunity to create some mischief had proved irresistible. He had hoped to scare her away from the house, and he would have been successful, too, if it hadn't been for that man.

Finally. She had switched off the light. The buttery glow peeping through the closed curtain was out.

He glanced at his watch. Four o'clock. The streets were still, the air hushed. This was the dreaming hour when people cried out in their sleep; the crisis hour when a fever might break or hope finally disappear. The hour when death's angel was walking, as his mother would say.

He picked up the gloves and pulled them over his fingers. He took the nylon stocking and pushed it into his coat pocket. He felt slightly ridiculous as he did so: the image of the stocking-faced intruder, his face squishily shapeless as though it had been pickled in brine for far too long, was such a readily identifiable menace from a hundred B-movies that he cringed. But it couldn't be helped. He did not wish her to know who was at her side when she entered those last desperate moments of her life. Call it superstition, but the image of his face should not be the last image she carries with her into her dream-death-sleep.

Earlier he had caught a glimpse of her as she had pulled the curtains shut. With pain in his heart he had recognized the nightdress she was wearing. It was not hers to wear. Just as it was not her life to live. She was usurping Alette's place; seeking to take her stead. It was obscene; it could not be allowed.

He gave a last look around him and walked to the door.

SHE HAD KEPT THE LIGHT BURNING FOR AS LONG AS SHE COULD, LIKE a child scared of the dark. But weariness had overtaken her and now she was lying on her back, staring into darkness, her feet and hands twitching involuntarily. The phone was connected. Soon her dreams would be wide open. She wanted Alette to contact her: there were questions she needed answered. But she was also afraid, so very afraid of what she might find if she walked into the nightmare Alette had planted in her brain.

What had happened to the dreams she and Alette had shared as children: dreams so rich, so dazzling, they could make you weep with joy. It came so easy then. It was an act as natural and sane as drawing breath. She never questioned the validity of it all; was completely uncritical about what was happening to them. All she cared about every evening while she waited drowsily for the moment of transition was that her dreams might lead her to experience feelings so magical and exhilarating they could never be replicated in real life. That, and the knowledge that they would be side by side: Alette the dream maker and she, Isa, the chronicler of their adventures. In those days she had kept a dream journal filled with sketches and descriptions as rich and complex as any Jungian Red Book. Of course, only a few years later she had destroyed that journal with her very own hands. Eric hadn't actually asked her to do so, but he had told her the journal 'creeped' him out. What was it Justin had said? Tests: Alette would set him tests to prove his devotion. Well, Eric didn't even have to. She had been quite capable of playing such a self-destructive little game all by herself.

She could feel her eyelids closing. She was so tired and this time the effort to keep her eyes open was too great.

Take my hand.

And without thinking twice about it, she did.

HIS THICK GLOVES WERE HAMPERING HIS EFFORTS TO PRY AWAY THE loose brick from the wall. As he took them off, he winced as a thorn on one of Alette's rosebushes scratched savagely at his wrist.

He pushed his hand into the dark hollow, his fingers searching for the keys to the front door. Something touched his palm; something soft, moist, and cold. He felt the hairs on his arms rise. But it was only a slug. A dead slug.

And now the keys were in his hand and he was walking up the shallow steps to the front door. This was where she would bid him good night, standing on tip toe, her hands pressed unsteadily against his chest, kissing him tipsily. The soft pressure of her lips, that low, slow laugh— they left him with no defense. She always blew him a kiss before closing the door. She never invited him in.

He fitted the key to the lock and the door opened silently under his hand. Against the right-hand wall were motionless shadows. Alette's coat. Her jackets. A gray felt hat.

He took the stocking from his pocket and pulled it over his face. He placed his foot on the bottom stair and looked up to where the staircase spiraled away into darkness.

TAKE MY HAND. AND HER DREAM COLLAPSED IN ON ITSELF AND THE next moment Isa was searching for her keys in her coat pocket, catching sight of her reflection in the car window as she bent down to unlock the door. As she brushed the long coppery hair from her face, her eyes widened with astonishment.

Isa looked down at her feet and the shoes were not her shoes. She looked down at her hands and they were not square, capable-looking Isa hands, they were small, narrow hands with slim fingers. And Isa understood that Siena's warning had come true. Her dream had taken possession of her. *Alette* had taken possession of her. What is dream and what is reality? She didn't know anymore.

The car door was open but something was bothering her, and she hesitated. She stood next to the car slapping her gloves against her palm: back and forth, back and forth. She hesitated because she sensed a rage in the air. Something malevolent was out there—close by—biding its time.

But it was cold and the light was fading fast. If she were to get to London before dark she should leave now. Of course, she hadn't bargained on having to drive back to town today. If things had worked out as planned, she would be with Justin now and they would be making love.

Making love. What an innocuous description of an act that holds such danger for a woman; which is such a leap of faith. A lowering of the barriers—reaching out to him at your most vul-nerable—offering the soft part of the throat. It takes such courage. Men never understood that.

This afternoon Justin had said he never wanted to be with her again. In her mouth was the sad taste of rejection. But no use think-ing about that. About the humiliation and the hurt. As long as there was breath in her body—and even when there wasn't—she'd see to it that he would not be free of her. She'll return again and again; continue her war of attrition. All's fair in love and war and love is the greatest war of all.

The seat leather was cold against her thighs. She turned on the car heater and adjusted the rearview mirror. She pulled the seat belt over her shoulder, but for some reason the clip would not slide into the buckle. Something was blocking it. After several useless attempts to get it to work, she let it go and pushed the belt away from her.

Just as she was about to turn on the engine, her eyes were caught by a thick book lying on the passenger seat. She reached for it, puzzled. She couldn't recall seeing it there before.

As soon as she had picked up the book, she recognized it. It was Michael's. A yellow sticky was peeping out from the pages and on it he had written her name. He often did that: leaving volumes of poetry lying around—marking passages he wanted her to read. She used to find it sweet.

She frowned and opened the book on the page he had marked.

And here the precious dust is layd;
Whose purely temper'd Clay was made
So fine, that it the guest betray'd.

She sighed impatiently. It was one of those stylized poems cele-brating idealized love. Woman on a pedestal; abstract object of desire. For some reason she found the reverential tone vaguely sin-ister. She didn't recognize the name of the poet: Thomas Carew. But it was written in 1632, which probably made him one of the Metaphysical poets Michael so admired. Why he had such a fond-ness for their work—those intricate, densely woven little puzzles of death and eroticism—was beyond her. She wished for poetry "to dream" by; he preferred "strong lines" and dark, religiously tinted passion. But then his entire outlook on life was tinged with a gloomy, perverse fatalism. At first glance a man of almost aggres-sive sanity—he was, when you got to know him well, dis-turbingly fragile.

She looked back at the book on her lap. He had circled the very last stanza:

Learn from hence (Reader) what small trust
We owe this world, where vertue must
Fraile as our flesh, crumble to dust.

She tossed the book onto the edge of the passenger seat next to her and turned on the engine. She'd have to do something about Michael. It was getting out of hand. So needy, my God, he was so needy. His desperation was a clammy cloth smothering her heart. She couldn't stand it anymore. He was constantly hovering over her; sometimes she could swear he was following her around. There was a time when she had enjoyed being with him—to be honest, that kind of uncritical admiration was just what she needed after her breakup with Justin. And it had been an interesting flirtation at first. An unconsummated affair, but with enough sexual tension to set a house on fire. Then it became a drag. His excessive gratitude for any attention she showed him irritated the life out of her. And once boredom had set in, amorous play was of no interest to her anymore.

But she was nervous. Even though his voice when he spoke to her was still loving and calm, she'd look into his eyes and see a stranger moving within. And she sensed his anger: an unstable mix of adoration and disappointment on the boil. She had a bad feeling about him. But these days she had a bad feeling about everything. A sense of impending disaster was shadowing her. She did not know the source of the danger, but the sense of imminent peril impacted on everything she thought, everything she did.

When she had a feeling this strong, it was usually right.

And so she had felt compelled to get her affairs in order; to place the untidy strands of her life in Lionel Darling's capable hands so they could be neatly tied together. To make her plans for *after*. So strong had been the sense that she was running out of time, that she had placed enormous pressure on her attorney to get things sorted as soon as was humanly possible. As a token of her appreciation for his efforts she had bought him a gift: a quite beautiful leather wallet made from ostrich skin. On the day she gave it to him, she could see he was troubled. "Don't do anything foolish," he told her, and she suddenly realized he was worried that her haste, her anxiety, the parting gift were all signs that she was contemplating doing herself harm. "Rest easy," she told him, "I'm not about to slit my wrists." And she had teased him, made light of his concern, flirted with him a little as she always did. But she had not told him of the fear inside of her, which was growing with every passing day.

Only one thing, she knew, could stop the deadly, inevitable, and as-yet-unknowable march of future events. If she could win Justin back, the threat would disappear. She believed in that absolutely.

But it was not to be.

Outside it was sleeting. She turned on the headlights. The wind has come up and every now and then the car shook mightily. There was a lot of traffic on this road, not just cars but heavy trucks as well. But soon she'd be able to leave the highway and take the scenic route down. On the map it looked like a detour, but she knew from experience that it would allow her to bypass a big chunk of extremely heavy highway traffic. She'd better keep a sharp lookout for the exit sign . . .

He was sweating like a pig. Sweat was dripping into his eyes, and as he touched his forehead through the thin mesh of the stocking, it was slick and wet.

He paused for a moment to catch his breath. His legs were tired. The staircase in Alette's house stretched endlessly ahead of him. Somehow, every time he thought he had reached the top, there would be additional steps to climb. He reached out to steady himself against the banister, but the wooden railing shifted underneath his hand and the space around him contracted and expanded; the walls first closing in on him and then bulging outward with vertiginous speed.

At last he was standing on the landing outside her door. He placed his hand on the handle and pushed.

The door did not budge. Was it locked? He leaned his shoulder against the solid wood and jiggled the handle—trying to make as little sound as possible.

With a sullen, reluctant click, the door opened.

. . . KEEP A SHARP LOOKOUT FOR THE EXIT SIGN AND THERE IT WAS. She braked slightly and the glowing green needle on the speedometer started to fall as she took the off-ramp.

This road was quiet. She could see no other headlights ahead of her or in the rearview mirror. In summer this was a lovely road with several picnic spots and scenic outlooks on the way. On the other side of the embankment was a drop of at least a hundred and fifty feet, but tonight the fog and swirling mist made any view impossible. She cautiously steered the car around the first tight bend, touching the brake pedal lightly with her foot.

Her foot met no resistance. The car refused to slow down.

She tapped the brake pedal with her foot several times in quick succession, mindful of the slick surface of the road, but again there was no response from the car.

The speedometer needle was rising. She gripped the wheel tightly, trying to fight the panic. For God's sake, this couldn't be. She had had the car serviced only a week ago.

This is no accident.

She managed to take the corner, swinging the wheel sharply to the left, and the wheels skidded unpleasantly. And now the car was taking the straight, accelerating wildly.

Oh God. Oh God. No. Help me.

The headlights burning into the fog. Trees spinning blackly past the window. The sound of the distressed engine.

And didn't she just know it was going to end like this?

This is no accident. This is no accident. Over and over again the same words running through her mind like a mantra. When she had a feeling this strong, it was usually right.

The next bend was coming up. She turned the wheel desperately and felt the car sliding into a long skid. She turned the wheel in the direction of the skid, her foot pumping the brake pedal uselessly. Michael's book flew off the seat next to her and she felt it brush her leg. *This is no accident.* And his face was suddenly clear in her mind. Her executioner, the malevolent presence in the shadows. She knew who he was now.

The car crashed into the embankment, and as she hurtled forward, her head smashing into the windshield with a wet smack, she screamed out his name.

HE STOOD NEXT TO THE BED AND LOOKED DOWN AT HER. ISA WAS sleeping like one already dead. *Sleep bindes them fast; only their breath / Makes them not dead: / Successive nights, like rolling waves / Convey them quickly, who are bound for death.* He smiled. His mother was right. Poetry is such a good tool for comprehending intellectually what is understood instinctively.

He peered at her intently. He was able to see the evidence of tears on her cheeks. Pale skin, remarkably long lashes. He had noticed them the first time he had seen her up close. Sad, sad mouth.

He knew why, and the reason for her tears. She was grieving for that man. She was in the grip of obsession: her mind and thoughts infected by the sickness Alette had passed on to her. Little by little, she had slipped into Alette's life, becoming consumed by it. In a way, tonight he would be killing Alette for a second time.

He had tried his best. No one could accuse him of not trying to watch over her. Poor Isa. He had sensed that she was falling for Temple and had tried to warn her off. But she wouldn't listen. She was blinded by him. The virus had already contaminated every groove of her brain, every fiber of her heart.

Obsession was disease. It called for a sharp knife in an uncompromising hand. Soft hands make stinking wounds, as his mother always says.

Her hair seemed exceptionally dark against the white pillowcase. He picked up the pillow next to her. It was filled with the finest down, so soft and pliable it would mold itself to her face like a mask. When he placed the pillow over her mouth and nose, how much would she struggle? Would she try to scream as she strained for oxygen, her heels drumming against the mattress in muted frenzy, her arms flailing? His eyes fell on the telephone next to the bed and for a moment he considered using the telephone cord. It would probably be quicker that way, but the idea of it was immensely unappealing. Bulging eyes and protruding tongue . . . and him having to watch. No, no. That won't do. The pillow would be a more elegant way to go about it.

The illuminated hands of the clock on the bedside table stood at thirteen minutes to five.

THIS IS NO ACCIDENT.

The scream wouldn't stop. It was echoing in her head, over and over and over again: a jagged shard of insane sound slicing through the soft tissue of her brain. And Isa knew if the scream didn't stop soon she would get lost in it and she would be unable to find her way back.

And suddenly the scream changed into a ringing sound: monotonous, drawn out, *real*—a lifeline dragging her from sleeping to waking; from death to life . . .

She fumbled for the telephone receiver and placed it against her ear. *Isabelle wake up! Wake up! Watch out*—

The next moment the receiver was snatched from her hand and a fist slammed into her stomach. Intense pain flared through her body. She struggled for breath. He slapped her with the back of his hand so violently that her head flew to one side and she bit down on her tongue.

Her eyes focused on the face looming above her and her mind went blank with horror. The flattened features were grotesque and alien. But she knew who it was. Oh yes, she knew who it was. Her dream had made sure of that.

She tried to roll away from him but he dragged her back to his side of the bed. And again he hit her in the face. The fury behind the blow shocked her as much as the blow itself. Her mouth filled with the taste of blood from her cut lip and bruised tongue. He placed one enormous hand over her mouth and with the other he pinched her nose shut.

Her eyes bulged, the pain in her head was immense. She flailed her arms desperately. He shifted his hand on her mouth to get a better grip and reached for the pillow next to her. She pulled her teeth apart and bit down on his palm as hard as she could. For just a moment his hold relaxed and she jerked her head free, gasping for air.

"Fuck you," she screamed at him. There were tears in her eyes, she was weeping now, but if she were to die in her own snot and blood, she wasn't going to make it easy for him. She brought her head up sharply and butted him in the face. The blow made her skull shudder and she must have hurt him because he grunted and pulled back slightly. She jabbed her fingers at him, trying to push them into the jelly of his eyes.

But now he had both his hands on her shoulders and was pushing her down, pinning her one arm underneath her body. She struggled and screamed and her free hand scratched at him viciously. But the next moment she was choking as everything went black. He had pushed the pillow over her face; was leaning on her with his full weight.

She tried to roll over, but he was so heavy. She was fighting him but he was so strong . . . too strong. She was suffocating. The pressure in her head was unbearable. At the periphery of her vision were violent flashes. *Oh God. Don't let me die. Please don't let me die.*

No air. No air for her lungs. No—

SHE WAS LIMP UNDER HIS HANDS. FINALLY. SHE WAS MUCH STRONGER than he had imagined. And who would have thought she could put up such a fight?

He relaxed his grip on the pillow and put his burning palm

against his mouth, sucking at the spot where her teeth had bit into the flesh with such frenzy. Then he turned back to the quiet figure on the bed. He reached for the pillow that covered her face.

The ecstatic smell of roses, intensely sweet and piercing, made him pause. One moment the air was clear, the next moment it was soaked in fragrance. The pillow was light as thistledown in his hands but his arms felt suddenly tired. He was exhausted. He could hardly lift his hand, he was so tired. Was it because he missed her so? His red-haired angel. Soft as water, strong as steel; vindictive as all get-out. She had bested them all. She had wreaked havoc on poor old Temple and she had outwitted him as well. Her death had not ended her obsession; it lived on in her revenge.

He wished she were here. He wished he could turn around and there she'd be, smiling at him mischievously. In his mind came the image of her face, so startlingly strong, he felt tears come to his eyes.

Darkling I listen; and for many a time I have been half in love with easeful Death . . . Her lovely mouth was moving, words of beauty tumbling from her lips. *Now more than ever seems it rich to die.*

She was beckoning him.

THE SOUND OF THE FRONT DOOR SLAMMING SHUT MADE ISA OPEN HER eyes fully. She had kept them closed when she had felt the pressure on the pillow ease. Her every muscle had wanted to explode into action to get away from him, to breathe in air, but she had controlled herself, forcing her limbs to slacken.

She pushed the pillow away from her and sat up. The balls of her eyes ached viciously. Her arm felt as though it had been twisted right out of its joint.

The creak of the garden gate outside drew her to the window. She looked down into the front garden. He had just stepped out into the street, his hand was still resting on the gate. He stood quite still.

With a sudden movement he looked up and straight at her

where she was watching him from behind the window. He had taken off the stocking and she was able to see his features clearly. For one frozen moment they stared at each other, their eyes locked.

He turned his back on her and pulled the gate closed behind him.

Without giving herself time to think it through, she grabbed her jeans and the sweater she had worn earlier in the day and pulled them on. She slipped her feet into her shoes. As she ran down the stairs, her legs felt wobbly, as though they would not support her weight. Her entire body was hurting.

It was so quiet outside. There was not a cloud in the sky. The moon was painting the world white.

He was walking at a moderate pace, his arms swinging easily. She saw him tilt his head to one side and even at this distance she could see his lips move, as though he was speaking to someone at his side. He was smiling, and now he was holding his arm out with old-fashioned courtesy, as if to offer support to his invisible companion. His gestures seemed so eerily out of whack, for one moment Isa wondered if she had slipped back into a dream.

He rounded the corner. She could no longer see him. She started to run. Her shadow kept close to her side and the street lamps seemed to dim. And once again she asked herself: Is this real or am I dreaming?

She heard a squeal of brakes—metal upon metal—a strange, hissing sound and a damped thud. And as she turned the corner, looking in the direction of the sick sound she had just heard, she knew without any doubt that she was not dreaming at all.

EPILOGUE

And in the icy silence of the tomb,
So haunt thy days and chill thy dreaming nights
That thou would wish thine own heart dry of blood
So in my veins red life might stream again,

> —"This living hand, now
> warm and capable,"
> John Keats (1795–1821)

THE NEW OWNERS HAD MADE SUBSTANTIAL CHANGES TO THE farmhouse. The front parlor where Aunt Lettie used to receive visitors and where her knitting bee gathered every Wednesday afternoon was now a mere extension of a considerably enlarged living area. The kitchen had been spruced up: lots of sponging and stippling effects on the walls and stylish wooden cabinets replacing the old, chipped melamine units. Siena's room had been transformed into a workroom for the youngest son, who had a passion for building model airplanes. Only Uncle Leon's study looked more or less the same, except for the shelves now filled with floppy disks and stacks of computer paper instead of dusty, plastic ledgers. Mr. du Plessis was a progressive farmer and believed in technology not just in the field, but also in the office. He had kept some of the early records—she recognized Uncle Leon's handwriting on the spines of the books—but where once had stood a glass canned-fruit bottle bearing a grisly trophy was now a potted plant.

Mr. du Plessis and his wife had been more than kind to her when she had approached them and asked if they would allow her to scatter Alette's ashes on the farm. They had even offered her the use of the house for the weekend. They were to attend a wedding in Pietermaritzburg and did not expect to be back before late Sunday evening.

It was very hot. She had forgotten how suffocatingly hot the farm could be in the month of February. As she walked, her feet were clammy with sweat inside her shoes.

At the top of the ridge she stopped and placed her hand to her eyes. Behind her, in the distance, she could just make out the red roof of the house. The house looked tiny; a speck of ocher floating in a green sea of sharp-bladed sugarcane.

In front of her, at the bottom of the steeply sloping hill, was the entrance to Siena's secret place. Hidden behind that green cloak of creepers and trees and messily flowering shrubs was the Yoni stone.

She started her descent, her feet slipping against the steep side, a shower of shale creating a cloud of dust. She had to use both hands to push her way through the tough tangle of vegetation. The large-leaved creepers closed behind her.

The shadows in here were deep and the rays of the sun filtered down through many layers of leaves. Even so, the air was sultry and incredibly close. Her ears were deafened by the screeching of cicadas: a solid wall of hallucinatory sound.

The Yoni stone looked exactly the way she remembered it. It was round and large—almost as tall as she. Unmistakably female in shape, it had an exquisitely smooth surface and in its center a wide, tunnel-like cleft with curved sides.

The stone was a polished dolerite rock of the type found in the western Transvaal. How it had ended up here, hundreds of miles away, no one knew. Siena said that in ancient times the rock had been used as an altar stone in sacrificial offerings to "MaBona," the Great Mother: she who gives life and takes it away. The sacrificial fire was built inside the cleft. Usually a Yoni stone was accompanied by a rock representing the male phallus. But no other rock shared this space. The Yoni stone was all alone.

The cleft cut deeply into the rock. At its bottom it was dark. Isa placed her hand inside and wiped away the grit and tiny stones. She slipped her rucksack off her shoulder and took out the brass box.

She lifted the lid. Three pounds of fine ash and bone fragments pulverized to the size of granulated sugar. Precious dust.

I want to go home; I mean really home. I crave a truly blue sky.
I don't want the sun to shine, I want it to burn.
Please strew my ashes on the farm—in the cleft of the great
Yoni stone—you remember: Siena's secret place.

Isa lifted the box over the cleft and tipped it slightly.

For a moment she just stood there; not thinking, not feeling. Then she stepped back. She watched as a large, yellow caterpillar left its precarious foothold on a thin twig and waddled onto a fat, jagged-edged leaf. An ashy white stain streaked across the dead trunk of a tree and pointed to the bird droppings that had accumulated at its roots.

On the top of her rucksack was fastened a long cardboard tube. She opened it and extricated with care the single rose she had brought along with her. The stem was wrapped in moist cotton wool and silver foil. *Félicité Parmentier*. Exquisite petals and a fragrance that haunts the memory. She placed the rose on top of the stone. The creamy petals seemed to sweat and melt in the oppressive heat.

At the edge of the clearing, where the creepers grew thickly, she stopped and looked back. She could just see the top of the rose, a hint of white against the gray of the rock. She turned her back on it and left the secret place behind her.

It was a relief to breathe in fresher air, to see a horizon. For the first time since Michael's accident, she felt some sense of peace.

Michael. He had stepped in front of a large, red, off-duty double-decker bus only two blocks away from Alette's house. At that time of the morning the usually teeming high street was deserted and the bus driver had admitted to taking advantage of the absence of traffic by driving too fast. But he also swore that Michael had stepped in front of the bus on purpose. He insisted that Michael had walked into the path of the uncoming bus without any haste, keeping his eyes on the bus driver's face as he did so. And he was talking, the bus driver said. As though there was someone at his side.

Isa had corroborated his account. It had gotten the driver off the hook, although the police were still reluctant to call it suicide. There was no note. No apparent motive.

She hadn't told the police about Michael's attack on her: it would serve no purpose. As for her knowledge that he had killed Alette, and that Alette in turn had seduced Michael into taking his own life: she had kept that part to herself as well. What proof did she have? "It came to me in a dream?" She could imagine the reaction that would get.

The sun was losing some of its sting. She glanced at her watch. She had been away from the house for almost two hours. Justin would be waiting.

He had agreed to accompany her to the farm but had refused to be present for the scattering of the ashes. And she hadn't insisted. She was still so uncertain of her footing with him. The two of them faced a long journey ahead, and whether they could work through her guilt and his anger to arrive at the end together, she did not know. His anger was fearful, and sometimes deepened into despair, but by some divine grace it had not curdled into resentment.

"Why would you want to be with me?" she had asked him on the day he had returned to the house. She was busy packing the last of Alette's books into cardboard boxes, her hands dusty, her back aching, when the doorbell rang and there he was; eyes wary, lips tight.

He placed his hands on both sides of her face. She held her breath.

"Part of me says this relationship has been damaged beyond repair," he said. "But something about you moves me. Something inside me recognizes you." And for a few seconds the old Justin looked out of his eyes.

But then he dropped his hands and moved away. He spoke without looking at her. "When I met Alette, I thought she was this free spirit—a beautiful, strong woman. That was the person with whom I fell in love. And that was the pact between us. I would give her room to breathe, I thought, accommodate her independence. But this image she had presented to me was a lie. She never wanted room to breathe. She wanted a constant, cloying, stifling intimacy. Her neediness was fearful. If I so much as looked at another woman, she lost control. She was even jealous of my mother. She demanded constant attention and admiration. Do you know how tiring it is to be engaged in a never-ending courtship? It is impossible for the most devoted person to be continually loving, but any hint of criticism from me she'd blow up into a major crisis. And she had all these rules I had to follow. I was only allowed to read if she was reading. I was only allowed to listen to music when she was not around. If she entered the room I had to focus on her immediately and give her my undivided attention. She once destroyed all the documents on my table, because she felt they were more important to me than being with her. She made me get rid of some of my oldest friends because she saw them as competition for my affection. After the divorce, things became even more dire. She simply would not leave me alone. I couldn't even visit a restaurant anymore because she'd be sending me bottles of wine or making some or other extravagant gesture. It was painful."

His voice was suddenly tired. "You once said to me that if you love someone you love them regardless. Remember? I always thought so as well, so you can imagine how guilty I felt for falling out of love with Alette so easily. But she was simply not the woman she had pretended to be. And my God. She was manipulative. It was insidious, subtle but utterly relentless: this ability to maneuver you to go in the direction she wanted you to go."

He looked at her. "You lied to me as well, Isa. But you're not a manipulative woman: not at heart. You yourself were manipulated by a master of the game. I suppose, in a way, it creates a bond between us."

She waited, aware of her heart beating painfully in her chest.

He sighed. "Whether it can work in the long run, I don't know. We can try. Let's take it one step at a time." He had added, his voice remote, "No promises."

No promises. Well, for now that was enough. She dared not ask for more.

She and Justin together. How would Alette feel about that? A breath of wind, more imagined than real, chilled the sweat on the back of her neck. Over the past few weeks she had deliberately refused to think about it. She had been so busy—tying up all of Alette's affairs, selling the house—that it hadn't been that diffi-cult to close her mind to the thought. But now the apprehension and doubts she had repressed were thrusting their way up to the surface.

She still loved Alette, that would not change. And she recog-nized that Alette had warned and helped her on the night of Michael's attack. But Alette was indeed a master manipulator: an alchemist magician who could transmute reality and shape it to conform to her objectives. Someone who had no trouble getting people to follow her wishes. Until the day she collided with some-one who made a stand, who refused to be manipulated. Until the day she met Justin. And by striving to gain domination over Justin at all costs, Alette had set in motion events over which she lost control and which eventually destroyed her.

For a brief moment Isa closed her eyes. The time has come for her to make a stand as well and live her waking life free from her cousin's influence. They would never again meet in the dreaming world either. Their shared dreams were no longer the magical, lib-erating experiences of their childhood. Things have gone wrong and could not be set right again. She would never again take the hand. Since that last, desperate dream in which Alette had taken possession of her, Isa had adamantly shut her mind to Alette when-ever she closed her eyes to sleep.

"Alette." She spoke out loud. Her voice fell into the silence like a pebble into deep water. "It's over. Let it be."

She waited, but she sensed nothing. Just sun, fragrant earth, and rustling cane.

"I want him. I'll fight for him." Isa hesitated. "I'll fight *you*."

Nothing. Only the drone of a large bumblebee.

She was close to the house. She could see Justin waiting for her at the back door. She increased her pace, stretched her stride.

He was leaning against the door, his elbow and forearm forming a lopsided triangle. His head was turned to one side as though he was listening. And then she heard it as well and behind her eyes she felt a quivering nausea.

The telephone was ringing. A long-drawn-out monotonous sound. A curious sound, disturbing in its atonality.

Flat, strident: strangely off-key.